By Alison Lurie

FICTION

Love and Friendship
The Nowhere City
Imaginary Friends
Real People
The War Between the Tates
Only Children
Foreign Affairs
The Truth About Lorin Jones
The Oxford Book of Modern Fairy Tales (editor)
Women and Ghosts

NONFICTION

The Language of Clothes
Don't Tell the Grown-Ups

FOR CHILDREN

The Heavenly Zoo
Clever Gretchen and Other Forgotten Folktales
Fabulous Beasts

THE
LAST
RESORT

THE
LAST
RESORT

a novel

ALISON LURIE

Henry Holt and Company
New York

Henry Holt and Company, Inc.
Publishers since 1866
115 West 18th Street
New York, New York 10011

Henry Holt® is a registered trademark
of Henry Holt and Company, Inc.

Published in Canada by Fitzhenry & Whiteside Ltd.
195 Allstate Parkway, Markham, Ontario L3R 4T8

Library of Congress Cataloging-in-Publication Data
Lurie, Alison.
The last resort : a novel / Alison Lurie.—1st ed.
p.   cm.
ISBN 0-8050-5866-4 (hb : alk. paper)
I. Title.
PS3562.U7L37   1998
813'.54—dc21   97-42985

Henry Holt books are available for special promotions
and premiums. For details contact: Director, Special Markets.

First Edition 1998

Designed by Michelle McMillian

Printed in the United States of America
All first editions are printed on acid-free paper. ∞

10   9   8   7   6   5   4   3   2   1

For Doris

Manatees are slow-moving creatures that feed on aquatic vegetation in shallow coastal waters, estuaries, and slow-flowing rivers. They live singly or in small family groups. . . . Members of a group frequently communicate by muzzle-to-muzzle contact and, when alarmed, by chirplike squeaking. . . . All three species are declining in population.

—*The New Encyclopedia Britannica,* 15th edition

But there's a tree, of many one,
A single field which I have looked upon,
Both of them speak of something that is gone.

—Wordsworth, "Ode: Intimations
of Immortality"

THE
LAST
RESORT

1

At three A.M. on a windy late-November night, Jenny Walker woke in her historic house in an historic New England town, and sensed from the slope of the mattress and the chill of the flowered percale sheets that Wilkie Walker, the world-famous writer and naturalist, was not in bed beside her.

Often now Jenny woke to this absence. The first time, after lying half awake for twenty minutes, she tiptoed downstairs and found her husband sitting in the kitchen with a mug of tea. Wilkie smiled briefly and replied to her questions that of course he was all right, that everything was all right. "Go back to bed, darling," he told her, and Jenny followed his instructions, just as she had done for a quarter century.

After that night she didn't go to look for him, but now and then she would mention his absence the next morning. Wilkie would say that he'd had a little indigestion and needed a glass of soda water, or wanted to write down an idea. There was no reason to be concerned about him, his tone implied. Indeed her concern was unwelcome, possibly even irritating.

But since the day they met, Jenny had been more concerned about Wilkie Walker than anyone or anything in the world. He had come into the University Housing Office at UCLA where she was working after graduation while she waited to see what would happen next in her life. It was a misty, hot summer morning when Wilkie appeared: the most interesting-looking older man Jenny had ever seen, with his broad height, his full explorer's mustache; his shock of blond-brown hair, steel-blue eyes, and sudden dazzling smile. Dazzled, she heard him ask about sabbatical sublets for the fall. He wanted somewhere quiet with a garden—he liked to work out of doors if he could, he explained—but he also hoped to be within a half-hour's walk of the university. Which no doubt wasn't possible, he added with another radiant smile.

But Jenny was able to assure him that she knew just the place. And two days later, while she was still dreaming of Wilkie's visit and wondering if she could get leave to audit his lectures, he reappeared to thank her and ask her to have lunch with him.

It was only later that Jenny realized how unusual that had been, because at the time Wilkie Walker was extremely wary of all women. He had been married twice, both times briefly and disastrously ("I get on well with most mammals, but I seem to have difficulty with our species"). First to a sweet and graceful but totally impractical girl whom he compared to a highbred Persian cat ("all cashmere fur and huge sky-blue eyes and special diet, but she always had a slight cold, couldn't hike more than a mile without collapsing, and was terrified of most other animals").

Then, on the rebound, he had married a young woman who was equally good looking and much more competent and robust ("strong and healthy as an Alaskan husky"), but who turned out to be deeply hostile to men and especially to Wilkie. For example, when at a time of crisis he asked her to retype one of his articles, the husky not only growled at him but dropped his manuscript into the kitchen wastebasket, among eggshells and wet grapefruit rinds and crusts of rye toast.

At that first lunch Jenny knew that Wilkie Walker was someone she could, even should, devote her life to. And as she came to know him better she was almost shocked to discover how badly he needed this devotion; how much of his own life was wasted on inessentials. How often he had to set his work aside for tasks someone else (Jenny, for instance) could do for him much faster and more easily, for Wilkie had no natural aptitude for shopping or household repairs or balancing a checkbook.

And after they were married she did all these things and much more: happily, gratefully. Soon she became able to help Wilkie in many other ways: not only typing and proofreading his books and articles, but accompanying him on field trips, making notes, and taking photographs. At home she helped with library research, copying and faxing, finding illustrations (often her own photos), and creating tables and graphs. As Wilkie became ever busier and more famous, she kept his schedule of lectures and interviews and meetings, arranged airline tickets and hotel reservations, took phone and E-mail messages, and corresponded in his name with agents and editors and fans.

Usually now, when Jenny woke at night and found herself alone, she sighed, turned over, and slid back into oblivion. But tonight sleep didn't come. She lay in the antique four-poster bed listening to the windy scrape of bare twigs against glass, thinking that everything was not all right and neither was Wilkie. For months—since he retired last spring, really—his nights had been wakeful, and more and more often he seemed restless or weary during the day. Moreover, none of the things that he used to enjoy so fully seemed to please him now. For the first time since she'd known him, Wilkie had to be urged to attend concerts, lectures, or films. He didn't read most of the books and articles on nature and the environment that crowded into the mailbox, often accompanied by letters of gratitude and appreciation. More and more often he declined to serve on committees and boards, and he delayed returning telephone calls, even after Jenny had gently reminded him several times.

More worrying still, Wilkie hadn't finished his important new book, *The Copper Beech.* This, perhaps the culminating work of his life, was the portrait in depth of a great tree on the

Convers College campus; it would bring together all his interests: botany, climatology, ecology, entomology, geology, history, soil science, and zoology. Wilkie's agent and editor were excited about *The Copper Beech,* and it had already been announced in his publisher's catalogue. Every day Jenny expected her husband to give her the final chapter to type into the computer, and every day she was disappointed.

Besides this, and almost worst of all, Wilkie seemed to be losing interest in his friends and family. For over a month he hadn't been to the faculty club, and he wouldn't let her ask anyone to dinner. Last week when the children were home for Thanksgiving he had had little to say to them. He had less and less to say to Jenny too; also, for nearly a month he had not suggested making love.

Clearly something was wrong. And that being so, it was Jenny's responsibility to correct it. Perhaps, she had thought at first, her husband was ill but didn't realize this, because he had hardly been sick a day in his life. He had always refused, for instance, to acknowledge colds: when one showed signs of wanting to attach itself to him he ignored it until, defeated, it slunk away.

A month ago Jenny had persuaded Wilkie to have a medical checkup—first on general principles, then resorting at last to her usual last resort: the claim that it would make her feel better. Grumbling about the waste of time, reiterating his belief that people who weren't ill should stay away from doctors, Wilkie accompanied her to Dr. Felch's office and was pronounced to be in excellent health for a man of his age. Prompted by Jenny, he admitted that he occasionally got up at night, but declared that he saw nothing wrong with this; he refused to accept the term "insomnia."

Like almost everyone in Convers, Dr. Felch was somewhat in awe of Wilkie Walker, the town's most famous citizen. More for Jenny's sake than his patient's, perhaps, he wrote a prescription for what he called a "muscle relaxant," which Wilkie afterward refused to take. The trouble with most people today, he told his wife, was that their muscles were too relaxed, not to say atrophied.

Though Wilkie seemed to have forgotten the whole episode, one phrase Dr. Felch had used kept running through Jenny's head: "a man of his age." Wilkie's age was now seventy. Not for the first time, she recalled the uncomfortable conversation she had had when she first brought him home to meet her parents. Wilkie clearly hadn't noticed the slight hesitation in their welcome, and would have been surprised to hear what was said when his wife-to-be confronted her mother later in the kitchen.

"Darling, I do like him," Jenny's mother had insisted. "And of course I realize he's brilliant. He was wonderfully interesting about those South American bats. And I can see he really loves you. But—" She turned on the water in the sink, sloshing away the rest of the sentence, if any.

"But what?"

"Well. He has been married twice before, that always . . ." Under Jenny's hurt, resentful stare, her voice faltered. "And then . . . the age difference. You're barely twenty-one, and Wilkie Walker is forty-six, almost my age. I always think of what my mother said once: If you marry someone much older, you don't ever quite grow up. And when you're forty-six, Wilkie will be seventy. An old man.''

Jenny refused to listen. Wilkie Walker was not like other people, she declared. He had more energy and endurance and enthusiasm than most of her college friends.

Her mother, for whom tact was almost a religion, never brought up the subject again. But her comments continued to swim in the weedy depths of Jenny's mind, occasionally surfacing in a sharklike manner. "You see, you were quite wrong," she had felt like telling her mother on several occasions, the latest being her own forty-sixth birthday last spring. "Wilkie hasn't become an old man at all. When we were on that walking tour in Greece last month nobody could keep up with him except the tour guide." She did not say this only because, though her mother was still in excellent health, her father was now, after two heart attacks, all too evidently an old man at seventy-four: stoop-shouldered and short of breath, slow-speaking and slow-moving.

Remembering all this, Jenny lay listening to the wind scratch at the glass, recalling recent conversations with her two grown children over Thanksgiving vacation.

"I tell you what it is, Mom," Ellen had said as they were washing the dishes. "I think Dad has got a clinical depression."

Since her daughter was now a medical student, and like

many such students given to scattershot diagnoses, Jenny both believed her and did not believe her. "Oh, darling," she temporized. "I don't know."

"That's what I think," Ellen repeated. "I'm surprised his doctor isn't more concerned."

"Dr. Felch is concerned. He admires Wilkie very much."

"Everyone admires him very much," Ellen said. "That's not the point."

Billy (Wilkie Walker Jr.) was as usual less definite, but no more reassuring. "Yeah, I sort of agree with Ellen," he admitted the next day in answer to his mother's question. "Something's wrong. Dad seems to be moving around less, you know? Like he wouldn't come for a walk yesterday because it was too cold? I never heard that before; he was always dragging us out in the goddamnedest freezing snowstorms. Maybe you should go somewhere warmer this winter."

"Somewhere warmer?"

"Like, I don't know. Florida, for instance."

"Oh, darling. Your father would hate Florida." A glaring panorama of pink beach hotels and condominiums trimmed in neon and surrounded by artificial neon-green turf rose in Jenny's mind.

"I know, Mom. But you could try Key West. It's different from the rest of Florida. Sort of like Cape Cod with palms, that's what my roommate said when we were there on spring break last year. And there's supposed to be lots of writers and artists around that Dad could talk to."

Jenny lay in bed rehearing these voices, wondering if she ought to go downstairs, fearing that if she did Wilkie would not be pleased to see her. For a while she distracted herself from this anxiety with familiar, less pressing anxieties about her two beautiful and brilliant children. She pictured Ellen, who so much resembled Wilkie: tall, ruddy, and broad-shouldered—and also, since early childhood, always so sure of herself. Sometimes lately Jenny was almost frightened of her daughter. I wouldn't like to be Ellen's patient when she becomes a doctor, she thought: she'd be so sure she knew what was wrong with me. Then in the dark she blushed, ashamed of this disloyalty.

She imagined Billy, who had been such a beautiful, affectionate little boy, and now seemed somehow subdued and uncertain. Both of them were doing well professionally, but Jenny sometimes worried that Billy, isolated in the nearly all-male world of computer hardware, would never meet a nice young woman, and that Ellen would scare nice young men off. Then they would never marry and have children Jenny could love.

Jenny marveled at people who desired expensive manufactured objects like an indoor swimming pool or a Mercedes. She already had too many such objects to take care of. What she longed for no money could buy: at least one grandchild. And now, for Wilkie to be himself again.

Downstairs a thin, icy wind rattled the antique bubbled panes of the windows and sliced its way into the family room, but Wilkie Walker did not adjust the thermostat. He remained huddled in his forest-green L. L. Bean bathrobe in a corner of the sofa, watching the weather channel with the sound turned off and thinking about death.

Death was what Wilkie thought about most of the time these days. The death, over the past few years, of his three closest friends and colleagues; the slow, lingering death of the natural environment. The progressive destruction of the ozone layer, the slashing and burning of tropical forests, the poisoning of oceans, wars and assassinations in Africa and Asia, terrorist bombings, drug wars in great cities, the scummy sulfurous yellow-gray foam on Baird Creek behind his house, the raccoon he saw smashed on the road as he was driving home yesterday afternoon, and his own regress toward extinction.

If they could have heard his thoughts, Wilkie's thousands of fans and many of his remaining friends and colleagues would no doubt have shared his shock and sorrow, except for the last item. What was he complaining about, for God's sake? they might have said. For a seventy-year-old man he was in good shape. He was also a famous, perhaps the most famous popular naturalist of his generation: the most eloquent among those who had called public attention to our wanton destruction of the earth and its flora and fauna. His best-known and best-loved book, *The Last Salt Marsh Mouse,* had never been out of print, and there was hardly a schoolchild in America who had not read its famous first paragraph:

It is the year 2000. In the Zoological Gardens of a great city, a small furry pale-brown, bright-eyed creature clings to a dry stalk in a clump of artificial reeds and stares at the passing humans. A sign stapled to the other side of the wire identifies him as

Salt Marsh Harvest Mouse,
Reithrodontomys raviventris
"SALTY"

Salty is alone in his cage, though once he shared it with his parents and four older siblings. As far as anyone knows, he is the last of his family, the last of his race: the sole surviving salt marsh mouse on this earth.

More than anything else, it was this book and this passage that had made Wilkie Walker famous. *The Last Salt Marsh Mouse,* unlike its namesake, had thrived and reproduced profusely over the last quarter century; it had given birth to paperback editions, translations into sixteen foreign languages, innumerable excerpts in anthologies and condensations and simplifications for the juvenile market. There had been documentary film, television, and cartoon versions, sometimes with a tacked-on happy ending. "Salty" posters and T-shirts were available in science museums everywhere, and toy salt marsh mice, some moderately authentic as to size, color, and shape, and others distorted in a Disney manner, were widely sold. "Salty" had become a cuddly shorthand symbol for the threatened extinction of North American mammalian species. He had made Wilkie's fortune, and his name a household word.

But now, whenever Wilkie recalled this endangered rodent, he felt a shudder of self-hatred and despair. In spite of the hundreds of thousands of copies they had sold, his books had in some ways done more harm than good. Many salt marsh mice had been illegally kidnapped for sale as pets; others had been acquired by zoos that wanted to display this now-famous mammal. As a result, just as in Wilkie's worse-case scenario, Salty was now nearing extinction in the wild, and the world was going to hell in a nonbiodegradable plastic handbasket.

Last week, against his better judgment, he had given yet another interview to a student from the local high school newspaper.

"How many species do you figure you have helped to preserve, Professor Walker?" the child, a pimply girl, had inquired.

Wearily, Wilkie gave his standard reply, displaying his famous modesty, declaring that he had been only one of several working in the field. But other words screamed for utterance. I preserved the species Wilkie Walker, that's what I preserved, he had wanted to tell her. And not only this one specimen of the species, but hundreds, thousands of imitation Wilkie Walkers: noisy, posturing, sentimental amateur naturalists. He visualized them as half-human Yahoos: packs of ugly, hairy, ungainly two-legged goats in cheap outdoor jackets and boots, tramping heavy-hooved over the fields and woodlands of North America, crushing flora underfoot and frightening fauna, baaing, nibbling, preening.

It was clear to Wilkie now that if he had stayed with serious science he might have made some significant discovery. Instead, horrified by what was happening to the world around him, he had become a popularizer. A propagandist. He had brought upon himself the fate of all successful popularizers: he had made his point so well that it had become banal. Once his name had been used to describe and recommend the works of writers like Ed Hoagland and Annie Dillard; now their names were used to recommend his work. His books, at first popular with adults, were now read mainly by children and teenagers, and it was now mostly high school and college students who asked to interview him. If you're over seventy, he had realized belatedly, nobody important in the media wants to hear from you anymore. Their attitude is, Wilkie Walker? Is he still alive?

Once Wilkie had dined at the White House and been the featured speaker at important conferences, earning very large fees (often donated to good causes afterward). Now his typical honorarium had shrunk. He had been reminded of this a while ago by the brash young man with sideburns who had taken over the business of his former lecture agent, now retired. "Let's face it," this disagreeable youth had said, leaning confidently toward Wilkie across a table in a pretentious Italian restaurant and breathing garlic on him. "You're an established name, sure, but you're no longer the flavor of the month."

Wilkie's left hip, which he had injured five years ago climbing a cliff in New Mexico to observe jackrabbits, ached tonight: no position on the sofa was comfortable. He could picture how the bones must look, lumped with calcium deposits that grated against the adjoining muscles, tendons, and nerves. That hip would never totally heal now; probably it would get worse and worse, until he was permanently stiffened and crippled, permanently in pain.

Except he probably wasn't going to live that long. For six months he had been aware of an intermittent ache in his lower gut, and in October, in a graffiti-scrawled toilet stall at the college library, he had seen blood. He knew what that meant: cancer of the colon. He couldn't feel it yet, but somewhere in his bowels his life was diseased and bleeding away. When that fool Dr. Felch asked him if there were ever blood in his stool, Wilkie hadn't volunteered the information. He knew the odds; he had looked them up. He was determined never to be the weak, exhausted victim of a colostomy, weakened further by chemotherapy and radiation, dragging through what was left of his life with a plastic bag of his own shit strapped to his body. No. He would say nothing until treatment became impossible.

The trouble was, he couldn't put the fear and the pain and the fear of coming greater pain out of his mind. And this failure of courage and detachment pained and terrified him further. He was sick with self-disgust to think that when this planet and the animals that lived on it were in such desperate straits, he should be obsessed with his own declining health—and, worse and more shameful, his declining reputation. He was an animal too, and animals suffered and died, he told himself; that was what had always happened and always would happen.

His hip ached, ached. But he was not going to admit this to anyone, not even Jenny, not yet. For many years articles and books had portrayed Wilkie Walker as stoic, heroic, fit, and invincible; stories had been told of how in search of rare creatures he had survived Alaskan blizzards, tropical heat and storms, treks through remote jungles, frostbite, days without food, a dislocated shoulder, a broken wrist. Largely, these stories were true.

But Wilkie was no longer regarded as heroic by everyone. Many animal-rights activists now considered him weak and gullible, and his writings outdated and irrelevant. Ecological vandals who had tried unsuccessfully to enlist him in their cause now despised and bad-mouthed him because he wouldn't support or participate in the driving of murderous spikes into redwood trees or the bombing of animal research laboratories. As several of them had troubled to inform him, in print or in person, in their opinion he was not only a cowardly, cranky has-been, but a traitor to the environment.

All this was in Wilkie's mind, always. But he was resolved not to complain, especially not to Jenny. For as long as he could, he must be strong for her, because she was weak.

A troubled, complex expression appeared on Wilkie's face. For a quarter of a century he had loved Jenny more surely, more steadily than any other human being. But now he also resented her, because if she did not exist he would be free to leave the world by the nearest exit—in his current fantasy, the exhaust system of their Volvo station wagon. Because of Jenny all such exits were barred; he knew that psychologically she would not survive his self-inflicted death.

For Jenny he must live as long as he could and die as peacefully. He must save and shelter her now, as he had saved and sheltered her ever since, over a quarter century ago, they had met at UCLA. His first reaction, even stronger than his awe at her delicate pale beauty, was astonishment that such a creature—a creature of the woodlands and wild places, surely—should be living in Los Angeles. When he heard that Jenny had been born and raised in New England, he understood better. Later, when he learned that she had been unwillingly transported to Southern California by self-centered and ambitious parents, and then abandoned there, a spirit of ecological knight-errantry had suffused his romantic admiration. He swore to himself that, whatever it cost, he would rescue this beautiful, unique primate and restore her to her natural environment.

And in the end he had done so. Choosing among three possible endowed professorships, he had returned Jenny to an unspoiled New England town, bought her an unspoiled colonial house, and surrounded her with woods and fields and flowers. There was nothing he would not do for Jenny, Wilkie thought. She asked so little, was so content only to be with him. For twenty-five years she had made him almost wholly happy. Moreover, she had presented him with what most people would consider the three greatest gifts of his life: two healthy, handsome, intelligent children and (perhaps even more important) Salty.

It was Jenny who, when he had taken her to San Francisco at the end of his lecture series, had given a name to *Reithrodontomys raviventris.* Walking in a Bay Area park just after sunset on that first miraculous evening, Wilkie had spotted a rare salt marsh mouse and pointed it out to her. "Oh, Salty, you're beautiful!" Jenny had cried as the warm wind swept musically through the pale winter reeds and her long pale reed-colored hair. And the tiny bright-eyed creature, as if understanding, had paused on his tuft of grass to exchange with her a look of mutual appreciation.

It was not Jenny's fault that her gifts had turned sour in the end: that Salty had become a media cartoon; or that Ellen and Billy, once so wholly satisfactory, had grown into flawed and problematic young adults. It was no one's fault that Ellen should have inherited Wilkie's strong will and his tendency to take control, so much less charming in a woman; or that Billy should have inherited Jenny's physical slightness and her sensitivity to the opinions of others, so much less charming in a man. In his darkest moments Wilkie sometimes described Ellen to himself as a noisy, opinionated feminist and Billy as a sissy and a computer nerd.

The way it seemed to Wilkie now, as he crouched in the cold draft, clenching and grinding his jaw against the pain in his hip, only two possible futures were open to him. Either he would give up, tell some doctor the truth about his symptoms, begin taking mind-altering painkilling drugs, and descend into a blurry, shameful last act of life. Or he would get out, while it was still possible.

And it was, theoretically, possible. An accident on a field trip, for instance . . . He would have to leave Convers for that: there were no mountain cliffs here, no lakes he could not easily swim across, even if he could discourage Jenny from accompanying him as she usually did. Perhaps an automobile smashup, one that wouldn't injure other people? When the snows came, some night when the roads were dark and icy . . . But if no one else was involved, there might be doubts about his intention. And how could he be sure that it would not end in a fate far worse than his slowly dwindling life: brain damage, a coma, paralysis?

Upstairs Jenny was still awake. At last she slipped out of bed, pulled a long robin's-egg blue robe over her lacy white cotton nightdress, and padded barefoot down the wide, chilly oak stairs.

"I couldn't sleep either," she apologized. "Goodness, it's cold in here."

"I hadn't noticed," Wilkie lied, watching his wife as she turned up the thermostat, thinking how graceful she was, how beautiful, with her pale, fine regular features and her silky pale-beige hair, still only lightly touched with silver, waterfalling over her shoulders.

"Do you know, I was wondering," Jenny began, perching on the arm of a wing chair. She paused, waiting for the go-ahead.

"Yes?"

"I was thinking about that awful cold I had for so many many weeks last year. I was wondering if we might go somewhere warm for a while this winter. It would be so nice to escape all the viruses that I know are on their way to Convers now, just looking for me."

Wilkie said nothing.

"It doesn't have to be abroad," she added. "There are parts of America that don't have winter." She glanced at the silent television screen, which obligingly showed a weather map of the United States banded in rainbow colors, the wavy bottom strip a glowing red. Wilkie hardly saw it; instead he recalled a recent interview in a local TV studio where he had learned that what one sees on the screen is a lie, a construct: there is no real map projected behind the weatherman, only a blank wall toward which he gestures. That's what I'm doing now, he had thought at the time, gesturing at a blank wall, while people imagine I see something there.

"I was wondering, what if we were to take a place in Key West for a month or two," Jenny continued. "Molly Hopkins still goes there every winter, doesn't she?" Molly was the widow of a professor of American history who, though older than Wilkie, had been one of his closest friends.

"I believe so," her husband said in a neutral, considering voice. Key West, he thought. An island, surrounded by the deep kind drowning sea— Afterward everyone would assume it had been a sudden cramp, or a freak undertow—

"I wondered if Molly might know something about houses to rent in Key West."

He should have known better; some people might say that too, Wilkie thought. Why did the old fool try to swim out so far? they might say. Well, so what?

"I could write to her there. Or even phone." Jenny glanced

back from the weather map to her husband, and caught her breath. What she saw in the flickering television light was someone she hardly recognized: an old, exhausted-looking person in the grip of something between desperation and despair, his eyes squeezed shut as if in pain, his jaw set.

But then Wilkie shifted his position, turned away from the ghastly blue glare toward Jenny, smiled slightly at her, and was himself again. "Well, why not, my dear?" he said. "If that's what you'd really like."

2

Mid-December in Key West. Bougainvillea foamed over white stucco walls in Christmas-ribbon colors, palms swayed in the soft breeze, sand sparkled like Christmas tinsel in the sun. Streets and shops and restaurants were crowded with adults dressed like children at play, in colorful shorts, T-shirts, sneakers, and sandals. Their garb was the outward sign that for these few days or weeks they were free to enjoy and indulge themselves, like kids on vacation. They had no responsibilities or chores: they did not cook for themselves or make their own beds. They stayed up late at night, and ate when they liked, preferring the childish foods disapproved of by parents and health experts: cheeseburgers, hot dogs, sodas, chips, fries, pizza, and candy.

During the day many of them were at the beach: splashing

in the warm ocean, or lazing in the warmer sand, watching the slow waves lick the shore. Others dawdled along the streets, gazing into shop windows or licking ice-cream cones. The more athletic were jogging, riding bikes, throwing balls, and tossing Frisbees, or out at sea: windsurfing, sailing, snorkeling, deep-sea fishing, or scuba diving. At night they could be seen dining in open-air seafood restaurants, or sitting in bars listening to loud, rhythmic music and exchanging loud, rhythmic comments.

Though most tourists accepted the occasional comic misadventure, it was important to them that overall their vacation should be pleasant. When you spend money on a holiday you are essentially purchasing happiness: if you don't enjoy yourself you will feel defrauded.

There are dangers, though, in enjoying yourself too much. "Real life," when you return to it, may seem painfully drab and confined by contrast. But this is usually temporary and bearable. More serious consequences faced those tourists who did not go home, who enjoyed the freedom and pleasure of Key West so much that they stayed on longer and longer.

What happened then, inevitably, was that these temporary children started to grow up. They bought property, joined volunteer organizations, took jobs, or invested in some local business. As homeowners, workers, or proprietors, they began to view tourism from the other side. When they saw plastic debris washed up on the shore, or homeless people sleeping in alleys, they had the impulse to do something about it. They began to take positions on local issues; they not only read the local papers but wrote to the editor. Some became active in politics, or even ran for office. They agitated to save the reef, change the zoning laws, and permit cruise ships to tie up on Mallory Dock more often or never.

Meanwhile, because they now had jobs and meetings to go to, they stopped wearing shorts and T-shirts and sandals, and changed into shirts and slacks, perhaps even into skirts and suits. For them Key West was no longer a playground. It had become the "real world"—a world in which they were real adults.

Molly Hopkins, the widow of Wilkie Walker's old friend, was one of these ex-tourists. For thirty years she had been coming to Key West every winter: at first only for Christmas and Easter vacation; later, after her husband retired, for the six months and one day that made them official residents of a state with no income tax. At present Molly lived in Key West from October through April, and socialized mainly with other winter residents, or with full-time citizens like Lee Weiss, whom she was visiting on this warm afternoon in early December.

Once, Lee Weiss herself had been a tourist. Twenty-five years ago she had come to the island on impulse for a week's vacation from an oppressive marriage. As a direct result of this interlude, she left her husband. She returned the next season, then stayed on. Eventually she became the owner of a successful women's guest house, and one of the island's semisolid citizens. When she wanted to relax and enjoy herself in a carefree, childlike manner, she left town—usually in August or September, which is hurricane season and the low point for tourism—and went to Europe or to New England.

In the high season, from mid-December through mid-April, Lee had many cares and responsibilities. Now, as she sat on the vine-shaded front porch of Artemis Lodge with Molly Hopkins, she felt that this burden had just been increased.

"Oh, hell. How could you do that?" she exclaimed, sitting forward and letting her natural-fiber knitting slide to the floor. "Don't you know what kind of a reactionary shit Wilkie Walker is?"

"No, not really." Molly, who was reclining on a wicker chaise with her hair fluffed out against the flowered cushion, gave a little yip, almost a sigh. As she aged, she bore a greater and greater resemblance to the Hopkinses' long series of Maltese terriers—especially the last one, Lulu, whose death three months ago still devastated her whenever she recalled it. Molly had the same big brown eyes, pug nose, mildly eager expression, and sparse floppy white curls.

"Didn't you ever read that disgusting book of his, *The Natural Animal*?"

"I don't really remember it. . . ." Molly's voice trailed off. How exhausting young people are today, she thought. In fact Lee was over fifty, and though her Polynesian tan, wavy black mane, and ruffled magenta mumu suggested vigor and sensuality, at second glance she looked her age. But to Molly, at eighty-one, Lee seemed young, as almost everyone did now. There were so few grown-ups around, so few sensible people left alive in the world.

"Made homophobia respectable, that's what he did," Lee growled, staring at the dramatic orange and vermillion blossoms of the trumpet vine that partially veiled her veranda from the street. "He's quoted everywhere by those Family Values creeps. Prize-winning scientist states, etcetera . . ."

"But that was years ago. I know he doesn't think that way now."

"Yeah? Did he take it back in print?"

"I'm not sure—"

"Then it doesn't count."

"Honestly, it didn't occur to me that anyone would mind," Molly said, surprised by the persistence of her friend's reaction. Usually Lee flared up and simmered down fast. "And it's not as if he were living here."

"Yeah, but he's staying in Jacko's front yard. How's that going to work out? And it's not just Jacko, I mind for every gay person on the island. Including myself. That goddamn book of his nearly destroyed me as a person."

"Really?" Molly restrained herself from asking what else Lee could have been destroyed as; she had recently resolved to stop protesting the contemporary misuse of language. "I should have thought that would be difficult."

"Now it would, sure," Lee admitted. "But you didn't know me back in college. Well, hell, I didn't know myself. When I discovered I was attracted to women, this teacher I thought was so great gave me Walker's book. Said it would help me. So I read how I was sick and unnatural, because animals aren't queer. According to Walker, whatever animals do is natural and good. Homosexuality is a disease; it's got to be treated and wiped out. And then he goes on about how we've got to preserve some scruffy old mouse that's no use to anybody." She lapsed into brooding silence.

"You know Wilkie Walker hasn't been well lately," Molly remarked eventually.

"Oh yeah? What has he got?"

"I don't really know. But his wife said she thought he ought to be in a warmer climate this winter."

"Jesus." Lee slammed her glass of iced tea onto the wicker coffee table. "All right, let him be in a warmer climate. He's got the whole state of Florida to chose from, not to mention the rest of the Caribbean. Why should he have to come to Key West?"

"I suppose someone recommended it. It's where a lot of writers go, after all."

Lee made a hostile noise. "So when does he hit town?"

"January second, I think."

"Ugh. Less than a month away." Her angry grin showed square white teeth. "God, it's going to be disgusting. I can see it now. You'll have a dinner party for him, and then people like Roz Foster will take him up because he's famous, and he'll be everywhere. Sneering at gays and holding forth on our threatened environment and giving little inspirational talks to the Friends of the Library on Bubba Beaver or whoever his latest animal character is. And that backlash bitch his wife too."

"Oh, Lee." Molly sighed again. "Jenny's not a bitch. She's a perfect lady."

"Yeah, well, it comes to the same thing sometimes. I've read about her too; she's always mentioned in those interviews. The happy fulfilled wife and mother, the devoted secretary and research assistant. And some smarmy quote. 'I see my role in life as making it possible for Wilkie Walker to be truly productive.'" Lee raised her voice to a shrill, whispery caricature. "Sorry. But when I think of that type of female I get riled up."

Molly shook her head slightly. Did I ever take such inconsequential things so hard? she wondered, as Lee began a review of the unliberated beliefs, statements, and actions of these females, much of which her friend had heard before. Perhaps when I was in my teens, she decided; but I was rather ashamed of it even then. I had been brought up to believe that except at the worst moments of life you didn't curse or carry on. Because if you did, nothing would be left for those moments. It was like that old rhyme of Dr. Johnson's:

> *If a man who turnips cries*
> *Cries not when his father dies,*
> *Is it not a proof he'd rather*
> *Have a turnip than his father?*

Molly had cried for her father, and miserably, wrenchingly, month after month, for her husband. But for two years now she had not cried, except in private when her arthritis was at its worst. She couldn't imagine getting seriously upset because someone she didn't want to see was coming to Key West. The world was full of people Molly didn't especially want to see, but she recognized that they had as much right to spend the winter here as she did.

"So what's been happening with you lately?" Lee asked at last.

"Oh, nothing really." Molly smiled briefly. She recognized Lee's question as not so much an expression of interest as a friendly willingness to listen rather than talk for a while. But Molly had always found it boring to speak of her own life. After over eighty years she still did not understand why people enjoyed talking about themselves so much—even insisted on it—and were so eager to repeat facts they already knew. Sometimes she wondered if they were not wholly convinced that they existed and had to keep proving this.

"Look, I'm sorry I flew off the handle about Wilkie Walker," Lee said, apparently taking Molly's silence for rebuke. "I know you weren't deliberately planning to make things unpleasant for me."

"No. I wanted to make them easier for Jacko, that's all," Molly said. "He's been trying to rent Alvin's house ever since those people from New York canceled, you know."

"Yeah, I know," Lee admitted, her tone shifting to one of concern. For years her friend Perry Jackson, who was also a year-round resident of Key West, had made his living partly as a landscape gardener and partly as the caretaker of the estate of a former lover, a rich, fussy, tiresome old man called Alvin. He had the rent-free use of a one-room cottage on Alvin's property, and was enthusiastic and knowledgeable about plants. Last month, Jacko had tested HIV-positive.

"How's he doing?" Lee asked. "I haven't seen him since Sunday, but he's due here this afternoon."

"Oh, he looks fine. It could be ten years, you know. Or more."

"He told me he's thinking of flying to Europe in July or August."

"I'd go now, if I were him," Molly said slowly.

"Jacko wouldn't do that," Lee protested. "He wouldn't let us all down that way in tourist season. And besides, it's winter now over there."

"All the same, I'd go fairly soon," Molly said. "While I was well."

"You think he's getting sick? Oh hell—Has he—Did he say?—" Her voice faltered.

"No, not at all. It's just that one never knows. It could be ten years, or it could be ten months." In Molly's mind, death appeared as a sort of invisible flying red dinosaur, like the one on a red rubber stamp marked AIR MAIL that she sometimes used. Or rather, considering everything, there was probably a whole company or battalion or army of flying red dinosaurs. These stupid, greedy reptiles cruised forever over the Earth, occasionally and randomly swooping down to snatch someone in their long carnivorous jaws. Sometimes, since they were not only stupid but clumsy, they dropped their victims again in a more or less damaged condition (heart disease, stroke, cancer, diabetes, fractured hips). But, drawn by the scent of blood, they would be back.

Molly herself was one of those whom the flying dinosaurs had snatched up and dropped. As a result she now had bad eyesight, a wonky heart, and crippling arthritis. Not too long from now, presumably, the dinosaurs would return for her. When her arthritis was worst, she hoped it would be soon.

One raw icy day last spring, when she was just back in Convers and winter was supposed to be over, she had stood on her porch staring at the foul frozen heap of dirty snow the town plow had dumped across her driveway again, and felt in her aching wrists and knees the exhausting, probably impossible labor of shoveling it away so she could reach the supermarket. Then she had raised her eyes to the heavy ashen sky that promised still more snow. "All right!" she had called aloud. "Come and get me now, why don't you?"

But usually Molly wanted the flying dinosaurs to stay away a little longer, because the world was full of things she didn't want to miss: an upcoming party, a new detective story by Tony Hillerman or Susan Conant, a Thai restaurant that had just opened, a visit from a granddaughter back from an archaeological dig in Ireland. Also, always, there was her curiosity as to what would happen next. For her, both Convers and Key West were full of interesting characters and ongoing soap operas, and her children's and grandchildren's lives were like long-running, richly populated comic strips. Would Captain Tony run for mayor again? Who were the man and woman seen making love in the empty lot behind the glass shop on Simonton Street at noon? Would her son be transferred to his west coast office, and if so would his wife refuse to leave her job, as she had threatened? Would her niece Clarissa marry the self-proclaimed Druid she had recently met? It would be a shame, really, to miss the next installment.

"Hey, here's Jacko now," Lee said.

A white pickup truck had just pulled into the driveway of the Artemis Lodge. Stylized green flames flowed backward across its hood, and the inscription on its door read GREENFIRE GARDENERS. From it, a beautiful young man emerged. He had curly dark hair, aquamarine eyes, an athletic physique, and a deep golden tan. It was impossible to tell from his appearance either that he was ill or that he was gay.

Molly looked at him with concern. Like everyone who knew Jacko, she was always watching him now for signs of illness. So far there had been none, but the anxiety of this surveillance had begun to show in the watchers, producing the look of eyestrain and narrowed, focused vision that Molly remembered in plane spotters on Cape Cod during World War II. Meanwhile Jacko, perhaps consciously, seemed determined to prove their watch unnecessary. A month ago he might have taken the porch steps casually; now he bounded up them two at a time.

"Hi, how's it going?" he asked. "Hi, Molly!"

"Oh, fine," Lee replied flatly. "Except I hear you've just rented Alvin's house to a world-class homophobe."

"A homophobe?" Jacko took this in slowly. "You mean Wilkie Walker?"

"That's right." Lee nodded sourly. "He thinks we're disgusting and unnatural. He wrote a whole book about it."

"That was years ago," Molly protested. "Twenty years at least."

"You said he was a famous scientist," Jacko protested, glancing at her uneasily; he liked celebrities, and would sometimes announce their presence in Key West to his friends.

"Yeah, so what?" Lee growled.

Jacko did not reply, but Molly could almost see the words LOOK, I DIDN'T KNOW ANYTHING ABOUT THAT, I JUST NEEDED A TEN-ANT passing through his mind as if on the illuminated bulletin board in Times Square, and being denied utterance. Avoidance of the unpleasant was one of his basic instincts.

"Hey, is it okay if I let Marlene out?" he asked, gesturing at his truck, where a plump white cat with green eyes stood with its paws on the sill.

"Oh, sure. Those two women from Montreal with the allergies went home Sunday, thank God."

Released, the cat followed Jacko back up the porch steps and leapt onto the low back of a wicker rocker, where it sat upright, waving its tail as the chair swayed.

That would make a good picture, Molly thought in spite of herself, for she had given up art. Every few weeks lately she made up her mind not to draw anymore: it was too hard to see the paper, too awkward and painful to hold the pen. Besides, there was no point in it. *The New Yorker,* under its new management, wasn't buying her vignettes; and her dealer was politely dim about sales possibilities, definitely discouraging about a show. But then something would catch Molly's eye: a spider and her web in a shop doorway, a bearded monkeyish man with a live monkey on his shoulder, a sweet-lime tree swarming with ragged black and white children.

"I just want you to know, I'm not coming to your house while those people are on Alvin's property," Lee warned Jacko.

"Really? That's too bad," he said in a neutral tone.

"And don't you ask me to meet them, either," she told Molly. "If I see them I'll spit on them."

"Oh yeah?" Jacko said. "Mrs. Walker too?"

"Yeah. Because in a way she's worse than him. She's a traitor to her sex. If she has any sex, which I doubt. And Walker's a creep, take it from me. You're going to wish you'd never rented Alvin's house to them." Lee laughed angrily, but Jacko did not respond; he merely smiled with the tolerant confidence common among physically beautiful people, who know that they make a contribution to the scene simply by being there.

"I tell you what, though, Molly," she added, laughing more easily. "Maybe you could get rid of them, the way you did with Seymour."

"Really, Lee," Molly said. "Who says I got rid of Mr. Seymour?"

"Hell, I don't know," Lee replied. "Everybody. They say you scared him out of town somehow."

"It wasn't like that at all." Molly giggled slightly. "I only gave him a little push."

"She told him the tap water was full of poisonous chemicals," Jacko volunteered from the porch railing, where he had assumed a graceful, watchful pose which echoed that of his cat. "All sweet and concerned, she was. She explained that it didn't bother her that chemical poisons were slowly building up in her body, because she wouldn't be around for long, but she thought he ought to know."

"That wouldn't work with Wilkie Walker," Lee said. "Where the environment is concerned, he's probably convinced he's the expert. Nothing anybody else says would make a dent in his mind." She scowled. "So how long are they staying?"

"It's not settled. Two, maybe three months."

"Ugh, really? Isn't Alvin coming down this winter?"

For a long moment, Jacko didn't answer. He shifted his posture and rubbed his sea-green eyes. "I don't know," he said slowly, and then in a rush, "I don't see why it has to be such a fucking big secret. Alvin is—He's in the hospital with a stroke; he might be dying, that's what his secretary said when she called this morning, and please don't tell anybody."

"Oh, I'm sorry," Molly and Lee exclaimed simultaneously. Neither of them liked Alvin, but he was a Key West institution, and they were unsettled, as they would have been by the sudden demolition of an ugly but historic local landmark.

"It just doesn't seem right," Molly added with a helpless gesture.

"Yeah." Jacko glanced from one to the other, registering their embarrassed inability to express real sorrow. "It's rough. I'm going to miss him. Well, I guess I'll start on those aralias."

As Jacko disappeared around the side of the guest house, carrying a pair of clippers and a trash can, Molly and Lee looked at each other.

"Alvin isn't all bad," Lee declared finally. "He always writes a check for AIDS Help, even though it's not for much, considering the kind of money he has."

"He gave a hundred to the Everglades Fund last year," Molly said. "A lot of rich people who come here don't even do that."

Having discharged the obligation to speak only good of the dying, they turned to more pressing matters.

"Yeah," Lee said. "But the real question is, suppose Alvin does die, what happens to his property?"

"I think he has relatives," Molly offered. "There's a brother, or maybe it's a sister. They've never been down here, though, as far as I know."

"If they sell the place, they could get a lot for it," Lee suggested. "Or somebody could buy it for a condo development. There's the big house, with that separate apartment over the garage, and Jacko's cottage. And you could make over the pool house; it already has two dressing rooms and bathrooms and a wet bar."

"Maybe whoever buys the property will keep Jacko on as caretaker," Molly suggested.

"Well, hell, they should," Lee said. "He practically created that fantastic garden out of crabgrass and marl." She lowered her voice. "But what happens if Jacko gets sick?"

"When."

"What?"

"Not if," Molly said wearily. "When."

"I suppose so. What a bitch," Lee muttered. "You know Jacko has no health insurance," she added. "He was joking about it last fall; he said it brought on trouble, made you careless. He said that after his friends signed up they fell off ladders or got ringworm. Talk about stupid."

"Probably he couldn't afford health insurance," Molly suggested.

"Yeah. Probably not." Lee picked up her glass, in which the ice had now melted. "He never got himself tested for HIV, you know," she said. "They did it without asking when he cut his arm replacing a window in Alvin's greenhouse."

"I know." Molly sighed.

"I can't relate to that," Lee said. "I couldn't take not knowing. Hell, it'd be on your mind the whole time, right?"

"I suppose it would," Molly said. The knowledge of approaching illness and death was often on her mind, though as seldom as she could manage. Think positive thoughts, she kept telling herself. Concentrate on the things you can like and enjoy.

For a few moments they were silent. Molly observed the warm wind as it ruffled the trumpet vine; she heard birds trill and insects buzz in the tall poinciana tree that shaded the street in front of Artemis Lodge with its sprays of delicate leaves.

"It's so pleasant in Key West," she sighed. "It doesn't seem as if anything really awful could ever happen here."

"I know," Lee replied. "That's what I used to think too."

3

In midafternoon the oversized pool behind the oversized house shimmered turquoise in the January sun. Since it had been built in the 1940s, before Mosquito Control, the pool and its adjoining pool house were enclosed in a giant cage of wire netting. Many tropical flowering plants and white-painted metal chairs with tropical-flowering cushions shared the enclosure, and mango and orange trees provided a lush, jeweled shade at one side.

Jenny Walker lay in one of the double-width lounge chairs, laxly turning the pages of *Harper's,* at loose ends. The phrase was her grandmother's, and was associated in Jenny's mind with a sense of guilt and with her grandmother's cream paisley shawl, its fading, mystically patterned cashmere unraveling into long tangled fringe.

At home Jenny was never at loose ends. Even when she wasn't working with Wilkie, there was the house and three acres of lawn and garden and woods to look after. There was shopping, cooking, mending, errands, letters to write; people coming for lunch, tea, and dinner, and to interview Wilkie; the cleaning lady and the gardener; the bills and investments. And, whenever there was time, her sewing and knitting and weaving and tapestry projects.

But here, after the initial flurry of unpacking, stocking the refrigerator and pantry, and getting the computer, printer, fax, and answering machine set up, suddenly there was almost nothing for her to do. The caretaker, a pleasant young man called Jacko who lived in a cottage on the property, cleaned the house and tended the exotic flowers and shrubbery. She had no loom or sewing machine here, and it was far too hot to work on the tapestry cushion she had brought, or the Kaffe-Fasset wool sweater. And often she didn't even have to shop or cook because they were eating out.

What was most disturbing was that for the first time Jenny was also free of her real task in life. For years, whenever anyone asked her what she "did," she had replied patiently: "I help Wilkie with his work." "Our work," she might have said if she were less modest, for Wilkie's books were full of sentences, and even paragraphs, that she had composed. In *The Copper Beech,* for example, much of the chapter on the uses of beechwood and beechnuts had been transcribed verbatim from her research notes.

Wilkie recognized the importance of her contribution: every preface he had written from *The Salt Marsh Mouse* on ended with a warm tribute to "my wife, Jenny, without whom this book could never have been written." Occasionally other people recognized the literal truth of this statement: the copy editor of *Wolves of the West,* for instance, had declared at one point that Jenny's name ought to be on the title page with her husband's, not just in the preface. If Jenny agreed, this rather angry young woman had said, she was going to tell Wilkie and his editor so. "Oh, please don't do that," Jenny had exclaimed. "I don't want it, really. Besides, even if the research is mine, most of the ideas in the book are Wilkie's."

She knew that in the 1990s many people found her attitude strange. "Jenny's a walking anachronism," a loud-mouthed, temporarily tipsy acquaintance had said last year when introducing her at a college reception. "She devotes herself full time to her husband, like a Victorian wife." And years ago her daughter, Ellen, in junior high school and in the first rush of intoxication with feminism, had asked her, "Mom, don't you ever want to have a real job, and earn some money of your own?"

"No, darling," Jenny had said. "Because no job I could possibly have could be as important as the work I do with your father."

But now Jenny found herself wishing that she did have some kind of outside job. Since they'd arrived in Key West, Wilkie hadn't asked her to do any research, and she still hadn't been given the final chapter of *The Copper Beech* to edit and type into the computer. She also couldn't persuade him to answer even the most pressing business letters or return phone calls. "Let it wait awhile. We're on vacation, for Christ's sake," he kept saying.

Yes, Jenny thought, as she lay in the speckled shade by the lukewarm pool; but in the past she and Wilkie had worked just as hard on vacations. Often her computer could hardly keep up with their output of letters, essays, lectures, reviews, and books. Every morning after breakfast they would plan the day's work, and Wilkie would often erupt from his study several times a day to add to the list. But over the last few months these discussions had slowed, slowed now to a complete stop. Most days there was nothing at all for Jenny to do. Wilkie still retired after breakfast to the guest bedroom she had set up as his study, sometimes requesting delivery of a sandwich and coffee or iced tea at noon; sometimes descending for a brief, almost silent lunch, then reascending with the *Times* under his arm. At five he reemerged and walked to the beach for his daily swim.

When they met people, Wilkie was almost his old self; often he talked freely and at length, volunteering information and opinions. But if they didn't go out in the evenings a dark weight of silence settled over the luxurious tropical house. Wilkie, once so warmly communicative and confidential, spoke to her less and less, and sometimes hardly responded to her questions or comments. And when Ellen or Billy phoned he seemed to have almost nothing to say to them.

Something was wrong, dreadfully wrong—but what? When Jenny, trying to shield her growing anxiety under a light tone, asked Wilkie how he was, how he was feeling, or how he liked Key West, he always smiled perfunctorily, hardly glancing at her, and said "Fine, thanks." The last time, though, when perhaps she hadn't kept her tone light enough, Wilkie almost grated out these words, adding, "Why do you keep asking that? If I weren't fine, wouldn't you be the first to know?"

"Yes, I guess so," Jenny had stammered.

What made everything worse was that in the past few days Jenny had realized that she herself was not fine. For one thing, she almost couldn't bear this rented house, with its luxurious but exaggerated and rather vulgar contemporary decor. Most of the furniture seemed to have come from two stores on Duval Street that specialized in expensive camp. There was far too much chrome and leather everywhere, too many mirrors, and too many large-scale glaringly colored representations of tropical flora and fauna, especially flamingoes. Jenny had put some of the smaller monstrosities, like the phallic dark-red wax anthuriums, away in a closet. But there were others she couldn't do anything about, such as the giant coffee table in the sitting room: a thick ice-green sheet of glass supported on the heads of two grinning plaster monkeys, which must weigh half a ton.

When the furniture wasn't vulgar it was unfriendly, and encouraged unfriendliness. The free-form orange leather sofa was overstuffed and hard, like sofas in motel lobbies; the folding screens painted with exotic flowers and birds blocked the view of what other people in the house were doing, and the indirect lighting and heavy silk-shaded lamps made their expressions obscure. On the king-sized "floating platform" bed Wilkie and Jenny slept far apart, like strangers, and the bed didn't sag or creak when he got up at night, so she wasn't always aware of his absence.

Even the soundproofing, which was supposed to be such an unusual advantage in a Key West house, was unfriendly. Back home in Convers, even if Wilkie's study door was shut Jenny could hear him moving around inside, sometimes playing tapes of waves or bird song as he worked. Here, when he went into the study after breakfast, it was as if he had totally disappeared.

What was Wilkie doing all day shut in that upstairs room with its camp cherry-vanilla color scheme and distant view of the sea? From material evidence, she knew that he filled in the *Times* crosswords and the Sunday acrostic; presumably he read the rest of the paper and some of the magazines whose change of address she had conscientiously arranged.

Perhaps Wilkie was napping in there, since he was still sleeping poorly at night. Or perhaps he was writing and rewriting *The Copper Beech*. But if so, why was he so silent now, so withdrawn? Once they had talked easily, continually, and when Wilkie was working on a book or an article or a lecture, which was practically all the time, he had shared his ideas with her and often incorporated her suggestions. "You're my ideal reader," he had told her more than once. "You appreciate everything that's really good. And when you don't understand something, it means I'm not making myself clear." Now there were days when they hardly spoke.

Maybe Wilkie was having writer's block, Jenny thought. He'd never had it before, but according to an article she'd read it could infect anyone anytime, and mostly you just had to wait it out. But meanwhile, what was she supposed to do all day? What was she actually doing?

Essentially, nothing. Wandering around the huge unfamiliar supermarkets, or lying in this antimosquito cage reading some magazine or novel, occasionally sploshing back and forth in that box of overwarmed water. No doubt Wilkie had noticed her idleness. Hadn't he said just yesterday (after denying again that there was anything wrong or anything she could do for him) that she ought to get out and see the sights, meet some people?

Used as she was to following Wilkie's directions, Jenny hadn't yet really followed this one. Though she'd loved going to strange parts of the world with him, she hated being a solitary tourist in her own country. She'd tried it one day here: walking through the Hemingway House alone, and then sitting alone among families and couples on a glass-bottomed boat while the tour guide described the sea life swirling vaguely and promiscuously below their feet. She knew long before the day was over that she deeply disliked the public aspect of Key West: the homogenized "tourist attractions," the raucous bars whose loud music and loud customers spilled out onto the pavement, the shops crowded with neon-pink seashells and T-shirts with extraordinarily vulgar slogans printed on them. The half-dressed tourists who thronged Duval Street, drinking and eating and smooching, not only offended her aesthetic sense but reminded her that Wilkie had hardly touched her since they'd arrived.

Even here, lying by the pool, Jenny wasn't comfortable. The humid air was cloying; the giant potted hibiscuses—six or seven feet tall, some of them—with their huge red and shrimp-pink blooms, made her feel small, as if she were one of those miniature people in that children's book, *The Borrowers,* that her son, Billy, had liked so much. And after all she was a kind of Borrower here, living in someone else's house, among someone else's outsized furniture, lying inertly by their outsized pool— A pool potato, that was what she was turning into.

Jenny sat up abruptly, dislodging the magazine, which fell to the ground in a flurry of white pages. At least she could get some exercise, she decided. She would walk down to the beach and go for a long vigorous saltwater swim, just as Wilkie did every day.

Hot and impatient by the time she reached the ocean, Jenny plunged across the warm, coarse sand past the various cautionary signs that were posted there. She'd seen them before, including the amusing one that forbid "intoxicating beverages and dogs." So she barely glanced at and dismissed a new hand-lettered placard that announced in red capitals:

DANGER: MEN-OF-WAR.

Taking a breath of warm, salty air, she strode into the cool salt waves. Yes, that was more like it! As soon as the water lapped over her knees she began to swim vigorously away from shore, her ponytail of pale hair streaming out behind her. The exertion, the cool caress of the heaving aqua-green sea, felt wonderful. Why hadn't she come here before, instead of plowing back and forth in the overgrown concrete bathtub behind their house?

She turned onto her back and lifted her wet head. Pale sky above, wide aquamarine sea below, punctuated with white gulls and distant white handkerchief sails. And though the temperature of the water was perfect, there were no other bathers in sight; only sluggish tourists lounging or prone back on the sand. How indolent they look, Jenny thought, taking another strong stroke through what felt like a floating mass of seaweed.

Aow! A searing pain fastened itself on the back of her upper leg. Jenny screamed, tried to stand, and sank. She swallowed saltwater and came up choking and splashing, spitting ocean, gulping, thinking Sharks!, crying out against the burning biting sensation that grew worse every second. "Aaoo! Help!" she screamed.

"Here. Hang on to me."

Somehow a long-haired woman had appeared close beside her. She had her strong arms round Jenny, was pulling her toward shore.

"Swim, damn it!"

"My leg," Jenny choked. "I can't—"

"This way . . . Okay, you can touch bottom now."

Jenny felt with her good leg and stood. Weeping, coughing, sputtering, leaning gratefully on her rescuer, she staggered through the last small waves and limped onto the sand.

"My leg," she gasped. "I don't know what— I'm sorry—" She bent sideways, trying to see the wound. "Was it a shark?"

"No, you just ran into a jellyfish," the woman said. "Come on, I have what you need." Supporting Jenny closely and warmly, she helped her up the beach.

"Wait here just a sec. Yep." From the capacious basket of an old bicycle, she brought out a jar labeled Adolph's Meat Tenderizer. "Okay, let's see. Where does it hurt? Yeah, it really got you."

Jenny twisted round and looked over her shoulder. There was no bite, no blood; but the back of her left thigh and most of the quarter-moon of buttock exposed by her new high-cut pale-blue bathing suit was an inflamed scarlet.

"Right. Hold still." The woman sprinkled Jenny's rump liberally, as if she were planning to roast it. "You'll feel better in a moment."

This kind, strong person is crazy, Jenny thought through her tears and pain. I've got to get away from her, find a doctor. "That's all right, I'm all right now," she lied . . . and then, surprised, realized that the fire was easing. "Hey, it is getting better, really. Thank you. What's in that jar?"

"Meat tenderizer, like it says." She held out the jar. "It's papaya enzyme, actually. I always carry it just in case. They say you can use a ripe papaya too, if you have one handy."

"I didn't know— Thank you." Swallowing the last of the saltwater, Jenny looked at her now evidently sane rescuer. The woman seemed to be about her own age, but half a foot taller and more squarely built, tanned and striking-looking in an almost Gypsy style. She had thick, streaming-wet, dark hair and was wearing a fire-red T-shirt and cutoff jeans, now drenched with saltwater and clinging to her generous figure. "How did you—"

"I was out on the pier, I heard you scream. What the hell were you doing in the water, didn't you see the sign?"

"Sign?"

"Men-of-war." She pointed.

"Men-of-war is jellyfish?"

"Yeah. Where the hell have you been all your life?"

"In New England, mostly." Jenny answered the rhetorical question. "I only got here about two weeks ago, I didn't know—men of war—I thought that meant battleships."

"You thought they'd put up a sign warning swimmers of battleships?" Her laugh, like her body, was strong and warm.

"I didn't know," Jenny repeated, beginning to feel cross and embarrassed as well as grateful. Then, ashamed, she added, "I mean, I heard there was a navy base here, so I thought— I'm sorry. My husband will think I'm a total idiot."

"Don't worry about it. How do you feel now?"

"Much better, thanks." Jenny's thigh and hip still stung, but no more than a moderate sunburn.

"Can you manage by yourself, do you think? I have to get

back to the guest house so my desk clerk can pick up her kid at day care."

"Yes, sure. I'm fine, really."

"Okay. Here, take this. Have a shower when you get home and then put some more tenderizer on."

"No, I couldn't—"

"Don't be dumb, you'll need it. I don't know where you're staying, but somebody there should have warned you. Next time you come to Key West— Have one of these." She dug in her bicycle basket again and produced a printed brochure.

"Thank you. Thanks for everything, you really—" But the woman had mounted her bicycle and was riding off. Jenny turned the brochure over and read, in rustic capital letters, the words ARTEMIS LODGE.

In the pleasant study his wife had arranged for him—the last of many such studies, he thought blackly, and the least functional—Wilkie Walker sat brooding, waiting. There was nothing else for him to do here: no reason to spend all day imprisoned in the hot half-dark with the blinds lowered to shield his desk from the burning, indifferent Florida sun. But nevertheless his presence here was necessary. It was essential that he appear to be normal, and working normally, so that no one, especially not Jenny, should ever suspect that the death he was planning was anything but a tragic accident.

Though there was nothing to do in the study, Wilkie felt no wish to leave it and explore Key West. In his present state of mind the idea of such an expedition was exhausting, irrelevant, even repellent. For him the whole world was smudged and darkened. The bright scenery outside registered on his consciousness only dimly and dully, as through a clouded, dirty strip of film like the one he had held up to his eyes as a small child during an eclipse of the sun. The less he had to see of it the better.

He had been right to come to Key West, though, Wilkie thought. It was best for bad events to take place in neutral surroundings, so that they would not contaminate a house and a town thickly silted with good memories. Besides, in Convers he was constantly threatened with interruption from ex-colleagues and ex-students, not to mention possible visits from his offspring.

Christmas with Ellen and Billy had been hard. Knowing that he wouldn't see them again, Wilkie had forced himself to spend time with the children, to speak with them in ways that they would remember as calm and upbeat and concerned in a fatherly way with their rather uninteresting lives. He didn't enjoy the process and—he suspected—neither did they. For one thing, though he had tried not to say much about it, they must have seen that he was depressed by their choice of professions. He had approved of Ellen's wish to become a doctor; but why should she choose a specialty like neurology, instead of pediatrics or obstetrics, where her knowledge might some day be of use to her family and community? And now Billy had declared an interest in what he called "computer art"—in Wilkie's opinion, an oxymoron.

Already, unless the ocean currents had brought in jellyfish, as they had today, Wilkie went swimming every afternoon to establish a routine and prepare for his tragic accident. All that remained now was to determine its optimum time and place. Late in the day would be best, he had decided, when visibility was poor and there were few other swimmers. Perhaps just after sunset when the light was dimming, the wind strong, the glass-green surf churned and choppy. It would be important to make sure that there were no boats or windsurfers near: he didn't want to be rescued ignominiously.

As for the location, there was a choice of four places, two of which Wilkie had now ruled out. The long state beach was always thick with tourists and too shallow—he would have to wade at least a quarter of a mile before the water was over his head. The city beach was small, usually crowded, and overlooked by buildings. He was hesitating now between the two other options. At Fort Taylor there were often real waves, and occasionally a good strong undertow. But it closed at sunset, which meant he would have to swim out to sea sooner, increasing his chance of being seen and "saved."

The county beach at the end of Reynolds Street had the advantage of being within walking distance, and there was a pier, so he could get into deep water fast. The only problem was that this pier was a favorite location for sunset watchers. Most of them left once the show was over, but a few sentimental couples sometimes lingered; he would have to wait till they'd gone, or were focused on each other.

Only two things delayed Wilkie's departure now. Most important, he had to finish his last (perhaps his best) book, *The Copper Beech.* All that remained was deciding on the final chapter. The actual Copper Beech was still in its prime, and would probably outlive his children—and grandchildren, if any. But for dramatic and didactic purposes Wilkie Walker's monumental biography, like all great biographies, must close with the death of its subject. There were three possible endings; they had already been roughed out and lay on his desk in three numbered folders.

In the first version of Wilkie's final chapter the great tree suffered a lingering and pathetic death: dropping its foliage early, losing its limbs, becoming weaker and more susceptible to insects and disease. As it aged it was gradually deserted by the squirrels and chipmunks and birds that had long made it their home. Then one spring it failed to put out leaves, and stood as a mute gray skeleton among its green companions.

In his second version the Copper Beech was destroyed by hostile human forces: air pollution, acid rain, and a damaged root system due to the digging of trenches for pipes across the campus, a nuisance that was constantly occurring at Convers College. Wilkie had also considered having the Copper Beech chopped down to make room for some hideous new building or parking structure; but this was not only painful to contemplate but most unlikely, considering the symbolic status of the real tree on the Convers campus.

The third possibility was for the Copper Beech to be the victim of natural disaster. Wilkie had contemplated and rejected having his vegetable hero struck by lightning: according to some authorities, beeches actually attract lightning far less often than other trees. He had also ruled out the idea of a tornado—unlikely in northern New England. Instead, the great tree would fall dramatically (perhaps melodramatically?) in a great hurricane.

Wilkie had been aware almost from the beginning that in a sense this book was his own story: the king of the forest fallen. The real Copper Beech, after all, was the most notable tree at Convers College, and was often (like Wilkie Walker) pictured in its catalogue and alumni magazine. He recoiled from the prospect of its ugly, slow, and undignified death as he did from his own. If he were to carry out the symbolic parallel, a sudden tragic accident would be most appropriate. On the other hand, this meant giving up the chance of making a final telling attack on ecological stupidity and vandalism.

The other thing that still held Wilkie back was that there was nobody in Key West for his wife to turn to afterward in her grief and confusion. Molly Hopkins and her friends were all too old and shaky to be depended on for practical help, and when Wilkie was gone there ought to be someone both competent and kind for Jenny to lean on. Often he had been on the verge of asking Molly if she knew of anyone like that in town, but he hadn't been able to invent a plausible reason for the inquiry. And probably Molly wouldn't know anyone anyhow. Her circle of acquaintances resembled a retirement home: everyone in it was old, and many of them were visibly sick and dying. Others, no doubt, were invisibly sick and dying, like him.

Wilkie had had a horror of retirement homes; he had sworn to himself that he would never enter one. But in coming to Key West, he now realized, he had done exactly that. For younger people the island might be a holiday destination, or offer seasonal employment. For the old it was nothing more than a tropical version of Skytop, the awful upmarket "elder community" that had recently appeared on a hill near Convers. Its name alone disgusted him. No doubt it had been chosen to subliminally suggest that all its residents would go to heaven—most unlikely, in Wilkie's opinion, when he considered some of those whom he knew.

A similar calculated cynicism appeared to underlie the financial arrangements of Skytop, disguised in mealy-mouthed good-think language. When you entered the "community" you purchased an apartment or town house for an exorbitant price, almost twice what it would cost on the open market. Then you paid a monthly maintenance fee which was double the standard rent for a similar dwelling unit anywhere else. After you became unable to "live independently," you moved into a hospital wing that was part of the complex, and your apartment or house was resold. You and your heirs received nothing.

Essentially, therefore, the proprietors of Skytop were gambling that you would become disabled or die quite soon; the longer you lived and occupied your apartment—or a room in the hospital wing—the less profit for them. Not a safe proposition for residents, one would think. Wilkie Walker did not envisage a concealed staff policy of euthanasia, but wouldn't there be, sometimes at least, an unconscious bias in that direction?

Several retired professors of Wilkie's acquaintance had moved into Skytop, and when visiting them he had been appalled by their blind complacence as well as their increasing self-centeredness. It was clear to him that though Skytop resembled an upmarket motel, it had deeper parallels to an expensive internment camp. If you lived there, you couldn't help but be aware that every so often one of the inmates would be taken away to die slowly in what was euphemistically called a "nursing facility." You wouldn't know when your turn was coming, but the longer you stayed, the more likely it would become that you would be chosen. And of course eventually everyone would be chosen.

If you didn't die at once, you would be brought back to your luxurious cell terrified and exhausted and damaged, and everyone would be formally nice to you, the way people were nice to Molly's friend Kenneth Foster after he got out of the hospital last week. But the men and women in white coats would come for you again, and again. Finally you would not return.

A little later there would be a tasteful memorial service, with flowers and music and speeches and a printed program. After that, to judge from Wilkie's visits to Skytop, you would be forgotten quite soon. In a few months nobody would even mention you; new prisoners would have arrived to fill the luxurious cells.

Anything but that, he thought; anything. His accidental

drowning would be hard for Jenny and the children, but the shock and pain would pass, and they would remember him always as strong, vigorous, productive, and competent—not as a weak, whiny, damaged invalid. And for this memory to be intact, he must swim out to sea for the last time soon. He would have no trouble doing this: his hip hardly bothered him at all here, no doubt due to the warm weather. But more and more often the sudden sharp pains in his lower bowel came at night, and twice since they'd been in Key West he had seen splashes of fresh blood on the flowered "bathroom tissue"—a horrifying watery red.

He must not swim too far out, since it would be best that his body should be found, to end all speculation that he had vanished on purpose or been murdered. And, irrational as that might be, he did not want to lie on the ocean floor, nibbled disgustingly by fishes. He wanted to be buried in the plot he had bought in the Convers graveyard, under a granite stone and a towering fir, not far from the grave of his old friend Howard Hopkins.

Possibly, before this, there would be an autopsy. If so, the coroner might find the cancer Wilkie knew was there; but of course no one would realize that he had been aware of it. The most that might happen would be that someone—the Episcopal minister in Convers, for instance, at the memorial service— might speak of God's providence in sparing Professor Walker a drawn-out, painful death.

It must be soon. Already, Wilkie realized bitterly, he had

ceased to be reliably competent in one important area; soon, no doubt, he would lose his sexual drive completely. In his mind he heard a voice that had been silent in the world for nearly sixty years: the voice of his Scottish immigrant grandfather, Matthew Wilkie, after whom he had been named. The words were ones he had heard many times in his childhood, whenever—always reluctantly—he had to leave his grandparents' farm and take the bus back to the city. But now they had a darker reverberation. "Willie-Boy," his grandfather's voice said, "it's time to go."

If no appropriate friend turned up by the end of January, he decided, Jenny would just have to depend on the children. Neither of them was ideal for this role, but together they might approximate the ideal: Ellen would be competent, and Billy would be sympathetic and kind.

And of course back in Convers there would be many friends to step in and support Jenny. They would help her to go on with what was left of her life, and gradually to take on the many responsibilities and duties she would have as Wilkie Walker's widow and literary executor. With the help of his lawyer and literary agent, she would manage. She had an orderly mind: she knew where everything was filed and which articles he would want reprinted. She would say the right things to the right newspapers and fend off predatory journalists. She would refuse all access to that illiterate, bossy woman from Indiana who wanted to write his "inspiring life's story"; she would work closely and efficiently with the professor in

Maine whom Wilkie had already chosen as his official biographer. She would know instinctively which papers this young man should see and which should be held back.

About Jenny's grasp of their personal finances he was less certain. Some years ago, when he first began to plan for retirement, Wilkie had tried to speak to her about their future. Since she was a woman, and twenty-four years younger than he, he had explained, the statistical odds were that he would predecease her by thirty-one years. Jenny didn't want to hear about it. "Don't talk like that! You're going to live forever," she had insisted, her voice becoming shaky. When he said that they had to discuss these things sometime, she'd cried, "Oh, but not now!" and made an excuse to leave the room.

Practically speaking, he ought to raise the subject again, to talk with Jenny about investments and annuities. But that was unsafe now, since it would suggest that he had foreseen—or worse, planned—his death.

The county beach would be best, Wilkie thought. He would leave from there on February 1. This would give him time to decide about his last chapter and prepare a final draft. There was no reason to hang around after that. There was nothing for him to do here in Key West, nothing for him any more in this world.

4

On the tree-shaded deck of Molly Hopkins's Key West house, the American poet Gerald Grass, who was once a favorite student of her husband, Howard, sat drinking iced coffee. When Molly first met Gerry forty years ago he was a handsome, good-natured, sincere, likable young man who, many thought, resembled the English poet Stephen Spender. Possibly under the influence of this resemblance, Gerry had also become a poet. Now, though perhaps (as Howard would have put it) not quite on the first team, he had published widely, taught at many colleges and universities, and received his share of awards and grants. Though his blond curls were graying, he was still handsome, good-natured, sincere, and likable.

Like Jenny and Wilkie Walker, Gerry had sought Molly's advice about housing, and as a result he and his current girlfriend were now occupying the apartment over the garage of Alvin's house.

"The place is great," he said in reply to her question, helping himself to another cucumber sandwich, of which he had already had more than his fair share. "I really have to thank you. I'd just about given up on Key West rentals after that last time. You remember: there were no towels, no soap, no toilet paper, no lightbulbs, nothing to eat or drink. All the landlord left us was fleas. Turned out they had three cats and two dogs." Gerry laughed.

"Yes, I remember. Howard drove over with a care package for you that first night."

"He was so great about it. God, I miss him."

"Yes," Molly said a little tightly. She liked Gerry very much, but didn't want to break down in front of him.

"You know, I haven't run into you in New York lately," Gerry remarked. "Do you ever go there now?"

"No, I haven't been in years," said Molly, who had once loved the city but now hated it. For her it was a city of death. Not only had Howard died there, but most of the people she had known in New York were also gone. Other editors and art directors were running the magazines that had published her drawings; if she went into the offices where she had once gossiped and laughed and drunk too much coffee and opened her portfolio, strangers would be sitting at the desks. Strangers would be living in all her friends' apartments, and if she knocked on their doors they would not welcome her. The last time Molly went to the city she felt as if she had got into a parallel universe in which she did not exist and perhaps had never existed.

"I don't like it much now," Gerry said. "The place has become totally commercial. I'm glad we came here instead. And it was great to see the Walkers again. He's a wonderful man, you know? And she's a remarkable woman." He helped himself to another chocolate meringue. "A real wife. I thought they didn't make them anymore. Classically beautiful, well educated, intelligent, fantastic gourmet cook. And besides that, she keeps their accounts, drives the car, answers Wilkie's letters, and does all his research. And whatever he believes, she just naturally goes along. For instance, I just found out she's never had a fur coat, to protest animal rights."

"Really?" Molly, who still owned two—an ancient but beautiful Brazilian otter and a rather frivolous but amusing ocelot, both now in storage—thought back. It was true, she had never seen Jenny in fur.

"And I would bet she's totally faithful." He paused, looking at Molly.

"Yes, I should suppose so," she agreed.

"God, if I had a wife like her I could do anything."

"Unfortunately, she's taken," Molly said, adding ice to her glass and voice. She remembered something that Howard once said about Gerry, that the only reason he'd never made it into the first rank of American poets was that he was a copycat. If someone he admired began writing sestinas or waterskiing or keeping a travel journal of a trip to Scandinavia, Gerry wanted to do it too.

"You know, I need someone like that," Gerry confided. "The way it is now, my life is clogged up with errands. Sending out manuscripts, scheduling readings, phoning for plane reservations, packing and unpacking, balancing the checkbook, paying the mortgage, getting the computer fixed and the grass cut, going to the supermarket and the drugstore and the cleaners. It weighs you down."

"Couldn't your girlfriend do some of those things?" Molly inquired.

"Tiffany?" Gerry grinned. "Tiffany is worse than useless. Yesterday I was working on a new long poem, it was really going well, so I asked her to drive over to Fausto's for milk and tea. She came back with condensed milk and powdered iced tea mix." He laughed. "And then she said I should have gone myself if I was so goddamned fussy."

"I thought she was rather nice," Molly said. "Very cute, too."

"Cute." Gerry laughed again, less happily. "I've just about had it with cute."

In the sunny, cluttered kitchen of Artemis Lodge, with its long scrubbed-pine table, comfortably sagging wicker sofa, bright feminist wall posters, and hotel-size blender, Lee Weiss was unpacking groceries from the Waterfront Market. She wore a brilliant fuchsia mumu appliquéd with large purple flowers, and was humming a country-western song: "Please Help Me, I'm Falling."

There were five double rooms and a single in Artemis Lodge, four with private bath. From mid-December to mid-April they rented for from $100 to $150 a night, or $500 to $700 a week, continental breakfast included. During these months the guest house was almost always full. Even with taxes, insurance, laundry, cleaning, gardener, repairs, and a part-time desk clerk, Lee would have done well financially with only two-thirds occupancy. The only problem was that she kept reducing or even waiving the rent for friends or acquaintances, and sometimes for women she'd never met whom friends and acquaintances claimed were ill or in crisis and needed to be in a warm, relaxed place like Key West.

As she stripped the cellophane from three bunches of red and orange carnations, Lee heard the slam of the screen door and then rapid footsteps. It wasn't the tentative approach of a customer, or the guest she expected for lunch in half an hour, but someone familiar with the house, and in a hurry, almost bounding down the hall toward her: Perry Jackson.

"Well, hi there," she said—surprised, since it wasn't his regular gardening day.

"Lee, darling, I had to come over, I've got the craziest news." Jacko leaned against the kitchen door frame in faded cutoff jeans and a dark-green T-shirt, assuming a pose that might have been photographed for a fashion page. He was also fashionably thin: thinner than a month ago, before he had what he described as "a dumb nothing cold"—a cold that had caused much anxiety among his friends. "You won't believe it."

"Okay, I won't." She grinned and slammed the freezer on a quart of coconut ice cream. "Tell me anyhow."

"Alvin's left me his house."

"Shit, really?"

"Really. I just had a call from his lawyer in Chicago."

"Hey, that's fantastic!" Lee laughed with pleasure. "You want something to drink? A beer?"

"Beer would be great."

"You mean the whole place?" She popped open a can, which foamed up excitedly as if in sympathy. "Or just your cottage?"

"Everything. It was in his will, the lawyer read me part of it. 'To Perry Jackson, the only man who ever really loved me for myself, I leave my property at 909 Hibiscus Street, Key West, Florida, and all the buildings and contents thereon.' "

"Wow." Lee opened a beer for herself. "You know though, that's kind of sad. What he said."

"Yeah. I figure that's how it is a lot of the time for rich people. They can't believe anybody really likes them, specially if they've got nothing much else going for them." Jacko ran one hand through his perfect dark curls.

"I guess so," Lee agreed, thinking that in Alvin's case this view might have been correct. "Anyhow, it's great." She put a carton of milk and two of half and half into the fridge.

"Yeah, but the truth is," Jacko said after a moment, looking down and rotating his beer can.

"What?"

"The truth is, it makes me feel kind of crappy. I never loved Alvin, not the way he meant. I was impressed by him at first: I knew I was a lightweight, and he was so heavy in the world. So sure of himself, so much in control. If he wanted to go to Bermuda or somewhere, and there wasn't a convenient flight, he'd charter a plane. I was blown over by how cool he was about things like that. And about being gay. And of course by all the sophisticated people he knew, the places he'd been. But even when we were first together he was hard to get on with sometimes, y'know what I mean?"

"Yeah, I know," she agreed, suppressing the impulse to say more, to use words like "self-centered," and "crabby."

"And then, later on, I was really pissed at him. When I quit law school and moved here I thought, wow, I'm set for life." Jacko looked down, contemplating the little dark hole in the top of his beer can.

"Y'know, there's advantages in loving an older man," he continued. "I can't say I didn't see them. You skip all those years of dead-end start-up jobs, living in cheap apartments, opening cans of cheap chili. But there's disadvantages too. His friends are all older; they think of you as a bimbo, and either they ignore you or make passes."

"Mm," Lee said.

"And then Alvin had so much money, much more than I realized at first. There was a lot of competition for my job, from younger and younger guys. So one day I was just, what do they call it, deaccessioned? Desized?"

"Downsized," Lee said.

"What got to me was the way he acted when he came here afterward. If he was alone it was okay, but mostly he brought along some new boyfriend, and then it was like I was just the hired caretaker. You know. 'We're going out to dinner at Antonia's now, could you clean up the bathroom and bedroom, please.' I wouldn't say anything, but I'd sulk, and curse them behind their backs." Jacko sighed and shook his head. "And now all this property. I was thinking, maybe I shouldn't take it."

"For God's sake," Lee exclaimed. "Are you out of your mind? You made Alvin feel loved, that's what counts. Anyhow, he wanted you to have the place. You've got to go along with that."

"I guess so." Jacko slid onto a kitchen stool. "But you know, by his lights, Alvin was decent to me. I always liked plants and gardening, so he hired me to keep the property up, do the landscaping and maintenance and repairs. He introduced me to friends who needed a gardener or a caretaker, and pretty soon I had plenty of customers. And he never asked for the cottage back; I've been living here for years rent free."

"In exchange for the work you do on the place, you mean."

"Well, yeah. You know Alvin, he liked to get everything cheap."

"He was a tightwad," Lee said.

"Yeah. But I owe him a lot. You can't imagine how ignorant I was when we met. I'd never seen an opera, and I thought espresso was some kind of air freight. I'd been in two plays by

Shakespeare in high school, and never knew he was bisexual. I was a dumb Oklahoma hick."

"Really?" Lee said a little skeptically, setting two tomatoes on the window ledge to ripen.

"Really." Jacko grinned. "Shit, you know, I can't take it in yet. I figured what I'd probably get from Alvin's lawyer was a letter telling me to vacate the cottage by the end of the month." He laughed.

It was what Lee had expected too, knowing Alvin, but she did not say so. Instead she unpacked three dozen assorted croissants and brioche for her guests' breakfasts and began wrapping them in plastic to keep fresh. "So what will you do with the property?" she asked. "You think you'll sell the place, or part of it?"

Jacko shook his head. "No, what for? Anyhow, it could take up to a year to settle the estate, that's what the lawyer said. After that— I don't know. Just play it as it lays, I guess." He drank again, set the can down. "The first thing I'm going to do is get rid of that hideous night-blooming cactus in the front yard."

"Yeah?" An awkward, thorny, barren-looking gray-green vegetable monster, nearly eight feet tall, appeared in Lee's mind. "You didn't plant that yourself?"

"No way. I don't see the point of something that's ugly three hundred and sixty-four days a year. It came with the house. Alvin wouldn't let me take it out, he had some kind of weird attachment to it." He laughed. "And then I'm going to invite my mom down to visit, so I won't have to go to Tulsa this spring."

"Good idea," Lee said. Jacko visited his mother twice a year, attempting (not always with success) to get into and out of town without seeing his other relatives, most of whom violently disapproved of him and his way of life. "I'd like to meet her."

"Sure, we'll fix it up. I just have to clear out one of the dressing rooms in the pool house and put in a bed."

"Can't she stay in the apartment over Alvin's garage?"

"Not now. It's rented to this famous poet from California. Gerald Grass, his name is."

"Never heard of him," said Lee, who, though she read sporadically but with enthusiasm in women's literature, made no attempt to hear of any male poet.

"So you're a property owner," she added presently, putting a bag of jumbo shrimps and ice into the refrigerator.

"Will be, anyhow." Jacko's smile brightened, dimmed. "The only thing is . . ."

"Mm?"

"I wish I hadn't been tested, that's all. I'd be on cloud nine now."

"Mm," Lee repeated noncommittally. In her view, ignorance was never bliss. She visualized Jacko's cloud, not as they are usually portrayed in art, but as she had seen them in the White Mountains: a thick pale-gray mist, blocking visibility. If it were me, I'd have taken the test soon as I could, she thought.

"Some of my pals think I should have had it done years

ago," Jacko said, demonstrating, as he sometimes did, an apparent ability to read minds. He looked away at the dry pods of the women's tongue tree shaking in the breeze outside the window.

"Well, yeah. I can see that."

"I can't. I had a professor at the U of O who was always going on about how knowledge is power. But the way I figure it, with good news you ruin the surprise. And if it's bad, why find out before you have to?"

"I'd like to know if there was bad news," Lee said. "Nobody wants to live in a fog."

Jacko shrugged, smiled slightly. It was not his habit to contradict anyone. "Could be," he said vaguely. "Anyhow, it could be worse. I could be twenty."

"I guess that's so," Lee said, frowning, thinking of kids she knew around town who were twenty, or not much more, and already ill or, in one case, dead.

"The way it is now, by the time I go, I'd be finished anyhow. Once you hit forty, forty-five, it's over, even for me."

"Over, that's crazy," Lee protested. "Hell, I'm fifty-two; my life isn't over, not by a long shot."

"Yeah, but I want to be remembered as young and beautiful." Jacko grinned casually, as if he were kidding. "I don't want to watch myself turn into an old queen, going to bars and cruising the young guys. People saying, You won't believe it, but he used to be really hot. I don't want to turn into a sick, ugly old man like Alvin. And mean. I'd be mean."

"Aw, come on, Jacko," Lee said, laughing. "You could never be mean; it's not in you."

"Listen," he told her. "If I was old and sick and ugly, I'd be mean, you'd better believe it." He laughed. "I'll tell you one thing: I'm not going to hang around till I'm like poor Tommy Lewis, shoved along the street in a wheelchair, hooked up to a breathing machine. Soon as I know it's over for me, I'm out of here." He smiled easily. "So how's business?"

"Good. Full up. I lost two more flamingo beach towels yesterday, that's all. It was those women from Southampton in the big balcony room."

"Yeah?"

"It's always that way. It's the rich guests that lift things. They figure, cute towels, it won't matter to her, what's a few dollars?"

"You could send them a bill."

"Yeah, I might do that. Sometimes people pay up, if they think they want to come again. Or they could decide to stay somewhere else next time. Maybe I'll just write it off as a tax loss." She smiled.

"You're looking good today, you know," Jacko said.

"So are you," Lee replied, though with less emphasis; Jacko always looked good. "Well, the thing is," she added, trying and failing to suppress a wide, embarrassed smile, "I've got some news too. I think I'm in love."

Jacko raised his eyebrows. "Hey, really? Anyone I know?"

"No."

"One of your breakfast and bed-me types." Jacko grinned. It was not unknown for Lee's guests to propose an erotic fling, often with the same slightly embarrassed sensual hopefulness with which they asked for extra pillows, or an egg with breakfast. Now and then she obliged them.

"No."

Jacko registered Lee's expression and the shift in her grip on a bottle of tonic, as if it were about to become a weapon. "Sorry," he said. "So do you want to tell me about it?"

"Yeah, sure. I—" She sat down at the kitchen table, took a breath, paused.

"Okay; how did you meet, for instance?"

"Well, hell, it was kind of ridiculous. And kind of romantic. Day before yesterday, I rode my bike down to the city beach for a swim, but the jellyfish sign was up, so I just walked out along the pier. Nobody was in the water except this one woman, and then she started to scream. So I went in and helped her out onto the beach, and shook some tenderizer on her leg, where she'd got stung. She's got beautiful legs, so long and white and smooth, and this goddamn amazing long silky hair, not blonde but the palest pale brown. She was terrified, shivering all over. She didn't know about jellyfish; she thought she'd been attacked by a shark or something."

"So you rescued her, and she fell into your arms."

Lee gave Jacko a fast, furious look. "Of course not. She thanked me, and I rode back home. I didn't know if I would ever see her again in this world, but yesterday morning she turned up here to thank me, with a beautiful white moth orchid. You can see it right out that window." She pointed.

"Oh, yeah. Lovely," Jacko agreed. "It's a sign, don't you think, the flowers people give you? This car dealer I once dated, he sent me one of those orchids that look like a bunch of big brown spiders, very rare and expensive, according to him. I should have figured out then I was the fly, but—"

"You know, it kind of reminds me of her, that long spray of creamy white flowers," Lee interrupted, gazing out the window.

"So then what happened?" Jacko sighed.

"Nothing. Well, everything, maybe. I don't know. She's coming to lunch today. We haven't even kissed yet, but there's time. She's down here for two months, renting a house near Higgs Beach. I don't know if she's ever had a serious relationship with a woman, but I'm hoping she's open to it." Lee, still contemplating the spray of orchids, fell into a daze.

"Mm," Jacko prompted.

"She's a lot like me in some ways; she admires the same films and books, she knits and weaves—she got really excited when she saw my loom. I think Key West is going to be great for her, she's spent every winter freezing up in New England somewhere. The only problem is, she's married. But it sounds like that relationship is more or less dead. He's much older than she is, a retired professor."

"Ah?"

"Another thing that's kind of romantic, I don't even know her last name yet. Just Jenny."

For the first time, Jacko did not smile sympathetically; instead he frowned. "You said her husband's a retired professor, a lot older?"

"Oh yeah. Like twenty or thirty years, maybe. She can't be much over forty."

"And they're down here for the first time, in a house on Hibiscus Street?"

"Yes— How do you know that? Have you met them somewhere?"

Jacko looked at the floor, out the window, toward the front hall, and finally at Lee. "I guess I better tell you," he said.

"Tell me what?"

"I know your girlfriend's last name." Jacko looked away again, cleared his throat. "It's Walker. Jenny Walker."

"Walker?" Lee frowned.

"They're living in Alvin's house."

"How do you mean? You mean, she's— Oh, shit."

"You said you always wanted to know bad news," Jacko bleated, moving back as if anticipating violence.

"That's okay." Lee set her jaw. "Hell, I should thank you. You've probably saved me a lot of grief."

"I hope so. Hey, I'm really sorry."

"No sweat," Lee said as casually as she could manage. "There's other fish in the sea."

"That's right," said Jacko, for whom the oceans had always teemed. He smiled, relieved.

With some difficulty, Lee suppressed her true reaction to

Jacko's news for the remainder of his visit. But once she was alone, her face darkened. Jenny Walker, she said to herself. The first woman I've seen in four years that I could really love. So beautiful, so gentle, and she's read all of Willa Cather. Except she's married to Wilkie Walker, so probably she thinks like him about everything. Probably she votes Republican and thinks all homosexuals are sick.

I might as well phone now and tell her not to come to lunch, Lee told herself. A whole pound of jumbo shrimp that I went all the way to Stock Island for, wasted. Goddamn it to bloody hell. She turned to the cupboard, took a chipped breakfast plate out of the stack, and flung it at the cellar door, where it smashed with an explosive crunch.

It's like some awful kind of retribution, Lee thought. I said that if I met Wilkie Walker's wife I was going to spit on her. And by God, I did spit on her too, when we were at the beach. I was sprinkling the tenderizer on her leg, and I wanted it to work faster, so I spat on my fingers and rubbed it in. A vivid image of Jenny's upper leg and half-exposed haunch: white, smooth, cold from the sea and flushed with streaks of red, appeared in her mind. Yes, she thought.

No. You can't, don't love her, Lee told herself, opening a cupboard door to get the broom and dustpan. It's just cognitive dissonance. The theory that you naturally overvalue someone you've helped, because the more wonderful they are, the more wonderful and important it was to help them. Nobody wants to think they've rescued some uptight homophobic Republican from panic and jellyfish.

But hard as she tried, Lee could not superimpose upon Jenny the role of uptight homophobic Republican. Okay, she was that self-satisfied old bastard Wilkie Walker's wife. She was also beautiful, intelligent, and desirable. That, years ago, she had married Wilkie Walker did not prove the contrary; other intelligent women had made similar mistakes.

As she gathered the fragments of crockery into the dustpan, memories gathered in Lee's mind. She recalled how under the influence of her freshman English teacher and Wilkie Walker's stupid book, she herself had married before graduating from college, in order to get over her "neurotic attraction" to women. To make everything worse, she had chosen a conservative Presbyterian from rural Ohio who shared Walker's view of homosexuality as an unfortunate disease, as if she wanted to reinforce her guilt and her determination to become "normal."

With a sigh, Lee recalled some of the things her husband had said about what he called "deviants," even before their marriage, and his discomfort when two obviously gay men were shown to the table next to theirs in a restaurant on their honeymoon. She remembered his political views, and the expression on his face as he politely suggested that her Brooklyn relatives would not enjoy a vacation in the country—assuming, that is, that as urban Jews they would have no appreciation of rural WASP America.

She recalled how awkward his family had made her feel when she visited Ohio: the embarrassed twitch of their features when she did not know the name of some common flower or tree. No doubt if she were to become better acquainted with Jenny she would soon see these expressions again, on Jenny's face.

But on the other hand, possibly she wouldn't see them. Possibly Jenny wasn't in complete agreement with Wilkie Walker. After all, she hadn't said anything positive about him: only that she couldn't have supper with Lee because she had to make dinner for her husband, and that she could come to lunch anytime because he worked in his study all day and usually had a sandwich at his desk. Also, that day at the beach, Jenny had said that her husband would think her a "total idiot" for having misread the sign about men-of-war.

Perhaps Jenny wasn't totally an idiot about her husband, at least. Perhaps, even, she was in the state of growing discomfort and disillusion Lee remembered so well from her own marriage. Maybe what she needed was help in resisting the clinging, stinging jellyfish personality of Wilkie Walker. Maybe Lee could rescue her again, from him.

Opening the fridge, Lee removed the jumbo shrimp and put them in a saucepan with half a glass of white wine and a handful of fresh herbs. She'd have to go very slowly. Jenny might agree with everything Wilkie Walker thought and said. She might be completely happy with him. But if she wasn't . . .

Years ago, broke and battered and bruised by marriage—at the end, literally as well, though she had to admit she'd got in a couple of good licks herself at the time of the final breakup— Lee had despaired of vengeance on the homophobic WASP world. Back then, a twenty-six-year-old lesbian graduate student and single mother from Brooklyn had no power in that world. But now— Well, now we would see.

She turned off the stove and removed the lid from the pan, exposing the shrimp, now no longer gray and hard-shelled and icy-cold, but a delicious pale, steaming pink.

5

On a warm day in February, in Alvin's postmodern chrome-
yellow and chrome kitchen, Jenny Walker confronted the remains of last night's dinner party, her first in Key West. Every
horizontal surface was covered with the plates and cups and
glasses and flatware and cooking pots for eight people, all
coated in the dried remains of homemade cheese dip, seafood
bisque, lemon chicken, tropical fruit salad, cheesecake, three
kinds of wine, and mixed drinks.

It hadn't been Jenny's idea and wasn't her usual practice to
leave the dishes. But after their guests had gone Wilkie had
insisted on her coming to bed, hardly giving her time to put
away the leftovers—something he'd not done for years.

That was wonderful of course; but it was also one more example of the erratic behavior of her husband over the last few

months. He was sleeping irregularly again: almost every night, if Jenny woke he would be gone. Once when she mentioned this the next morning, and asked again if there were something on his mind, he had almost exploded. "I really wish you wouldn't keep asking that," he'd snapped in a tone that made Jenny recoil and recall the birthday crackers that used to frighten her as a child. "You worry too much, you know," he had added, less explosively and with an indulgent but impatient smile, as if he were speaking to a fearful child. It was the manner he had toward her often now, as if he knew something she didn't know, perhaps something awful.

But though Wilkie was so strange with her, so disconnected, he seemed to be getting back in touch with the rest of the world. He had started reading his correspondence and accepting invitations to write articles, to lecture and attend conferences and serve on panels—and now without any of the concern about fees and travel expenses he had irritably voiced last fall. "It doesn't signify, darling. I can afford it, after all," he said when Jenny pointed out that the letter about the symposium in Washington didn't mention airfare.

Wilkie had also agreed to last night's dinner party; and during most of it he had been affable and animated. He was full of ideas and opinions—some almost extravagantly upbeat, as with his extended praise of Molly's deceased husband; others sardonically downbeat, as when describing the future of the northeastern woodlands. But soon after ten, when they were sitting over brandy and decaf, he lapsed into a preoccupied silence that caused their guests to rise and say that they must be getting home.

Wilkie continued to spend most of the day in his study, but now Jenny knew he was working, since on Monday morning he'd sent her to the library for books. It was a bizarre selection, however, even a disturbing one. The volumes on the diseases of plants, animals, and humans, and those on death and dying, presumably meant that *The Copper Beech* would be a tragedy, a warning to the world; that its last chapter would expand to mention many other losses and extinctions. But what explained the books on the Gulf Stream and ocean currents, or those on wills and copyright law?

She would find out soon, because yesterday, just before their guests arrived, Wilkie had revealed that *The Copper Beech* was almost finished. There were a couple of changes he still had to make, he said, but in a few days the manuscript should be ready for her. "Oh, that's wonderful news!" Jenny had cried out, and kissed him impulsively, almost laughing with joy and relief. He had not kissed her back.

It's not that he's angry with me, she tried to tell herself as she scraped dried seafood bisque off Alvin's expensive and hideous green and orange art-deco crockery. It's just that he's been working so hard, even harder than usual. After all, he's been finishing a great book—perhaps his greatest book. Probably that was why he'd been so strange and distant. That was why, for weeks, his silence and absence had weighed on her like stone, and why whenever she moved nearer in bed he had shifted away.

But now, perhaps, all this was over. Last night Wilkie had embraced her eagerly and almost rushed her into the bedroom. Breathing hard with pleasure and anticipation, Jenny had helped him peel off her chiffon party dress printed with pale-brown leaves and ferns; she had tousled his hair as he bent to kiss her breasts, rubbed against him, done all the private, affectionate things she had been longing to do for weeks.

In the end, as had sometimes happened in the last few years, her pleasure had been more complete than his. No doubt the gin and wine and brandy Wilkie had drunk, the lateness of the hour, and the labor of finishing his book were responsible. And this morning, when he'd looked so cross and hardly spoken to her, he was probably just hungover. But none of that was important, Jenny told herself. The important thing was that they had made love again, and that *The Copper Beech* was almost finished.

And once it was finished there would be so much for her to do: the final draft to edit; notes and quotations to go over; illustrations to find; captions to write; correspondence with Wilkie's agent, editor, and lecture agent— Their life together would begin again; it would be full and satisfying again.

They'd been through a difficult time, Jenny admitted that to herself now. Their daughter, Ellen, had probably been right: Wilkie had been depressed, or at least very preoccupied. And Billy had been right too: it had been good for Wilkie to come to Key West. And for her too. The excuse she'd used had turned out to be true: she hadn't had a cold since they arrived. Besides, she'd made an interesting new acquaintance.

No, not an acquaintance, Jenny thought: Lee Weiss was already a friend. It was surprising, because Lee was so different from her other friends, but Jenny was starting to like her as well as or maybe even better than most of the women she knew in Convers. It was a different kind of relationship than any she had at home though, because it had nothing to do with her being Mrs. Wilkie Walker. Lee, in fact, didn't seem very interested in Wilkie, probably because she didn't care about nature and the environment. Really, if you were honest about it, you'd have to say that Lee was an anti-environmentalist, the first one Jenny had met in years. There were lots of them around, of course, but naturally the Walkers didn't see much of them.

Lee was open about her opinions—her prejudices, Wilkie would have called them. When Jenny mentioned that her husband had probably done more than anybody in America to save endangered species, Lee wasn't impressed. "The thing is," she'd said, "I grew up in Brooklyn. The main endangered species there is *Homo sapiens*. And *Femina sapienta* even more."

But surely, Jenny protested, rather shocked, it was possible to care about both people and animals.

"Maybe," Lee said. "But that's not usually how it works out in real life. Like for instance, suppose there's this kind of ugly inedible fish that's only found on the reef off Key West, and you tell me you're trying to save it from extinction. Okay, why not, I say. But then I find out you want to ban fishing and snorkeling, the way some morons here are proposing. You do that, and half the guys who work on the charter boats will be out of a

job, and that includes good friends of mine. I figure the important thing to save right now is people."

As Jenny heard these heretical remarks, made with smiling
ease in Lee's kitchen over a wonderful lunch of fresh shrimp and
avocado salad, her mouth fell open, and she felt unable to reply.

"You know what my mother used to say?" Lee had continued. "She said that nobody's supposed to care as much for
people they never met as for their own family and friends. And
I figure that goes double for fish."

It was rather awful, the way I didn't protest then, Jenny
thought as she finished loading the dishwasher and poured
green environmentally-friendly detergent into the plastic cup.
All I said was that I couldn't really agree with Lee, and then I
let the subject float away. Why wasn't I more forceful, more
definite? If Wilkie had been there he would have been surprised, maybe even angry. He would have thought I was a
coward.

And in fact, after that Jenny had hardly mentioned Wilkie's
ideas to Lee. But it wasn't cowardice, she told herself as she
heaved another stack of food-encrusted pots into the sink. It
was because I knew my arguments wouldn't convince her of
anything—not yet, anyhow. Until we know each other better,
they'd only make her unfriendly, maybe even turn her away
from me.

Another thing that made Lee different from Jenny's friends
in Convers was that she not only wasn't part of a couple but
didn't seem to mind. Lee had been married once, but the mar-

riage hadn't worked out or lasted very long, though she had a grown daughter in Boston. Then she'd lived with a woman for a while, but that hadn't worked out either. Right now she didn't seem to be involved with anyone, or want to be. She's been unlucky in love, and now she's given up on it, Jenny had thought when she first learned this, whereas I've been lucky and am married to a famous man. But Lee didn't seem to feel unlucky or sorry for herself the way Jenny's divorced or widowed or never-married friends in Convers did, or show any sign of envying Jenny's life. "Finally I'm living the way I want to," she had said.

It was satisfying in a way to know somebody who didn't value her more because she was married to Wilkie. Most of the time Jenny could never be absolutely sure of this. In fact, she thought, except for Lee Weiss, the only people in the world who I'm sure like me without reference to Wilkie are my parents and my children—and our cleaning lady in Convers, who really doesn't like Wilkie at all, because of the run-ins she's had with him over moving papers on his desk.

It wasn't that most people schemed or expected to profit from Jenny's connection to Wilkie. But she'd noticed long ago that if she met someone on her own, quite soon they would start talking about how much they admired his work, and how they would love to meet him. And when Jenny's new friends met Wilkie, whenever he was in the room they would look at him and not at Jenny, and they would address most of their remarks to him. If the friend was a woman, sometimes she would sit close to Wilkie and kind of coo at him in a very irritating way.

It was restful to be with somebody who would never act like that. Lee had not said once that she'd like to meet Wilkie, and when Jenny had invited her to last night's dinner party she had declined, giving the excuse that she had to stay at Artemis Lodge in case guests showed up.

"Oh, that's too bad. But maybe you can come another time," Jenny had consoled her.

"Sure, maybe," Lee had replied, and somehow at that moment it became clear that she had absolutely no desire to meet Wilkie Walker. She doesn't care anything about him, she's my friend, all mine, Jenny had caught herself thinking childishly. And considering Lee's opinions about environmentalism, it was maybe just as well that they should never meet.

It was always fun to see Lee. She knew so many amazing stories about Key West: its history, and the crazy characters who had once lived here, or still did. The Last Resort, Lee said people called the place. Not just because it was at the end of the Keys, but because it was where you went when other places hadn't worked out.

Lee had been a therapist before she bought Artemis Lodge. "Yeah. Certified Ph.D. in counseling," she had admitted. "But I burned out after a couple of years. I finally realized that I could spend the rest of my life sitting in a box in Brooklyn Heights all day long, forty hours a week, with a different unhappy person coming into the box every hour. And most of them I couldn't really help because they were stuck in some destructive New York job or life situation, the same way I was. Besides, sooner or later most of them came down with transference. They began to project and thought they were in love with me, or they hated me, or I was their mother.

"I started to feel like a big waterlogged sponge. Not the kind you buy at Fausto's, but the ones divers bring in here, dripping with weepy saltwater and gritty sand. When I came to Key West for a week's vacation that first winter I thought, hey, this is what all those poor schmucks need: a little light and sun and air. Then I thought, hell, that's what I need too."

Having been a therapist came in useful, Lee said, when neighbors or guests got difficult. "It's simple," she had explained. "All you do is, you just repeat the last thing they said, and it makes them think you're sympathetic and sort of defuses the situation."

Because Lee had been a therapist and didn't want to meet Wilkie, Jenny felt she could talk about him without being disloyal. She hadn't said much yet, just a bit about the way he'd been for the last few months and that she was worried. "Yeah," Lee had commented. "It sounds like there's something on his mind."

It was easy to talk to Lee about anything. She was interested in things Wilkie naturally wasn't, even before he got so strange: novels and art, cooking and decorating and sewing and crafts. Lee had a big loom set up in her bedroom, and she had catalogs and patterns for all sorts of things you could make in a warm climate with cotton and silk and rayon chenille yarns. She'd taken Jenny to a shop on Duval that carried these yarns, and lent her a pattern for a sweater.

Besides, Lee was so attractive; it was pleasant just to look at her. That shouldn't make a difference in how you felt about people, but it did. It was lovely to watch someone who moved so gracefully, and had such glowing butterscotch tanned skin and such thick, shiny dark hair, with red sparks in it when she sat in the sun on her wide front porch.

"Hi there."

Jenny glanced up from the pot she was scouring. In the open doorway to the patio stood Tiffany (Tiff), the current girlfriend of the poet Gerald Grass, whom she and Wilkie had known slightly for years. They often met at official events, and she'd heard him read at a couple of pro-environment rallies where Wilkie had spoken—except it wasn't reading really, it was more like chanting. The last time, Gerry had accompanied his chanting on Indian drums decorated with beads and feathers. He was sometimes interviewed about poetry and social protest on television and by newspapers and magazines, and shown in photos with folk singers and rock stars.

In general, Wilkie approved of Gerry. He might be a little naïve and theatrical, but his heart was in the right place. Jenny, however, could not quite forget that ten years ago he had left his wife, whom she really liked, replacing her with a series of younger and younger women.

Since last week Gerry and Tiff had been renting the apartment over the garage in the compound, and they had been at last night's dinner party.

"Oh, hello." Jenny turned off the faucet. She was not especially pleased to see Tiff, who appeared to her as pretty in an obvious California-blonde way and amiably uninteresting. At the party she had hardly spoken, but she had drunk a lot of very good Chardonnay.

"Hey, that was a really great lemon cheesecake you served last night," Tiff said. "Where'd it come from?"

"Well, here, I guess," Jenny admitted. "I made it."

"Really? God, I could never do anything like that." She gave an almost teenage giggle. "I figured it must be from one of those fancy food catalogs. I mean it was that good."

"Thank you," Jenny said, smiling to take the edge off her tone of voice, which reflected the belief that her cheesecake was probably better and certainly fresher than any catalog cheesecake.

"Gerry would love it if I could cook like that. But I can't do anything except kiddie food. You know, like hamburgers and spaghetti," Tiff added, taking Jenny's smile as an invitation to enter and perch on one of Alvin's chrome and yellow plastic kitchen stools. "And even then sometimes I burn stuff. But what I say is, if he wants a chef, he should hire one, right?"

"I guess so," Jenny agreed neutrally.

"You can't have everything, I tell him. He says sometimes he took up with me for my looks, but I think it was really to get his taxes done for free." She giggled.

"You do Gerry's taxes?" Jenny asked, surprised.

"Sure. I can do anybody's taxes. I'm a CPA."

"Really." Jenny looked at Tiff again: her tight red scoop-neck T-shirt, tight white shorts, and gold frizz of hair.

"Except now I'm on vacation, so don't ask me anything."

"I won't," Jenny said, drawing back.

"I'm sorry. I didn't mean that like it sounded. It's just that usually everybody I know is after me for free advice this time of year. And it gets worse in March and April. I mean, it would be all right if I was still working, then I could just tell them to call me at the office."

"Mm-hm," Jenny murmured vaguely. She turned on the water again; then, realizing that this seemed unfriendly, turned it off. In the resulting awkward silence she remembered Lee's technique. "You would tell them to call you at the office," she therefore repeated experimentally.

"Yeah. Except after I moved in with him last year Gerry made me quit my job. He said he couldn't stand to share me with a computer. He has to have my full attention, he says." This last sentence came out heavily charged with negative feeling.

"He has to have your full attention," Jenny murmured, glancing again at Tiff and trying to see her as an appropriate companion for an established American poet in his fifties. It occurred to her that if there was anything less suited to this role than a domestically incompetent sexpot, it was a domestically incompetent CPA.

"Yeah. I thought that was so great once, when I met him at this party in L.A. The kind of film people that were there, the guys I mean, all they ever want to do is talk about themselves. And if they look at you they never focus above your tits, you get to expect that."

"You expect that, in Los Angeles," Jenny prompted sympathetically, remembering early experiences of her own. Lee was right, she thought; her technique works.

"Yeah. But Gerry was different. He was just as handsome as any of the actors there, but he looked right into my eyes; I thought that was so great. Only now I feel kind of surrounded."

"You feel—" Jenny paused and swallowed the rest of the repeat as it occurred to her that after all she was not Tiffany's therapist.

"But that's how men are, y'know. The more important they think they are, the more of your time they demand. I mean, look at you, right? Like Mrs. Hopkins said, your husband is a full-time job for you."

"Mf." This time, Jenny's murmur was not an assent. She recognized Tiff's tone; it was that of a standard-issue feminist. She would have recognized it sooner if Tiff had been dressed or spoken differently.

Now and then over the years, especially after the children were in school full time, many well-meaning and ill-meaning people had tried to suggest that Jenny was sacrificing a possible career to the demands of a chauvinist pig male. They lectured her, they lent her books, they invited her to join groups of women who got together to complain about their husbands. Jenny had been to one of these groups, where she had discovered that in some cases there was much to complain of, and also that when she herself didn't complain, the other women thought she was silently boasting.

Theoretically, as a modern, enlightened person, Jenny supported the women's movement, and occasionally had been persuaded to send a check to NOW. But in fact feminism had done nothing for her except make her chosen life seem peculiar and estrange her from her friends. She could agree with them that there was no reason why most men shouldn't help with household tasks and child care. But Wilkie Walker was not most men: he was unique, irreplaceable. The work they did together might change, had changed, the world. Jenny didn't want to be forced to abandon this work in favor of some theoretical "career."

This conviction, unfortunately, had come between Jenny and many women who might have remained or become her close friends. But when they cooled toward her, or failed to warm, Jenny forgave them. They didn't understand; they were married to ordinary replaccable men, men whose jobs could be done by someone else if necessary.

"Anyways, it was a great dinner." Tiff resumed, perhaps registering Jenny's silence, and backtracking. "And you were so sweet to that old guy who spilled his wine on the sofa."

"Oh, that was nothing. Wine doesn't stain if you put enough salt on it right away."

"Yeah, really? I never knew that. But you were awfully nice about it anyhow. I wish I could be like that, but I get so goddamned sick of the wrinklies sometimes. Oh hell, I'm sorry. I didn't mean your husband. But all these boring old writers Gerry knows that are always hanging around, and either they act like I'm not there, or they try to come on to me in this kind of slow, creepy way. Sometimes I feel like I'm going out of my mind. I mean, I guess you must run into the same thing, right?"

"Well, sometimes," Jenny admitted reluctantly. In fact, only last night, when she was serving up the cheesecake, an elderly art critic named Garrett Jones had come into the kitchen, praised her cooking, put his arm round her in a too-friendly way, and given her a sloppy kiss. She hadn't protested, because Garrett had obviously had a lot to drink and was only the Fosters' temporary house guest; but she hoped she would never meet him again.

"And the women are worse. They act friendly, but mostly they're just interested in Gerry. Half of them, the old ones, resent me because I'm not Cynthia—you know, his ex-wife. And the others resent me because I keep them from cuddling up to him. Well, I bet it's the same with you."

"No, not exactly," Jenny said, irritated by this caricature of her own recent thoughts. She lowered another stack of dirty pots and pans into the sink.

"And then when I tell Gerry how it is, he says I'm oversensitive, or I'm being paranoid. Sometimes I think he's getting to be like all the other old farts."

"Really," Jenny said, this time allowing a definite chill to enter her voice. She turned on the water again.

"I don't hafta put up with that, I told him. I don't hafta hang around if he isn't ever really there for me, right?"

"I suppose not," Jenny said. She opened the faucet further, causing some of the warm dirty water in the sink to splash onto her white sundress.

"Well, anyhow," Tiff said in a weak voice over the noise of water drumming on aluminum. "I guess I better be getting back. I expect I'll see you around."

"Yes," Jenny admitted without enthusiasm. "I expect you will."

When he reached the corner of Reynolds Street, Wilkie Walker turned for a last long look at the house. The structure was nothing to him—a vacation rental, anonymously Floridian, surrounded by a white stucco wall cluttered with thorny purple bougainvillea. But behind that wall were the two things he cared most about in the world: his book and his wife.

He had made the right decision about the manuscript, Wilkie told himself as he stood on the weed-cracked sidewalk under a coconut palm. He had wavered for a while last week after reading a deeply infuriating letter requesting—in fact, ordering—him to vacate his emeritus-professor office at Convers for six months so that the building could be enlarged to accommodate a computing center. For several days he had played with the idea of revenging himself by accusing the author of this letter—not by name, but so that everyone at the university would recognize him—of the death of the Copper Beech. Slowly and fatally, its root system would be killed by the construction of some such ugly nonsense.

But in the end Wilkie had dismissed this idea. He must think of the survivors: his family, his friends, his critics, and his readers. Some, no doubt, would make the connection between himself and the Copper Beech. If he portrayed it as destroyed by human stupidity, they might think that Wilkie Walker believed that he too had been driven to his death by hostile and ignorant persons. This was partly the truth, but it would make him seem weak, perhaps even somewhat paranoid.

Whereas if the Copper Beech were toppled in a great storm, all anyone could suspect was that Wilkie was gifted with precognition, since trees do not commit suicide. Today, therefore, he had moved the final version of this ending into a central position on his desk with the finished manuscript, and put the others away. As he did so he felt some regret at having to discard the other two versions, both of which contained excellent passages—some of the best he had ever written, in fact. But he knew he had made the right choice.

About Jenny he was less easy. He had planned to make their last days together memorable and intimate, to make her happy in every way—even agreeing to the dinner party she'd proposed to give. But he had had to forgo the long, intimate, relaxed conversations he had imagined their having here in Key West. The trouble was that whenever they were alone together Wilkie was assailed by the impulse to hint at some of what was on his mind. There was even the danger that he might suddenly weaken and tell her everything, as he had more or less done for so many years. At the same time he had become aware of an irrational anger at Jenny because she didn't know what was on his mind—irrational, because he had done all he could to prevent her knowing.

And since he had been successful, and Jenny didn't know what was on his mind—didn't even guess—she did things that irritated him. She kept trying to direct his attention to meaningless national and local events, or to supposedly humorous newspaper stories and cartoons. She proposed social and cultural events, and wanted him to speak to his children on the phone. Just yesterday she had been pestering him to go with her to some film, reading the reviews out loud and telling him that some new friend of hers said it was wonderful. For a moment Wilkie had felt almost hostile to his wife. When he looked at her across the breakfast table she no longer resembled a transfigured human version of a salt marsh mouse. Instead she reminded him of another creature far from the threat of extinction, rather increasing in numbers every year: *Sorex arareus,* the common or garden shrew, with its shrill little twittering voice.

But that was only the impression of a moment. It had been deeply painful today to leave Jenny without a sign, and in his mind he had tried out many last speeches: casual phrases that after the fact would reverberate with meaning. In the end he had resisted the impulse, fearing he might break down, and only called out "I'm going for my swim now." "See you soon, then," Jenny had called back, hardly glancing round; and he had replied, choking up, "Right."

His last words—his last word—to Jenny had been a lie. But a necessary one. What would happen now must seem a tragic accident. Why no, Wilkie Walker wasn't depressed, everyone must say: he was full of energy and plans for the future. Only the night before—

Yesterday he had planned to kiss Jenny casually yet fondly as he passed on his way to the beach, perhaps to compliment her intimately on the dinner party and what he had intended to follow it. That was what hurt, what rankled now more than the sharp occasional pain in his lower bowel. Not only his final words to his wife, but their final significant encounter had been false and meaningless. Last night, their last night together, he had planned to make love to Jenny. He had tried, strained, willed it with all his force—but all for nothing; worse than nothing.

"Darling, it doesn't matter. Really, it was lovely," Jenny had said when, muttering an angry apology, he had lain slack in her arms at last, a heavy, sweaty burden of inert bone and muscle and flesh. Wilkie discounted these words. Of course she would say that, out of politeness, out of love. Silently he had turned away from her and pretended to sleep.

In less than an hour he would forget all this, forever; but Jenny would not forget. That clumsy, humiliating failure would always be her last intimate memory of him.

He could wait a few days, try to make love again—earlier in

the evening, and sober. But suppose there was another failure? Also, today would be his last chance at the ocean for a while. According to the radio a massive cold front was moving in; temperatures would fall into the fifties tonight, and heavy rain was expected. If he went swimming tomorrow under such conditions he would be thought deranged.

Wilkie glanced again at the house where Jenny sat reading a book, unaware of what was to come. Besides great shock and loss, she would have many duties. For instance, she would have to cancel all the articles, lectures, and conferences that would be the proof of Wilkie's intention to live on. Fortunately, she had now made a friend in Key West, some woman who had been a therapist in Brooklyn and now ran a guest house here. Neither of these attributes recommended her to Wilkie Walker, but they had advantages. This Lou? Lil?—something like that— presumably knew the local scene, and also had professional training in dealing with crisis and grief.

"Hi there! Wilkie!"

Dimly, he became aware that someone was shouting his name. As he turned, the waving figure far down the street was recognizable as Gerry Grass, who was occupying an apartment in their compound and had come to dinner last night. Wilkie's first thought was that he was being recalled to some emergency. But as Gerry galloped nearer it became clear that he was grinning, wearing Hawaiian-print swim trunks and carrying a towel—in fact, that he intended to accompany Wilkie to the beach.

Wilkie's first impulse was to turn and run. He had over two

blocks' lead, and could reach the ocean well before Gerry. But how would such a flight sound when it was reported to Jenny, and to the police? He felt a rush of rage and bitterness. Until now he had had nothing against Gerry, whom he had met before on many public occasions. He had agreed to the inclusion of him and his current bimbo in the dinner party—the more witnesses to his nonsuicidal condition, the better, he had thought.

"Going swimming?" Gerry inquired, panting up to him.

Wilkie agreed grudgingly that he was; to deny it and turn back would seem deeply peculiar. It occurred to him that in unconventionally seeking freedom from a painful and constraining future, one had to become more conventional than ever. Acts that might pass without comment if you continued to live became weighted with significance when they preceded your death.

Wearily, he began to stride down Reynolds Street toward the sea. Gerry loped alongside, making noises with his mouth. In the past Wilkie had regarded Gerry as a man of fair intelligence and sound views. Gerry had reviewed two of his books enthusiastically, and Wilkie had more than once quoted from Gerry's impassioned nature poems in his writing.

But since he had left his agreeable wife (a long-standing fan of Wilkie's) and moved to Southern California several years ago, Gerry seemed to have become something of a New Age ninny. Though Wilkie knew for a fact that he was pushing sixty, last night he had spoken of himself as "middle-aged," so as to seem to belong to the majority, just as some rich people speak of themselves as "middle-class."

"You swim every day? That's great," Gerry told him. "You know, I met a really interesting guy in L.A. last month who recommends it. He sees swimming as a form of active meditation; says it helps you to clear your mind and tune into natural rhythms."

Cretin, Wilkie thought, glancing sideways at Gerry. Previously, he had seemed a normal specimen of *Homo sapiens.* Now his athletic handsomeness suggested atavism. Was there not a tinge of the anthropoid ape in Gerry's sloping shoulders, slightly prognathous jaw, and the dusting of gray-peppered curly hair on the rims of his ears?

"Hey, that's an unusual tree—it has two different kinds of flowers," Gerry remarked, stopping to drag down a branch. "What's its name?"

"*Hibiscus tiliaceus.* Mahoe, they call it here," Wilkie replied automatically, noting the low, apelike placement of the thumb on Gerry's hand. Genetic, or a throwback? "The flowers come in yellow, then turn dark red."

The serious problem was, how to elude Gerry once they got into the water. If he could put some distance between them fast enough, maybe he could still carry out his plan. Gerry was ten or twelve years younger; on the other hand, there was a stringy look to him; he didn't have the solid build and smooth muscles of a swimmer.

As they came in sight of the beach, Gerry shifted topics and began to complain of his lecture agent. The guy wasn't getting him interesting jobs anymore, and the fees had fallen. Maybe he needed to change agents. Who handled Wilkie? he wanted to know, and would he recommend this person?

"Well, that depends," Wilkie replied grudgingly, striding across the street. "We'll have to talk about it." You poor sucker, he thought. You're on your way down too. The world is getting tired of you, only you don't know it yet.

The sun was low in a pink sky as they reached the pier, and there was the usual complement of sunset watchers. Followed by Gerry, he descended the slippery wooden steps, plunged into the cool, foamy, bulging and retreating sea, and struck out for the horizon.

But though Wilkie put forth his best effort, his unwanted companion kept alongside with an awkward, splashy crawl. The problem was, he realized, swallowing a mouthful of thick briny water, that though he'd swum almost every day for weeks, he'd never gone very far. He had deliberately avoided increasing his speed and distance, realizing that the greater his endurance, the longer the whole thing would take, the more chance there would be of an unwanted rescue.

"Great, isn't it?" Gerry shouted.

Wilkie did not reply; it had become clear that if he showed any sign of drowning, Gerry would be close enough to officiously try to save him. For the first time in his life he felt the temptation to commit a capital crime other than suicide. Maybe I could take him with me, he thought. We're far enough out now; there won't be any witnesses. A quick choke hold from behind, and if I'm lucky we'll both go under. Let him find that unity with nature he was gabbling about last night.

A cold surge of excitement lifted Wilkie higher than the oncoming wave, then dropped him. The plan was too risky. If it failed, Jenny might be faced not with a tragic accident, but with a half-drowned husband accused of attempted murder.

Gerry, splashing onward, showed no strain, but soon Wilkie's breath was coming short; the waves felt icy as they slapped his head and arms. If he didn't turn back now, he could be in trouble. He might even, ignominiously, find himself actually being rescued by this fuzzy-minded anthropoid ape.

6

At the so-called Key West International Airport, on a cool, windy February evening, Perry Jackson (known locally as Jacko) was waiting for his mother's plane. The shabby lime-green cinder-block structure, with its airline and car-rental counters and racks of tourist brochures, was crowded. Beside the travelers, and people meeting them or seeing them off, there were taxi and van drivers, airline and car-rental and coffee-shop and gift-shop and janitorial employees. There were also a number of unemployed and unemployable persons just hanging out.

Except for the passengers, everyone was dressed casually; most in shorts or jeans and T-shirts. The T-shirts of the natives tended to recommend various off-island commercial products. Several departing tourists, on the other hand, wore T-shirts advertising local businesses or promoting Key West as a vacation spot (New Moon Saloon, Waterfront Market, Island Paradise, etc.).

Jacko, in a faded red T-shirt with the logo of a well-known plant food, leaned against the wall by Gate 2, which was in fact the only gate at the little airport. He was chatting with two acquaintances and looking casually beautiful but preoccupied. Three days ago he had been discharged from the Key West hospital after a short but intensely unpleasant episode of virus pneumonia. Antibiotics had wiped it away in forty-eight hours, but though he felt okay physically, his mind was troubled. This virus, he suspected—no, knew—was the first signal from the other and more fatal virus he carried. A signal from disease, from death. He pictured a small, very ugly man all in black, his pale face marked with purple splotches, getting off a black plane and walking toward him, through Gate 2.

Trying not to think of this, Jacko turned his attention to an acquaintance whose problem was snails in his ferns.

"Beer," he advised when the guy paused for breath. "You put out saucers of beer at night, and they crawl in and get drunk and drown. Blissfully."

"Aw, you're kidding me."

Jacko shook his head. For a bad moment, he visualized the viruses in his bloodstream as sluggish, half-drunk snails.

"What kind of beer?" Jacko's friend raised his voice to compete with a loudspeaker announcing the arrival of Jacko's mother's flight.

"It doesn't matter. Van thinks they like Miller's best, but mine'll drink anything. Hey, I gotta go. See you later."

As the passengers filed in they could be sorted into two distinct species. A few were local residents who had been away briefly: they were relaxed and healthy looking, lightly burdened with luggage and lightly dressed for Key West's perpetual summer. The rest were tourists from the north, pale and weakened by months of cold and darkness and hours of air travel. They were weighed down with carry-on bags, and struggling under layers of heavy dark coats and jackets and sweaters and scarves. Already, in the unaccustomed heat, some were beginning to sweat and look faint. They reminded Jacko of the homeless, hopeless people he had seen in northern cities, dragging or pushing their possessions and wearing their entire wardrobes.

Smiling, he stepped forward to embrace one of these sad souls: a small, pretty but faded woman in her early sixties, with curly gray hair and a sweet, anxious expression.

"Mumsie! You made it." In a traditional gesture, Jacko picked her up and swung her round—as he had first done, triumphantly, on his thirteenth birthday, when at last he was taller than his mother.

"Oh, Perry darling," she gasped as he set her down gently. "I was so scared you wouldn't be here."

"Of course I'm here," Jacko said, unruffled. His mother did not know that he was ill, or had been in the hospital, but sometimes she appeared to know things she had not been told. It was also characteristic of her to express small, senseless fears.

"It's just that so much can go wrong, you know, with airplanes. Oh, thank you. Barbie's got my little bag—" She gestured.

Jacko turned. Behind him stood a large, fair, sturdy young woman in an unbecoming powder pink quilted raincoat, whom he recognized with surprise and without pleasure as his cousin, Barbie Mumpson Hickock.

"Hi, Perry. Uh— I came too. Mom wanted me to kinda, you know, look after Aunt Dorrie. I mean, she thought— It was sorta a last-minute thing, see?"

"Yeah, I see." Jacko hardly smiled. "Well, welcome to Key West."

There was no point in protesting now, he thought as he led his relatives through the crowd to the baggage area, or asking why he hadn't been informed earlier. His aunt Myra, his mother's awful sister, had sent her daughter here deliberately. And not at the last minute either, whatever Barbie thought.

Again, as so often in the past, Aunt Myra had managed to off-load Jacko's boring girl cousin on him. His childhood memories were full of such incidents: scenes in which Barbie Mumpson, two years younger than he and congenitally clumsy, had cluttered up his life. Stumbling after him and his friends on hikes; getting in everyone's way in volleyball; and striking out on his team at family reunion baseball games. Through the years, her sad round face had been preserved at various ages in his mother's photograph album: often streaked with tears, or marred by mosquito bites, poison ivy, or acne.

"Now, Perry, you look after your cousin Barbie." That irritating command had echoed through the first ten years of his life, and the next ten were worse. As soon as he was in junior high Aunt Myra began demanding that Jacko partner Barbie at dancing school and take her to movies and the prom. Later he was pressured to invite his cousin to college basketball and football games and introduce her to eligible men from his fraternity.

"It's not really much to ask, darling," his mother (weakly parroting Aunt Myra) would say. "It's not as if you had a steady girlfriend."

Though Jacko liked or at least tolerated most people, this long forced association had turned him against Barbie Mumpson, especially after he began to suspect, in his last year of college, that Aunt Myra was scheming to marry them off. The idea terrified him, not least because he knew from experience that Aunt Myra usually got what she set her mind on. The dread of her somehow succeeding was one of the things that had driven him to leave Tulsa and move to Key West.

"So where are you staying?" Jacko asked Barbie as they waited by the baggage inlet.

"Gee, Perry, I d'know. Mom figured you could put both of us up in this house Aunt Dorrie says you've like inherited. I'm sorry."

"Well, I'm sorry too," Jacko lied. "I'm living in the gardener's cottage, same as always. Alvin's house is rented until April."

"Aw, I didn't know—" Barbie's voice trailed off, or was drowned in the sound of baggage being thrown into the luggage trough. "Maybe I can find a room somewhere. I don't need anything fancy; I can sleep on somebody's sofa—"

You're not going to sleep on my sofa, Jacko swore to himself as he carried his mother's two small bags toward his truck, leaving Barbie to drag her big one across the parking lot. I've got to have some privacy, for Christ's sake. Jacko's cottage contained only one large room, with an open sleeping loft above the far end and a kitchenette and bath below. Though he never shared it with anyone for long, he had occasional overnight or weekend guests.

Okay, Jacko told himself. You'll have to find someplace for Barbie to stay. Maybe Lee has a vacancy. His spirits sank as he contemplated the unlikelihood of this at the height of the season; the unlikelihood of finding a reasonable rental anywhere in Key West at eight-thirty on a weekend night. And if he couldn't find any place, tomorrow he'd have to buy a bed and move it into the other dressing room of the pool house.

Could it be that after all this time Aunt Myra was still scheming to throw him and Barbie together? She had known for fifteen years that he was gay, but Myra Mumpson often refused to recognize facts that did not fit into her system. No, he remembered with a sigh of relief, Barbie was married now; she'd been married for at least two years to some politician. His mother sometimes sent him clippings from the Tulsa newspaper showing Barbie and her husband campaigning or at official functions.

But if not that, what? Aunt Myra hadn't sent Barbie here just to look after his mother, for sure. Mumsie wasn't as hideously efficient as her sister, but she was certainly capable of flying to Florida on her own. So what the hell was his cousin doing in Key West?

Late the following morning Barbie Mumpson wandered out of the guest room of Molly Hopkins's Victorian gingerbread house in Key West, looking blurred and untidy, but better than she had the night before when Molly had taken her in. The weather had turned damp and drizzly, and the accompanying humidity had already given Barbie's blonde curls more bounce; her face, scrubbed of its chalky foundation, was agreeably freckled. Instead of the hideous beige polyester suit and spectator pumps in which she had arrived, she wore a plain pink gingham dress and sandals. Why, she's really quite pretty, Molly thought.

"Oh, hello. I'm sorry," she mumbled. "I guess I overslept."

"That's quite all right." Molly suppressed a sigh that was almost a yawn. She was tired and painfully stiff this morning—the result, no doubt, of having stayed up past her usual bedtime to wait for Jacko and Barbie. At her age, loss of sleep told on one. "Would you like breakfast?"

"Oh, yeah, sure. I mean, if it's no trouble."

"It won't be any trouble," Molly said. "You can make it yourself. I'll show you where things are."

"I'm sorry." Barbie trailed after her into the kitchen. "All I need really is a cup of coffee. And maybe some cornflakes or something?"

"There are no cornflakes," said Molly, who detested dry cereals of all types. "But there's coffee already made, and bread for toast in the fridge, here."

"Oh, thank you. I'm sorry, I'm so stupid. I meant to get up earlier, honestly."

"Why?" Molly asked, wishing her guest would stop apologizing. "You're here on vacation, aren't you?"

"Yeah— No—" Barbie took a loaf of raisin bread and a butter dish out of the refrigerator. "Well, I guess I am, sorta. But really I'm supposed to be thinking things over."

"Ah." Molly recalled what Jacko had said over the phone last night: "Hey, it's really great that you can put her up. But listen, I should warn you: Cousin Barbie can be a real drag. My whole life, till I got out of Tulsa, she was following me around whining. Everything always goes wrong for her, and if you give her the slightest encouragement she'll tell you all about it."

"It's, well, my marriage," Barbie continued without further prompting.

"Ah." In spite, or perhaps because of Jacko's warning, Molly felt a flicker of interest. "Would you like some juice?"

"Oh yeah. Thank you." Barbie poured, spilling a little, and drank, leaving an orange rim around her soft, rather large mouth.

"Here." Molly held out a paper napkin.

"Oh, thanks. I'm sorry. I'm not usually this helpless, really. It's just that I'm kinda in a state about Bob and everything. I mean, like Mom says, it's a serious responsibility."

"Marriage can be difficult," Molly remarked neutrally,

though she had not found it so; rather, she and her husband had
regarded it as a happy alliance against the world.

"Yeah— No— I mean, sure, I guess it is for everybody. But
for me it's a public responsibility too. I mean, my husband is
Bob Hickock." She paused, obviously waiting for recognition.
"Wild Bob Hickock, they call him."

Molly frowned. A country-rock star? A sports figure?

"Wild Bob Hickock the congressman," Barbie explained.
"He's only in his first term in Washington, but he's already
making a big name for himself. I kinda thought everybody—"

"I don't really follow politics these days," Molly said, suppressing the additional phrase *Thank God.* Not having to read
the *Times* seven days a week, with emphasis on the editorial and
op-ed pages, was for her one of the very few (perhaps the only)
positive results of Howard's death.

"See, Bob's going on to big things. That's what Mom says,
and she knows, 'cause her family has been in politics for like
forever. Bob could go real far, she says. He's a natural. When he
gets in front of an audience, they just about love him to death."

"Really."

"Everybody. Businessmen, or Boy Scouts, or old folks in a
nursing home, or whatever." Barbie, who was still holding two
pieces of raisin bread, looked round dimly.

"The toaster's over there."

"Oh, thanks." She fumbled with the controls. "See, the
thing about Bob is, he's really good looking. Six-five, and he's
got this great deep voice. And real curly hair and these sexy

eyebrows, sorta like two blond caterpillars. That sounds dumb. I mean, caterpillars aren't sexy, but you know, on Bob they are, believe me."

"I believe you," Molly said, though unconvinced.

"Mom told him she thought he should get them trimmed before he went on television, but Bob wouldn't. He really loves his eyebrows. Sometimes he kinda pets them, like this." As she demonstrated, Molly observed that Barbie's own blonde eyebrows were more or less vestigial.

"Well, it must be nice to be married to someone like that," Molly said, thinking how little she herself would have enjoyed it.

"I d'know. The thing is, I keep letting him down. I don't mean to, really, but—" The toast snapped up: she started, flushed.

"Here." Molly slid the butter toward Barbie.

"It's— Well, like there's this thing with food," Barbie went on. "See, when I was about fourteen I stopped eating meat. I've always loved animals, and it just like didn't seem right anymore, you know? But then about a month after we were married, we were at a thousand-dollar-a-plate barbecue, and this journalist asked if something was wrong with my steak, why wasn't I eating it? So I said why, and she put it into her newspaper. Mom was furious. She said, why couldn't you just have told the woman you weren't hungry, or you were on a diet?" Holding the lid of the English china butter dish, which had a cow on it, she looked at Molly helplessly.

"Why should you have done that?" she asked. "There's nothing wrong with being a vegetarian."

"Well, but there is sometimes, sorta. I mean, for a lot of people, in cattle country especially, if you don't eat beef it's an insult. It's sorta like, unpatriotic." Barbie giggled sadly. "The trouble is, when anybody asks me something, I don't think first, I just kinda tell the truth, you know?"

"I can see that might be a handicap for a politician's wife," Molly said. Becoming impatient, she took the two slices of toast away from Barbie, buttered them, and set them on a plate.

"Oh, thanks. I'm sorry, I'm so stupid today—"

"Why don't you pour yourself some coffee?" Molly suggested, pointing to the electric pot, which was more than half full. When her arthritis was bad, as it was this morning, she didn't try to lift the heavy, slippery glass container, but scooped the hot liquid out with a soup ladle. She was reluctant to demonstrate her method in front of strangers, even as inept a stranger as Barbie Mumpson.

"Oh, thanks." Barbie poured, then sat down heavily at the kitchen table with a mug of coffee to which she had added large measures of sugar and half and half. "Hey, this toast is yummy."

A child, that's what you are, Molly thought. "Maybe you should learn to tell an occasional white lie," she suggested in a neutral voice.

"Yeah, that's what everybody says." Barbie sighed. "Only I mostly can't think of any. But it's not just that."

"Mm." Molly lowered herself into a chair.

"It's—" Barbie chewed toast. "The thing is, everybody loves Bob so much, so naturally he just has all these opportunities."

He cheats on you, Molly translated. "I see."

"So then these things happen. Mom says it's my own fault. She says I don't know how to hold my husband's interest."

"Really."

"I've tried, honestly. I read all these kinda weird books, and I went to Dallas and bought this silver lace camisole and panties set that the saleswoman at Neiman-Marcus swore was the latest thing. You wouldn't believe what they cost. Only when Bob saw me he went into a laughing fit and said it looked like I got myself caught in a spiderweb."

"That wasn't very nice," Molly said, making an effort not to laugh herself, or even smile.

"No," Barbie said, as if surprised. "I guess it wasn't." She blinked fast, as if there were something in her eye, then swallowed. "What it is, see, there's this person called Laverna he knows. She's very glamorous, she used to be a showgirl in Las Vegas. When Bob was running for Congress he swore it was all over, and we were going to start a new life together in Washington. But then last month I found out Laverna was in Washington too, because I called up the number he left with his receptionist and she answered."

"Ah," Molly said, this time more sympathetically.

"Bob said it wasn't like that. He said, didn't I think Laverna had a right to visit our nation's capital, like any other patriotic American? I said yeah, okay, but what was he doing at her place at ten o'clock at night? Then I started to cry, and he said, 'Baby, you're hysterical. Why don't you go back to Tulsa for a while, get ahold of yourself?' So I bought a plane ticket and went on home."

"Mm."

"I was crying the whole time, the flight attendant kept bringing me Kleenex. I told Mom it wasn't any use, I wanted a divorce. But she says I should think it over for a while. And she thought I should get out of town, because she didn't trust me not to break down and blab to some journalist, like I keep doing. And besides, then there would be somebody to come to Florida with Aunt Dorrie. It was sorta killing two birds with one gun. Mom likes that kind of thing."

"She likes to kill birds," said Molly, who had begun to form a negative opinion of Barbie's mother.

"Yeah—What? No, it's a, what do you call it, a proverb."

"Really," Molly said, managing to keep her voice neutral.

"So what do you think I should do?" Barbie gazed wide-eyed at her.

"Well." Molly paused. For most of her life she had been considered an artistic and delightful lightweight, and people seldom asked for her opinion on serious matters. But once she became elderly, she was assumed to be wise—perhaps a survival from an earlier age, when simply to live into old age suggested that you were both shrewd and lucky.

"Mom said before I do anything drastic I'd better be sure. She says most men are like Bob. Eventually they run around on their wives, if they get the chance. She says I should think about my future, what it would be like without him. And there's no guarantee I would do any better next time, at my age."

"Really," said Molly, to whom Barbie seemed scarcely out of adolescence. "What is your age?"

"I'm thirty-six. And it's probably true what Mom says. I mean, if I leave Bob I can forget about ever living in Washington again and being the wife of a prominent person."

"If that's what you want from life," Molly said. Barbie, staring into space, did not respond. "So what will you do now?" she asked, as mildly as possible.

"I d'know. I've got to think about it. Mom says if I decide to stay with Bob, she'll tell him he has to treat me right."

"You think that'd have any effect?"

"Yeah, maybe. After all, Bob owes her. Once we were engaged, Mom got behind him in a big way. She raised a lot of money for his campaign, and got him some real professional staff and advance people."

"I see."

"Anyhow, she says we've got the upper hand now, because if people find out about Laverna it could really hurt Bob's career, especially on account of he has a lot of born-again-type constituents."

"You mean she would threaten to tell his constituents about

Laverna," asked Molly, in whose mind a less and less favorable picture of Myra was taking shape.

"Yeah. Well, probably she'd just tell the media, that'd be faster. But she says if Bob listens to reason, she'll get rid of Laverna for good."

"Really? How could she do that?"

"I d'know. But I guess she could if she wanted to. She knows people who can do things for her. She probably knows some even in Washington."

Molly stared at her guest. Was it possible that this naïve young woman was talking about the planning of a murder? "People who do what kind of thing?"

"Well, you know." Barbie chomped on her raisin toast. "I mean, it doesn't hafta be like something drastic," she added, finally registering Molly's tone and expression. "Mom says, with somebody from that kinda background, there's always a charge against them on the books somewhere, or something in their past they don't want to have come out."

"Really."

"Yeah. Like drugs maybe. Or Laverna could have been a hooker once, Mom thinks. Anyhow, she isn't the kind of person a congressman could marry, even if he wanted to. See, in politics you need a wife with a good reputation and the right connections."

"Like you," Molly said. She swallowed another sigh.

"Well, sorta. Except I keep doing things wrong, like I told you."

"It sounds as if your mother wants you to stay married," Molly suggested.

"Yeah, I guess so," Barbie admitted. "She said, if I wasn't sure, I could tell myself I was doing it for Oklahoma."

"Really!" Molly remarked, this time not troubling to keep her tone neutral. "And do you feel you have an obligation to Oklahoma?"

"I d'know." Barbie's voice trembled between a whisper and a wail. "I guess I do in a way. I mean, I'm not much use for anything else."

Molly did not contradict her guest; her response had shifted from sympathy to a weary impatience. Barbie was what her husband used to call an Eeyore, someone who deliberately chose to be helpless and depressed. Why should I feel sorry for you? she thought. You have everything I've lost: youth, health, beauty—at least a plump blonde all-American prettiness—and a future. "I'm going to lie down for a little while now," she said. "If you want anything else to eat, help yourself."

Later the same day Jacko parked his truck in front of Molly's house in Old Town. He had spent most of the morning buying a bed for his cousin Barbie, hauling it home, and wrestling it into Alvin's pool house. Then he had grabbed some lunch and gone on to one of his regular gardening jobs, while his mother napped.

"Hi," he said when Molly opened the door. "Barbie here?"

"Not now. She went on the Conch Train."

"Oh, for shit's sake." Jacko made a face. The Conch Train was a gasoline-powered imitation old-fashioned locomotive, trailed by four open cars painted yellow. Actually there were several nearly identical trains, which all day took tourists round the island while the driver, through a loudspeaker system, described local sights.

"Come on in," Molly said soothingly. "She should be back soon. Would you like some iced tea?"

"No," Jacko nearly growled. "Oh, all right, why not? Sorry, I'm in a foul mood. It was great of you to let Barbie stay here last night, I don't even remember if I thanked you."

"Of course you thanked me. Here you are. Let's sit outside."

"The Conch Train," Jacko repeated, following Molly through the house and onto her side deck. "That's the sort of idiot thing Barbie would do."

"She was very eager to go," said Molly, who had never been on the train, though it passed her house continually. The day she and her husband first moved in, the loudspeaker had called the tourists' attention to a large tropical tree with loose, flaky bark that grew in their side yard. "On your left, just ahead, you will see a fine specimen of one of Key West's native trees. It is a gumbo limbo, but natives call it the tourist tree, because it is always red and peeling."

The first time Molly and her husband heard this joke they laughed. They heard it again soon afterward, and then at regular intervals until sunset. It did no good to shut the windows;

the loudspeaker was clearly audible through the uninsulated walls of the house. Polite calls to the Conch Train office over the next few weeks accomplished nothing; the woman who answered the phone appeared to think that Molly should feel honored to have her tree noticed.

After hearing the joke approximately every twenty minutes for two weeks, Molly and her husband discussed having the tree removed. But it turned out that the gumbo limbo was a protected species; any tree service that destroyed it would lose its license and be liable for heavy damages, as would the Hopkinses. An acquaintance suggested pouring bleach into the roots, but the gumbo limbo appeared to like bleach.

Finally, after getting permission from the Historical Preservation Society (a lengthy process), Molly and her husband put up a fence which cut off their view and darkened the yard, but concealed the trunk of the tree. On one memorable day at the end of the season, the Conch Train passed in silence.

"I got a room in the pool house fixed up for Barbie," Jacko said. "She'll be out of your hair soon." He set his glass down. "And in mine."

"Maybe she can entertain your mother while you're at work—take her to the tourist attractions."

Jacko shook his head. "Mumsie wouldn't like that. What she wants, as soon as she's rested, is to go round gardening with me. She's great with plants: most of what I know I learned from her."

"Will Cousin Barbie go too?"

"Not if I can help it. She'll have to take care of herself."

"It sounds like that's just what she can't do," Molly said.

"Yeah, really?" He laughed. "You know I warned you she'd have some sob story. So what's the problem now?"

"Well." Molly paused, wondering if she should repeat Barbie's confidences to this unsympathetic audience. But no doubt he would hear soon enough. "You have to feel kind of sorry for her," she began.

"Says who?" Jacko rejected the imperative.

"The problem is her husband, mainly. He's been having an affair with some Las Vegas showgirl. Barbie wants to leave him, but if she gets a divorce the scandal will hurt his political career."

"Why should she give a damn about that?"

Molly shrugged. "I don't know that she does, but her mother seems to."

"Yeah. She would." Jacko scowled. "Aunt Myra has an obsession about politics. Her grandfather was a senator, and she thinks every man in the family should carry on the great tradition. She practically railroaded me into law school, and she was furious when I quit. And when it came out that I was gay she wanted to send me to a shrink so I could get cured, and nobody would ever know. Then I could be a senator too."

Molly stifled a little sigh. Though it was not yet teatime she already felt tired. All these stories, all this emotion, she thought, as she had often thought before. When Howard was alive it had seemed natural; she had been part of it. Now she sometimes felt as if she were living in the epilogue of her own life, watching things happen to other people.

"I can't quite see you as a senator," she remarked, glancing at Jacko's purple T-shirt and frayed denim cutoffs.

"Damn right." He laughed. "Listen, I better be getting home; Mumsie's nap should be over by now. Tell Cousin Boobie to call when she gets back."

7

About a week later, in the front room of Artemis Lodge, Jenny Walker sat behind the glass-topped desk with its hotel register, stack of brochures, and vase of orange lilies. This was her third day as Lee's temporary morning guest clerk, and also her first paying job in twenty-five years. She would have been happy to help out for free, but Lee had insisted on the going rate. "Hell no. I'd feel like a cheapskate otherwise. Anyhow you're not doing me a favor, you're doing one for Polly Alter. She was wiped out, trying to work here and get ready for her show next month."

But really, Jenny had explained, Lee was doing her a favor. If she weren't here she'd be at home brooding. The day after the party Wilkie had frozen up again. He remained shut in his room every day, and when he came out it was as if he were there still. He was keeping the last chapter of his book back for more revisions, so there was nothing for her to check or comment on or type. When she'd asked again if she couldn't help somehow, he said that there would be plenty for her to do soon enough. His thin, distant tone made Jenny wonder, not for the first time, if he were angry with her about something. But when she diffidently suggested this her husband denied it. "Don't be ridiculous," he had said, in a way that seemed to contradict the denial.

There was something wrong, Jenny told Lee; something serious. Wilkie had never brooded over a book like this before, never shut himself away from her like this. His new editor had inquired about the progress of the manuscript again only yesterday, addressing his note to Jenny rather than her husband—of whom, she suspected, he was a bit afraid, as many people were.

Jenny, who knew now what it was like to be slightly afraid of Wilkie Walker, had tactfully delayed passing on this query until after supper, when he was usually in a more relaxed mood. But her tact had not been successful. A deep crease had appeared between his eyebrows, and he had used the phrase "damned interference." The interference referred to, nominally, was that of the editor; but as Wilkie growled the words out, the dark thought came to Jenny that they were meant for her. Somehow, her presence had become unpleasant to him, her speech unwelcome. Maybe it was because she'd suggested that they come to Key West, she told Lee. Maybe he hated it here, and blamed her.

Or perhaps it was something else she'd done, something she couldn't even remember. Or something that she was, that she couldn't help. And now the little fear that had haunted Jenny years ago returned: the fear that she was not worthy of a man like Wilkie Walker. Like his first wife, she was not really an intelligent person: she had never been more than a B+ student in college. Dishonestly, knowing it was wrong, giving herself the false excuse that it didn't matter, because Wilkie Walker would soon disappear from her life as magically as he had come into it, Jenny had concealed the weakness of her mind and her grades from him. And then he had asked her to marry him, and it was too late.

During their engagement, and for a while after the wedding, Jenny had dreaded that somehow Wilkie would realize how ordinary she really was. Now, in this ugly expensive house in Florida, this ugly fear had returned. In her anxiety, two days ago, Jenny had confided it to Lee. Suppose Wilkie had somehow discovered belatedly how ordinary and unworthy of him she was, she said. Because they had been together so long, he would probably say nothing about it. He would just slowly withdraw from her, as he had in fact done over the past few months. Perhaps also, in his deep disappointment, he might withdraw from their children, and even, eventually, from other people.

Lee had listened to all this attentively, seriously, as she always did. But when Jenny finished, instead of making some mild or reassuring comment, as usual, she had exploded.

"You're out of your mind," she said. "What the hell do you

mean, you're not worthy of Wilkie Walker? If you want to know what I think, I think he's damned lucky to have you, and if he doesn't realize that, he's a—" Lee paused, swallowing something stronger, and finished, "a complete booby. And you're not ordinary. You're one of the least ordinary people I've ever known."

Remembering Lee's warm, indignant expression as she had said this, Jenny smiled in spite of her confused unhappiness.

It was wonderful to know someone like Lee, even if she might not be right. That was what a real friend was, she thought: somebody who thought better of you than you did of yourself. Somebody you really liked; no, loved. Who loved you too, when the people who should love you didn't. "I feel as if I can tell you anything," she'd said to Lee two days ago, "and you'll never say Bad Girl."

"Same here," Lee had replied, grinning—though it was already clear to Jenny that if anyone said Bad Girl to Lee, she wouldn't give a damn.

Outside it was raining again, for the fifth day in a row, and the air was saturated with damp. It had been too cold and wet for a week to swim; and Jenny had left the house this morning in a heavy misty drizzle that blurred the palms along the street. Her hair, which she had washed before breakfast, still wasn't dry. She pulled the white elastic band off her ponytail and fanned it out over her white T-shirt, where it lay loose and pale and slightly wavy from the humidity.

Three hours times three mornings times twelve: a hundred

and eight dollars a week, the first money Jenny had earned since she was twenty-two. She didn't need it: the Walkers had a joint account, and Wilkie never questioned her spending. But the idea of those hundred and eight dollars pleased her. And it was so easy—just sitting here and answering the phone, taking reservations, dealing with any minor problems the guests might have, and handing out maps and information on tours and shops and restaurants.

According to Lee, Key West was in the midst of what she called "our regular ten-day winter." "Hell, I don't mind," she had told Jenny this morning. "It might chase some of the tourists away, but it gives me time to catch my breath before the first wave of college students hits town for spring break."

Only two of Lee's guests had been driven off by the weather, but those who remained were cross and disappointed. Pretending to be joking, they blamed Jenny for the rain. ("Will you look at it outside! How could you do this to us?")

All morning she had done her best to suggest alternate activities: a tour of the perfume factory or the aquarium; or, if it stopped raining, a visit to the dolphin sanctuary, or a kayak excursion among the mangrove swamps like the one Jacko's mother and cousin were going on today. But nothing seemed to interest Lee's guests. This disturbed Jenny, and when Lee returned at noon she said so.

"Hey, don't worry about it," Lee reassured her, smiling and tossing a sparkle of rain from her dense, dark hair. She was wearing a tangerine-orange nylon poncho that would have been garish on anyone else. "Who was grousing today? Was it Bitsy and her Oriental friend in Room Four?" She opened the screen door, pulled off her poncho, and shook it out onto the porch. How wonderful she looks, Jenny thought, how she lights up the room!

"Yes, them. And those two nice schoolteachers from Connecticut. They didn't want to do any of the things I suggested."

"That figures. Aw, don't look like that, it's not your fault, really. You have to understand that what some people come to Key West for is to do nothing. They could goof off back home, of course, but their superegos won't let them. Especially the New England types."

"Oh, Lee." Jenny looked up, almost blushed. "That's not why I came, honestly."

Lee gave her wonderful, deep laugh. "I know that. I'm not talking about snowbirds like you. There it's mostly fear of winter, I suppose."

"I did rather fear the winter," Jenny said, and paused, recalling that what she had feared most was the effect the darkening days and falling temperatures might have on Wilkie's state of mind. But she had resolved not to mention her husband today: she didn't want to become a one-note whine.

"Well, you're safe from winter in Key West," Lee said in an odd, thick voice. "Luckily for me." She leaned forward and for a moment rested her warm hand on Jenny's bare shoulder and brushed Jenny's face with her warm mouth.

"It's lucky for me, too," Jenny replied as the phone began to ring. The places on her shoulder and cheek that Lee had touched seemed to glow as if a match had been held to them.

Actually I don't always feel safe in Key West, she thought as Lee spoke into the phone; but I do here. That's odd, because the guest house is full of strangers. But they're all women; that makes it safe. ("It was one of the best damn ideas I ever had in my life, only renting to women," Lee had confided last week. "No serious violence, no piss stains on the bathroom floors, no high decibel beer parties, and if women do get drunk they usually don't smash up the furniture.")

"Okay, you keep track of the weather forecast and let me know." Lee hung up and cleared her throat. "Another customer who wants me to guarantee sunshine," she said, and laughed. "See, the problem is most people can't admit that they want to do nothing on vacation. That's because according to the moral system most Americans buy into, it's sin: the sin of laziness and sloth. But at a resort the rules are changed. As long as it's hot and sunny, especially if you're near water, you can take off most of your clothes and lie around doing nothing for hours at a time, and it doesn't count. Sloth is redefined as 'sunbathing,' even if you put a towel over your face and slather yourself with total sunblock. So naturally if it's cloudy, they complain."

"I guess that's true." Jenny laughed.

"Sure it is. Take a look next time you go to the beach, or pass a motel pool. Most people aren't in the water, they're flat out around it. They could save the airfare and room fees if they would stay home, turn off the phone and TV, and lie down in the bedroom, or out in the yard if it was warm enough. And in the evening they could go to expensive restaurants, just like they do here."

"If you did that where I come from people would think you were sick," Jenny said. "I mean, you know, mentally."

"Oh, absolutely. And I'm all for it. If everyone realized how dumb and unnecessary sunbathing was, not to mention what it does to your skin, I'd probably go broke." She laughed. "Hey, let's have some lunch. There's some pretty good fish stew left from last night, and I can make a salad."

"Oh, I can't, not today," Jenny said. "I have to get back. Maybe next time."

"Sure," Lee said. "Well, see you Monday."

I could have stayed for lunch, Jenny thought as she descended the steps of the guest house. The truth was that she had been afraid to stay for lunch; afraid that she would start complaining again about Wilkie, and boring Lee, who was already bored by him even though they hadn't met. And afraid of showing how important Lee was to her, because what if she didn't feel the same way? After all, Lee had lots of friends in Key West; she couldn't possibly love and need Jenny the way Jenny loved and needed her.

It had been raining off and on for days, and the effect on the landscape was depressing. Key West needs sunshine to look its best, Lee had said, and she was right: in bad weather the island seemed drab and shabby and makeshift. Now the quaint little white-painted gingerbread houses were exposed as peeling and gray; most of the bright flowers had been beaten down into the earth, and the luxuriant tropical trees hung over the badly paved streets like clumps of heavy wet spinach.

Because Key West is built on coral rock, Lee had explained, rain drains off very slowly. This morning when Jenny walked to work there was water collected dirty-gray around clogged gutters everywhere, splashing pedestrians like her whenever a car passed. In some places, for instance at the corner of United and Simonton, the streets were two to three feet deep in muddy runoff, and filled with soggy floating debris and with stalled rental cars whose engines had flooded.

Instead of going home Jenny headed for the Key West library, a large pink stucco building surrounded by dripping exotic foliage. Usually it was more or less empty, but today the rooms were crowded with people who would otherwise be strolling past the shops on Duval Street or at the beach. There was also an identifiable population of homeless persons: men and a few women who, in order to avoid the police, normally slept during the warmth of the day on a bench or under a bush in some park, and stayed awake at night when it was cool. Half a dozen of these people, driven indoors by the rain, were slumped on library chairs, pretending to read newspapers or magazines, or blatantly dozing.

Jenny pulled off the stiff, sopping-wet London Fog raincoat that she should never have brought to Key West. It was not only too formal, it didn't keep out the tropical rain, which seemed to come from all directions at once, including the horizontal. She shook out her damp hair, then, hesitantly, approached the circulation desk.

Back in Convers, the staff of the college library always fell all over each other to help Jenny—once even literally, when Mrs. Ormondroyd and one of her assistants collided coming out of the stacks behind the charge desk, both carrying books for Wilkie. Here it was very different. The collection was much smaller, and most of what Wilkie wanted had to be ordered on interlibrary loan. The staff was polite, but it had soon become clear that obtaining items for a temporary resident on a permanent resident's card wasn't their top priority. Jenny was not too surprised now to hear that nothing she'd requested had arrived.

Wilkie wouldn't like that, she knew. In the past he had always been tolerant when a book or a fact was temporarily unavailable. But lately he had developed a nervous impatience, a demand that what he wanted should appear immediately. "You tell them Professor Walker has to have it now, this week," he had said this morning about some book on tides, ocean currents, and navigation in the Keys—a topic unrelated in any way Jenny could think of to *The Copper Beech*.

It wasn't fair, Jenny thought. She was doing everything she could, everything Wilkie asked her to do, just as always. But now she was doing it without joy, and without the rewards. In the past Wilkie had always been lavish with praise and compliments for everything from her creamy scrambled eggs to her discovery of a lost footnote. "Darling, you are a wonder," he used to say, sometimes more than once a day. But now he was withdrawn and unappreciative. And ungrateful: on Wednesday when she came home with a magazine he wanted he had snatched it without even thanking her.

In Key West, even when she had specifically asked that a book be held for Wilkie, it was sometimes reshelved. Hoping that this had happened now, Jenny made her way through the stacks to the shadowy corner where the Florida Collection was kept. But the gap on the top shelf was still there, which meant that when she got home Wilkie would be angry. He would have the face she had seen more and more often lately: the one she had seen this morning over breakfast, in the heavy wet light from the patio: the face of a detached, disapproving man, who didn't even answer when she asked him to please pass the key lime marmalade. "I think he's tired of me," she had told Lee on Wednesday, and for the first time Lee had not been reassuring. "I suppose it's possible," she'd said. "Men are like that."

The fluorescent tube above the stacks, which was on a timer, went out, leaving Jenny in semigloom. She rested her forehead against a row of books and began to weep silently, sheltered by the curtains of pale, damp, silky hair that fell forward on either side of her face.

"Hey, Jenny? Is that you?" The fluorescent light buzzed on, and Jenny wearily raised her head. She saw a man perhaps ten years her senior in a waterproof green poncho. He was tall and loosely put together, with curly gray-blond hair, warm brown eyes, and large reddish ears. Focusing, she recognized him as Gerry Grass.

"Oh, hello," she managed weakly, pushing her hair back.

"Hey— Are you all right?"

"I'm fine." She swallowed a throatful of tears and then a dim smile, realizing that her face must be wet, her eyes red. "Well, actually I've got rather a bad headache," she improvised. "Sinus. This weather, I guess."

"Hey, that's rough. I know; I used to have what I told myself was sinus every winter when I lived in Ottowa. But I think now it was the boredom as much as the climate."

"Yes?" Jenny said vaguely. Go away, why don't you, she thought, and smiled in a perfunctory, discouraging way.

"It's weird, you know, the effect bad weather has here." Gerry continued, undiscouraged. "It rains for a couple of days, and everybody's depressed or angry or both."

Jenny looked at Gerry, wondering if this applied to him.

"I guess you heard Tiffany's left," he added, answering her question.

"No, I didn't know."

"Day before yesterday. I figured Wilkie would have told you."

"He didn't mention it," Jenny said, frowning, thinking, He doesn't mention anything to me anymore, he hardly speaks to me. "Left Key West, you mean?"

"Uh-huh. And left me. It's, like, over between us." For a moment, the young hippie poet that Gerald Grass had once been spoke through his middle-aged mouth, with a half-aggressive, half-pathetic roughness.

Don't tell me about it, Jenny thought. Leave me alone, can't you see I have my own troubles? But automatically, social rules kicked in. "Oh, I'm sorry to hear that," she exclaimed, wondering why this was the usual, almost the only possible polite response to news of any separation. Sometimes, as now, the natural reaction might be, Hey, congratulations.

"Yeah, well."

"I'm sorry," she repeated, though in fact she wasn't sorry Tiffany had left, or even surprised. The only thing that surprised her slightly was Gerry's evident grief. If I was living with Tiffany, Jenny thought, I would want her to leave.

"I guess it had to happen. The relationship was, as she put it, all fucked up."

"Please, could you be a little quiet?" It was one of the librarians, hissing at them from the end of the stack of books. "Other people are trying to read."

"I'm sorry," Jenny apologized again, lowering her voice, and realizing that this time she meant the phrase.

"Anyhow, she cut out day before yesterday," Gerry said, hardly lowering his.

"But you're staying on in Key West," Jenny murmured, moving sideways in an attempt to bring the conversation to an end.

"Yeah. For a while anyhow."

"*Please.*" It was the librarian again.

"Aw, hell. Look, would you like to have lunch somewhere?" Gerry whispered. "I have to hang around this end of town until the copy place finishes the manuscript I just gave them."

"Well—" Jenny began, forming a polite refusal in her mind as she contemplated Gerry's curly wet hair, his sad, wet expression. But at this moment an old saying of her mother's came into her mind: Whenever you feel dreadful, dear, the best cure is to do something for someone else. "All right. Why not?"

"Thassa white heron," the guide in the lead kayak droned in his flat central-Florida twang.

The dumpy little widow sitting behind him, weakly paddling, said nothing. But her niece Barbie, a big, soft-looking young woman in a pink sweatshirt with a picture of a raccoon on it, cried, "Ooh, really?"

Wilkie Walker, paddling the following kayak with Barbie's eager but awkward assistance, scowled. He was no ornithologist, but he knew quite well that the bird standing in the shallows to their left was not a white heron, but an egret. At any earlier period of his life he would have corrected the error, would have taken satisfaction in correcting it. Now he didn't give a hoot in hell. All he gave a hoot about was getting through the days and nights until the weather changed and he could take his final swim in the ocean. It wouldn't happen today, though, he thought. The rain had paused for the moment, but heavy cold whale-colored clouds still sagged low over the Keys.

Wilkie had never been especially attracted to aquatic mammals or plants: according to an amateur astrologer he had once had the misfortune to know, this was explained by the fact that he had no water in his chart. He had come on this trip not out of interest, but to kill time in hell. As cold wet day succeeded cold wet day, his nerves were wearing down, and so was his nerve. Sometimes he thought that if he had to sit in his study for another hour he would end his life in some weak messy way, involving gas or blood.

Yesterday afternoon, unable to stay in the study, he walked into the living room and found Jenny sitting on the sofa, knitting a lump of grayish yarn that, she explained, would one day become a sweater for him—a sweater, of course, that he would never wear. In a few days, after his tragic death, she would set it aside. But probably not forever. Jenny was a practical housewife: she disliked waste, and had never failed to complete any task she had set herself. It was not unlikely, it was even probable, that some day, perhaps months or even years later, she would take up that lump of yarn and complete the project. Someone else, probably their son, Billy, would wear the gray sweater.

But could he be sure it would be Billy? Jenny was still a relatively young woman. After his death she would still be beautiful, graceful, and charming, an admirable cook and housekeeper, a gifted researcher and editor. And she would be well provided for: he had taken care of that. Certainly she would have suitors. It was not unlikely that she would marry again, Wilkie realized—not out of passion, that wasn't her style—but out of affection, loneliness, and a need for companionship and protection. Jenny was, in many ways, an old-fashioned woman. It was one of the things he loved in her, and one that he had—he admitted—indulged and cultivated. But once he was gone, it would make her vulnerable.

A wave of cold, unfocused jealousy washed over Wilkie, causing him to flub his next stroke with the paddle and send a corresponding, though smaller, wave of cold saltwater back into the kayak and onto Barbie Mumpson. "Sorry," he muttered, glancing round briefly.

"Aw, that's okay."

Wilkie scowled. He realized that he was angry at everything and everybody—even his wife—because they were going to live and he was going to die. Right now, for instance, he was angry at Barbie Mumpson, and at her aunt, and at the tour guide. But most of all he was angry at Perry Jackson. It was Jackson, the caretaker of their rented house, who had inveigled Wilkie into today's excursion. Jackson's mother and cousin Barbie were visiting him, he had explained, and he'd set up a trip for them to the dolphin sanctuary on Sugarloaf Key and then a kayak tour of the mangrove swamps; wouldn't Wilkie like to go too?

It wasn't goodwill that had prompted this invitation, Wilkie thought now. What Jackson had wanted was somebody with a car who would drive his boring relatives up the Keys so he wouldn't have to go himself. And he, Wilkie, had agreed in order to get out of the study for a few hours.

Jackson's mother, Dorrie, appeared to be a harmless, quiet little woman. But Cousin Barbie had almost immediately revealed herself as a fan of the most gushing sort. "Wilkie Walker!" she had screeched with embarrassed excitement when they met. "You're Wilkie Walker, I mean you're really him, I can't get over it! You've been my hero ever since I was a little girl. I've read everything you've ever written— And now I'm actually going on a nature trip with you, I can't get over it!"

To break the flow of gush, Wilkie had announced that he didn't like to talk while he was driving—the last long drive he would probably ever make, he thought. He had also managed to avoid Barbie at the dolphin sanctuary, where they were shown round by one of the staff members whom Perry Jackson knew.

Barbie, of course, had insisted on revealing Wilkie's identity to their guide, a tall, attractive, athletic-looking woman named Glory Green in jeans and a cotton sweater, with a gray ponytail and no makeup—a familiar type to Wilkie. To Barbie's evident disappointment, Ms. Green seemed unexcited by this news. Possibly, Wilkie thought, she had never heard of him; or she didn't approve of what she knew. More and more often, after all, this was the case. Or perhaps it was just her cool, deadpan manner, even when describing the work of the sanctuary.

Barbie Mumpson, however, made up for this. She cooed sentimentally and oohed indignantly over the injured dolphins. She was horrified to learn their individual histories; how they had been disentangled from fishing nets, or rescued from commercial aquariums where they had been starved into performing tricks for the public.

Wilkie, standing a little apart, wearily observed Barbie's performance—as automatic in its way, he thought, as that of a performing dolphin. He had always had mixed feelings about places like this. Naturally he favored the preservation of species, and most of the organizations that worked to breed and reintroduce individuals into the wild had his full endorsement. But he had also seen some that were merely glorified zoos or theme parks—or worse, showcases for dubious fund-raising.

There was always a potential conflict of interest in any charity, since its director and employees depended for their livelihood on a continued supply of the unfortunate individuals it was supposed to help. Social agencies need clients; drug counselors need drug addicts, and it was the same with animal-rescue enterprises. If dolphins were banned from commercial aquariums and all nets were biodegradable, the sanctuary they had visited this morning might have to close. Meanwhile, when the supply of damaged individuals fell off, there would be a natural tendency to keep them in care as long as possible, to sentimentalize them and treat them as pets.

Wilkie had been slightly surprised to discover that Glory Green, unlike many nature guides, was apparently aware of these issues.

"Yeah," she had said in reply to Barbie's horrified enquiries. "It keeps happening. If it didn't, we'd have to shut down. . . . Nah, essentially we can't do anything about it. We have to wait until they're hurt bad enough that the fish shows don't want them anymore." Her tone was dark but restrained, as if she had seen so much cruelty to mammals that it had worn her out, the way it had worn Wilkie out.

"But then when the dolphins get well, they go back to the sea," Barbie proposed eagerly.

"Yeah, usually they do. All except Lady Edna." Glory Green gestured at a large, slow-moving dolphin who was nosing the rim of the pool nearby, slowly sinking and surfacing again, as if performing some old Sea World routine. "She stayed around too long and got hooked on the free fish. Now it's too late for her."

"Oh gee," Barbie said. "You mean she can't ever live in the wild again?"

"Nah." Glory shook her head. "She couldn't make it there, not now."

"Aw, that's so sad. Do you think she minds awfully?" Barbie's voice trembled. "Do you think she misses the sea?"

"I used to think that. But now I don't think we ever know what animals really feel." Glory glanced at Wilkie Walker with an expression that suggested familiarity with his early and more popular books, and possibly a critical opinion of them. "Sometimes I figure she probably doesn't remember much what it was like out in the ocean. This is all she knows. When I lived in Southern California I saw a lot of over-the-hill actors like that. Old hams, going over their tricks one more damn time, scared shitless to leave L.A. or take a regular job. You have to feel sorry for them." Again, casually, she glanced at Wilkie.

She has my number, even if she doesn't know it, Wilkie thought now as he paddled through the winding shallow streams of the mangrove swamp, trying as much as possible to tune out the drone of the guide's spiel. I probably couldn't make it on my own in the wild anymore either. I'm an old ham like that fat old dolphin Lady Edna. That's what I feel when I get in front of an audience now, that I'm just going through my tricks. It's time to go back to the ocean, and past time.

"Oh, the sun's come out!" Barbie Mumpson squealed as gold light broke through the heavy, sodden cover of cloud, flooding the shimmering aquamarine water and glossy, shining dark-green clumps of mangrove. "Isn't it glorious!"

Wilkie did not reply. To him, the scene looked false and glaring, like a child's picture book colored with cheap, waxy crayons. He would have preferred that the day remain cloudy, to match his mood.

Animals are lucky, he thought, not for the first time. Places like that dolphin sanctuary, at the most, maintain only a few individuals past their natural life span. But with humans, in the so-called civilized countries, the old, sick, injured, and incompetent are preserved. As a result the world is burdened with a population that in an earlier, more natural age would have ceased to exist years ago. Miserable, senile, ailing individuals are made to survive past their natural life span in some pathetic institution like the home for bony, sick old cows he had seen in India.

We are the holy animals of this world, he had thought then, worshiped and cared for even when we should be dead—would far rather be dead. That was what would happen to him, if he didn't get out in time. But he would get out in time. It could only be a matter of a few days at the most now.

"Oh, look!" Barbie squealed from the bow of the canoe. "What's that big thing over there by the tree, moving around just under the water?"

"Lessee." In the other kayak, the guide reversed his stroke. "I d'know— It could be a manatee." For the first time he spoke in a nonguide voice, with human interest.

"What's that?"

"Well, uh, it's a kind of big, you know, fish. Likes warm water."

"The manatee is not a fish, it's a mammal," Wilkie said impatiently, shaken out of his torpor. He eased the kayak gently toward shore. "It's related to the dugong of the Indian ocean."

"Oh, wow," Barbie half whispered as they drew nearer. "Look, Aunt Dorrie, do you see it? That sort of big golden-gray thing shaped like a, a giant baking potato, under the mangrove trees."

"I do, dear. Is it alive?"

"Oh, sure. I mean, I think so."

Wilkie groaned silently to himself. The last day of my life, quite possibly, he thought, and I have to spend it stuck in a Florida swamp with two stupid women.

"It's alive all right," the guide said, lowering his voice as they approached.

"It's awfully big, isn't it?" Aunt Dorrie whispered nervously.

"They can get up to over three thousand pounds, some of

them. But you don't hafta worry, they're vegetarians. Only eat seaweed and stuff."

"Oh, wow." Barbie breathed ecstatically.

Yes, it was definitely a manatee: a rather large one—in fact the first Wilkie had ever encountered outside of an aquarium. He could see its broad mottled gray-gold hide under the slow flow of tea-colored water, and the gentle movement of its tail fin as it burrowed among the grassy reeds.

As they drifted closer to the shore, almost silently now, something—perhaps the shadow of the kayak on the sand— startled the animal. With a sudden unlikely burst of speed, it shot away, trailing bubbles and turbulence, rocking the boats heavily.

"Yeah, that was a genuine Florida manatee," the guide said with some awe. "You don't see too many of those fellers around here, these days. When I was a kid, they usta be all over the place."

"Really?" Barbie said. "How come they left?"

"Wal. I guess they didn't exactly leave. They mostly kinda died out. They're sorta dumb, see. They kept getting snagged in nets, and cut up by boat propellers. That old feller there, you could see the scars on him."

"Oh, that's so sad," Barbie wailed.

"And then, they don't breed the way they used to. Or when they do a lotta times the pups get sick and die. Wal, anyhow, you saw one today." A note of stupid self-satisfaction had entered the guide's voice, as if he had planned the whole thing. "You can tell your friends back home— Hey, ma'am. You okay?" He addressed Jacko's mother, who had slumped forward in the bow of his kayak, letting her paddle trail helplessly in the salty swell.

"Yes, thanks— I—" Dorrie's voice said in a series of squeaky gasps; Wilkie could not see her face. "I'll be all right in a moment— a little sick—"

"Bit rough now. Wind's getting up," the guide agreed. "Wal, you hold on, okay? We'll be back at the landing in five minutes." He quickened his stroke, driving the kayak forward across the open, now choppy waters of the Gulf.

Dorrie said nothing; instead, she seemed to slump further. In the other kayak Barbie also stopped paddling and sat staring ahead.

"Are you seasick too?" Wilkie asked, trying and failing to sound concerned rather than irritated.

"Nah, I'm okay," she said. "And I don't think Aunt Dorrie's seasick either. It was what that guy said about the manatee babies dying, because she's so upset about Perry. Well, I am too, but it's not so bad for me, because I'm not his mother."

Don't tell me about it, Wilkie thought; but Barbie did not hear this silent request.

"She's been like that ever since Perry told us about his being so sick, last night. I mean, he's not really sick yet, but he will be, because that's what always happens if you're HIV-positive." Barbie lifted her paddle again and took an awkward stroke.

"Excuse me." Now it was Wilkie who had stopped paddling. "Are you trying to say that Perry Jackson, our gardener, has AIDS?"

"Well, uh-huh, yeah. Didn't you know? I mean, Perry said everybody down here knows already."

"No, not everybody," Wilkie barked. His immediate reaction to the news was fear—not for himself, but for Jenny. The man had been in and out of their house, cleaning, every week. It was quite possible that he had left some smear of blood, some secretion— But he mustn't be paranoid: the virus, he had read many times, couldn't survive more than a few seconds outside its host. Jenny was safe. It was Jackson who, like him, was under sentence of death.

"I feel so strange and confused," Barbie said suddenly, missing her stroke again. "I mean, I keep thinking about Perry, and I feel awful. But then I think how I saw a manatee, and I'm really happy. And I got to meet you, and that's so wonderful too. I know I'll remember this day the rest of my life."

Wearily, Wilkie glanced at his latest, and no doubt his last fan: her untidy blonde curls, her rumpled pink sweatshirt. An odd impulse, compounded of irony and goodwill, came over him. "Yes," he said. "So will I."

8

On the overcast, intermittently drizzly morning of the next day, Lee sat at her dining room table doing the accounts and trying not to think about Jenny Walker. There were plenty of other things to think about, she told herself. For instance, why was the laundry bill so low this week, and the phone bill so high? Or, why was she so low today, when yesterday she had been so high?

That was easy: for a moment yesterday Lee had been almost sure that what she felt for Jenny was reciprocated. She had come in from shopping to find that Jenny had located a doctor for a guest who had contracted pinkeye and soothed the feelings of several others who blamed Artemis Lodge for the bad weather. Gratefully, impulsively, she had leaned over the desk at which Jenny sat and kissed her, just missing her mouth. Her lips had touched Jenny's cool, smooth skin; her dark springy hair had mixed with Jenny's pale silvery mane, which yesterday was not caught back into a ponytail. Anything might have happened then, if the phone hadn't begun to ring.

I must speak out, she had decided as she fielded an inquiry about room rates. If Jenny's going to scream and run, it's best that she should do so now, before I care so much I'll never get over her. When we're having lunch, I'll say—

But Jenny, with her slow, lovely smile, had declined to stay for lunch, saying that she "had to get back." She hadn't finished the sentence, but maybe that was because, with her natural tact, she had intuited that Lee didn't want to hear her husband's name again.

The time before that, when Jenny was at the guest house on Wednesday, she had talked about him far too much to suit Lee. Over lunch she had begun dithering again about the mental and physical condition of this piggy, self-satisfied, egotistical man. Worse, Jenny had started blaming herself for Wilkie Walker's cold, sullen, and hostile behavior, and calling herself bad names, until finally Lee had been unable to contain herself and almost referred to him as an asshole.

Yesterday Lee hadn't had to hear the name Wilkie Walker even once. But she had already heard it several times today, because Jacko's cousin Barbie Mumpson seemed unable to stop mentioning it.

Barbie's aunt Dorrie, it had turned out, presented no social problem. Now that she'd recovered from the trip she accompanied Jacko to his jobs every day. Oh, no, she didn't mind the rain, Dorrie said: she was a gardener herself. Besides, she'd been, as she put it—with the bashful smile of someone using the slang of a younger generation—"blown away" by the possibilities of a frost-free climate. "I can't get over it!" she'd exclaimed. "It's like gardening on Mars, all these strange, lovely things. And all my houseplants are growing outdoors here, as big as houses!"

Barbie might have gone with them, but Jacko wouldn't let her. Since she couldn't go to the beach in this weather, and had exhausted the indoor tourist attractions, she had taken to hanging around Artemis Lodge in a disaffected and helpless condition.

"Listen, if she gets to be a drag, throw her out," Jacko had told Lee. "Tell her to go sit in a coffee shop, or something."

Instead, Lee had put Barbie to work. She was strong, willing, and in spite of her protestations of helplessness, good with her hands. Already she'd repaired Molly's temperamental toaster, and this morning she had restrung the blind in the blue room at Artemis Lodge. "I get it from Dad," she had explained. "He could fix just about anything. Like he used to say, if you really take the time to look at something, you can probably figure out how it works."

"Oh yeah?" Lee laughed. "Maybe you can figure out my dishwasher. Half the time it won't drain."

"Okay," Barbie said seriously. "Anyhow, I can try. Have you got the manual?"

"I'm not sure, I'll look around for it," Lee had lied, wondering if she should take the risk.

"I mean, probably I can't, but you never know. I took this vocational test in high school, and it came back saying I should go into small appliance repair. Mom was livid." Barbie giggled. She was already looking better than when she'd arrived, Lee thought. Actually, in spite of her chunky build and unflattering clothes (ill-cut white shorts and a baggy lavender T-shirt), she was rather pretty.

Right now the room was silent, because Barbie was out of conversational range, on a stepladder in the dining room washing a tall Victorian Gothic window; but she was steadily edging her way toward Lee.

The laundry bill down by nearly half, and the phone bill up: two hundred and seventy-nine message units, and seven calls to Directory Assistance, plus taxes— Well, it could be that because of the cold and rain none of Lee's guests had gone swimming and brought back sandy tar-stained towels; instead they had stayed in the Lodge and got Jenny or Polly to call their travel agents, trying to change their tickets.

"You want me to do the windows in here, too?" Barbie asked.

Lee hesitated. "Sure," she said finally, "that'd be great," adding, to discourage conversation, "Seven times fifty-five is three eighty-five, and—"

"You know, I still can't get over it," Barbie announced, undiscouraged, as she hauled the stepladder toward the nearest window. "There I am, staying practically next door to Wilkie Walker. I was with him for hours yesterday, and he was talking to me just like he was an ordinary person. I'm so lucky. Mrs. Hopkins is even luckier, she's known Professor Walker for years, isn't that right?"

"I believe so," Lee said.

"She must have some great stories." Barbie gazed into the middle distance through a pane of glass smeared with chalky cleanser.

"Could be," Lee agreed, frowning at the phone bill. "All I ever remember Molly saying is that in college Walker was known as World War II."

Barbie stopped spraying. "World War II?" she said in the tone of someone mentioning a distant historical epoch—which no doubt it was for her. "I don't get it."

"Because of his initials. Wilkie Walker, WW. He was supposed to be hell on wheels."

"Professor Walker's not like that at all," Barbie protested. "And I bet he never was, either. That was probably just some dumb old joke. I wish you could meet him; then you'd see."

Lee did not echo this wish.

"Anyhow, he's not like that, no way. He's a very spiritual person. I'm kind of stupid sometimes, you know, and when I was paddling I kept heading us into the reeds, but he didn't yell at me or anything."

"Mm," Lee murmured, adding a column of figures.

"And he knew so much about the dolphins, and this rare sea mammal we saw. It's called a manatee."

"You saw a manatee?" Lee asked, attempting to divert Barbie from her praise of WW II. "What did it look like?"

"Well, it was kinda—kinda like a seal, I guess, only much bigger. Sorta tubby and pale brownish grayish, with a round face and bristly whiskers. And this sorta serious, wise expression— It looked a little like Professor Walker, actually."

"Really." Lee mentally compared the images of manatees she had seen in the Greenpeace store with recent photos of Wilkie Walker. "Yeah, I see what you mean." She laughed.

"He knew all about it too. It's not his specialty, but you know he's always loved animals and studied them. Even when he was a little kid. I was the same way myself, though of course I wasn't brilliant like him. I was always bringing home lost cats, and birds that had fallen out of their nest, and lizards and bugs. Mom used to get really disgusted with me." Barbie's tone slid down the scale from enthusiasm to something near depression.

"Mom's thinking of maybe coming to Key West, you know," she added.

"Oh, yeah?"

"Yeah. Or maybe she won't." Her expression brightened.

"It sounds like you hope she doesn't," Lee said.

"Well, uh. I mean, I know Mom wouldn't like it here."

"Oh? Why not?"

"Uh, well, you know. There's all these, you know, kind of weird people around. Anyhow, except for Oklahoma and Washington, Mom doesn't like most places. She thought Europe was sorta disgusting. And it would be real hard for her to get away now, she's so involved back in Tulsa."

"So probably she won't come," Lee suggested.

"I d'know. When she heard what the situation was here, she said she might consider it."

"Oh? What's the situation here?"

"Well, you know." Barbie swiped at a pane of glass. "I mean, Perry says everybody does in Key West, but we didn't have any idea back home."

"Any idea about what?" Lee asked with exasperation.

"I mean, about him being so sick."

Lee frowned and put down her pencil and calculator. "You're telling me Jacko's mother didn't know he's HIV-positive? I thought that was why she came."

"Uh-uh." Barbie rested the roll of paper towels on the top step of the ladder. "He just told her night before last. We were having ice cream in that Flamingo Crossing place you recommended. Aunt Dorrie just kinda fell apart. She dropped her cone and went all white and trembly, like she was the one who was sick or maybe even dying. Perry kept telling her it wasn't so bad. I mean, he feels fine now, and he still has lots of good cells in his blood. But it was like Aunt Dorrie couldn't hear him. She kept crying and there was mango ice cream all down her dress. It was awful."

"Yeah, I see." Lee imagined what it would be like to learn that her daughter, who was now becoming a city planner in Boston, had AIDS.

"She's been kinda weepy ever since. Yesterday when we saw the manatee Aunt Dorrie didn't hardly say anything, she was sorta out of it the whole time. And I guess she isn't really sleeping much, because last night and the night before, I could hear her walking around outside."

"Do you think she'd feel better if your mother was here?"

"I don't know. Maybe. I mean Mom is her big sister, and Aunt Dorrie usually kinda depends on her. And Mom's always on top of things. She's doesn't get confused in a crisis the way most people do. Like she puts it, she can see the big picture. That's why she's so successful in business and everything." Barbie sprayed another pane.

"I see. A kind of generalist."

"Well, yeah. Mom is like a general, in a way. She sorta goes right into a problem and finds out all the details and gets it organized. For instance last night she was asking me all this stuff about Cousin Perry, did he have medical insurance, when had he last been to the doctors, and what exactly did they say. Only I couldn't tell her anything really. Then she wanted to know about his place, where was it located, how many buildings there were, where Aunt Dorrie and I were staying, and how big was the pool. Like she wanted to visualize our situation in her mind, I guess."

"I see." The thought came to Lee that Barbie's mother, as a high-powered real estate agent, was anticipating the possible mortgage or sale of Jacko's property to cover his medical bills.

"Only I wasn't much use with that either. I don't organize

things like Mom does. She got kinda impatient with me, like she does." Barbie sighed and began rubbing the glass again.

"She often gets impatient with you." Lee frowned, irritated to hear herself falling into her therapist mode. She had promised herself not to do this with Barbie, who was obviously a dependent personality.

"The thing is, I'm a disappointment to her. I feel bad about that, because so many people have disappointed her already."

"Is that so?" Lee said skeptically. According to Jacko, Barbie's mother was a rich woman, a very successful real estate agent, and a powerful force in the local Republican party.

"Well, yeah. For instance Gary, that's my brother. Mom was keen for him to have a career in politics, but it didn't work out, because people, you know, voters, sorta didn't take to him."

"So what does he do instead?" Lee imagined Barbie's brother as a masculine equivalent of her: blond, innocent, clumsy, and lost.

"Oh, he's a big success in Tulsa. Oil leases and banking. He has a head for deals, he's like Mom that way."

"I see." Lee revised her image.

"And Dad disappointed her too. He was such a great guy, everybody loved him. But he didn't have Mom's business drive, and he wouldn't go into politics like she wanted him to. Then about ten years ago he was in this awful car accident, where a guy got killed. And then he went to England on a tour with his sister who lives in Fort Worth and he never came back." Barbie began to choke up.

"You mean he deserted the family," Lee said dryly, trying to head off Barbie's tears.

"Aw, no!" The maneuver worked: Barbie shifted from sorrow to indignation. "Dad would never have done that. See, he had this heart condition, and he just, he just went and passed away somewhere in England." Barbie's tone became weepy.

"But your husband's in politics, isn't he?" Lee said, to avert a serious rainstorm. "I think Jacko said he was elected to Congress. That must please your mother."

"Well, yeah. I mean, she was real happy at first. Only now she's kinda disappointed in him too, because of this woman—"

"I heard about it," Lee said. "Molly says that's why you came here, to think things over and decide whether to take your husband back."

"Yeah. That's right."

"So what have you decided?"

"I— Well, I guess I haven't yet."

Lee sighed, exasperated, as she had often been, by the indecisive weakness of straight women with obviously shitty husbands.

"I mean, maybe it wouldn't be such a good thing for him anyhow. It's like Mom says, I was supposed to be an asset to his career, but I've become a liability. Mom says he still really loves me. But I don't know if I should believe her."

"I suppose the question is, do you still love him?"

"I guess—" Barbie's voice wavered. "I mean, I used to, for sure. I couldn't believe my luck, that somebody so wonderful would want to marry me. But after Mom backed his campaign and he got into state government, he sorta changed. Things started to happen that I didn't like."

"Your husband began having affairs," Lee put in, to hurry the narrative along.

"No, not then." Barbie's voice wobbled. She looked down, trailing her cleaning rag. "At least, if he did, I didn't know. And he was still real sweet to me, mostly. But he sorta gradually got mean with other people."

"Oh? In what way?"

"Well. Like for instance there was this company, Tumble- weed Investment Consultants, that Bob was sorta involved in, that went bust." Barbie got down and began to drag the step- ladder to the next window. "It was his partners who were really running the firm, but after the news came out nobody could find them. So then people who had put money in the company started coming to our house. Bob wasn't home, but they said they would wait for him. It was August and real hot out, so I let them in and gave them lemonade. They started to tell me about it, how the Tumbleweed officials seemed so nice, and swore to them it was a sure thing."

Barbie stopped spraying the glass and sat down on the top step of Lee's ladder. "They were such sad people," she said. "One guy worked in the post office and had a retarded child, and there was this old lady schoolteacher who'd mortgaged her house to buy Tumbleweed stock. I figured Bob would want to do something for them, so I let them wait in the sitting room till he got home."

"I see. And what happened then?"

"It was real bad. There were about ten or twelve of them by that time, all over the sitting room and the den. Bob was smiley and polite, but I could tell he was real upset and angry. He kind of shooed them out of the house. He said afterward they were just taking me in, they were all frauds and whiners. They put up their money, he said, they took their chances. They could have bought a CD or something, but they wanted big fast profits, wasn't that right? So I said I guess so. Then Bob said, 'Do you think any of those guys would help us out if we were broke?' And I had to admit probably they wouldn't. Because that's how people are, mostly.

"Even after that I thought maybe we could do something, at least for a couple of them that were in real trouble. But Mom said it wasn't possible. She explained that Bob had to be really careful, because if he repaid anybody the others would want money too, that was only fair, and if we paid them all we would go bankrupt. Besides it would look terrible in the newspapers, as if Bob was admitting he was responsible for what happened to Tumbleweed, even though he hadn't known anything about it. Then people would vote him out of office, or maybe he'd get impeached, and all the important things he wanted to do for the state would go down the drain. Mom said, if anybody else came around I should just pretend I wasn't home. If I couldn't do it for Bob, she said, I should do it for Oklahoma."

"And did you take her advice?"

"Yeah." Barbie shrugged sadly. "But it was awful, you know. People kept on calling and coming to the house for weeks, it seemed like. The phone never stopped, and they would ring the bell and knock on the front door and shake the gate to the backyard. Sometimes they would climb over the wall and go round the house, looking through all the windows. I stayed away as much as I could, but I had to go home sometime. I started keeping the drapes closed, so the house was dark all day.

"But one time it got quiet, and I thought they had all gone, so I pulled back the white brocade curtains in the sitting room, and there was a man's face right there a couple inches from mine, with his nose flattened out against the glass. He looked like some kinda monster. I screamed, and he screamed back at me through the window. I shut the curtain again, so I couldn't see him, and then I just sorta sat there for I don't know how long. I was freaked out." Barbie sighed and fell silent.

"Lee? You home?" The front door thudded back, and Jacko came in, his yellow rubber poncho dripping with rain.

"I'm in here. How're you doing?"

"Great," Jacko said, with an ambiguous intonation.

"You look kind of wet. Would you like some coffee, to warm up?"

"Nah, I can't stay, Mumsie's still in the truck. Only I wanted to tell you the latest. Aunt Myra is coming."

"Really? When?"

"Tomorrow. When she gets an idea, Myra doesn't waste any time. Only what I'd like to know is, what the hell does she want here?"

Instead of answering, Lee, with a gesture of her head, indicated Barbie, who was now crouched behind the ladder, washing the lower panes of one of the windows.

"Well. Cousin Barbie." Jacko gave her a weary glance. "I get it," he said suddenly and even less pleasantly. "You little creep. You told your mom I was sick, didn't you?"

"I— Ah—" his cousin bleated, retreating further behind the stepladder.

"I should've known." Jacko laughed shortly. "That's why Myra sent you to Key West, isn't it, so you could spy on me."

"I didn't— I wasn't—" Barbie mumbled.

"Aw, shit. Well, she's not going to like it here, that's for sure," Jacko told Lee. "So why is she coming? And she's staying four nights at the Casa Marina; that's not cheap."

"Maybe she's worried about her sister," Lee suggested. Or her nephew, she added silently, giving Jacko a glance. In his shiny wet poncho, his curls diamond-dusted with rain, he looked as beautiful and fit as ever, but angrier than Lee had ever seen him.

"Not her," Jacko said. "The only person Myra ever worries about is herself. If she's coming to Key West, she wants something. Myra always wants something. The trouble is, you never figure out what until it's too late." He shrugged. "Well, I better get back to the house."

"Why don't you and your mother stay for lunch?" Lee said. "I have some curried squash soup in the fridge, and lots of cold chicken."

Jacko shook his head. "You're a pal, but no thanks. Mumsie is wiped out, and we're both soaked. I'll phone you later."

As the door shut behind him, Lee turned toward Barbie, who was still crouched in a heap by the window, clutching a bottle of Windex and a wad of paper towels. She did not look like a pretty young woman now: her appearance was rather that of an abused homeless person. Lee considered expressing disapproval of Jacko's attitude, then rejected this. Maybe Barbie had been sent to spy on him; how should she know?

"So what do you think your mother wants in Key West?" she asked instead, trying to make her tone sympathetic.

"I d'know." Barbie rose to her feet slowly. "Only I guess she'll get it, whatever it is. Mom always gets what she wants."

"Really?" Lee asked skeptically. "How does she do that?"

"I d'know." Barbie repeated dully. "She just does somehow."

We'll see about that, Lee thought. "Maybe Key West will be an exception," she said. "Anyhow, if you're finished with that window, come and have some squash soup."

9

For the first time in a week the sun poured like pale syrup over Key West. Again the island assumed its travel-magazine glamour: pulsating blue sky, ostrich-feather palms, scarlet and salmon red flowering hibiscus, bronzed and beaming tourists. Under this blue sky, rather slowly and painfully, Molly Hopkins descended her front steps and set out toward the restaurant where she had agreed to lunch. The fine warm weather had eased her arthritis, but she still walked with a limp. She would be a little late, as she often was nowadays.

Probably she should have driven, though it was only six blocks, Molly thought unhappily. Probably she shouldn't even be here in Key West, trying to manage alone. If she were home in Convers her cleaning lady, Sally Hutchins, would have taken care of everything during the last awful week. Sally, who had been working for Molly for over thirty years, would have come every morning, shopped for groceries, and gone to the drugstore, post office, and library. When Molly wasn't up to getting out of bed Sally would have brought her lunch, straightened her unwieldy pillows, and refilled the pink velvet-covered hot water bottle.

But there was no one like Sally in Key West: winter season provided so many jobs in the tourist industry for reliable people that anyone who didn't have one was probably delinquent or incompetent. Like nearly everyone she knew, Molly had a cleaning service. Once a week a posse of strange women, most of whom did not speak English, descended upon her house armed with mops and vacuums, and disappeared an hour later.

When Molly was ill in Key West she was dependent on friends, which embarrassed and depressed her. Two days ago, for instance, she had had to ask Lee Weiss to open a can of black bean soup because her own hands simply could not turn the crank. Maybe it was time to give up Key West and stay home through however many winters remained to her. Long, cold, icy winters, they would be, during which she would be housebound and crippled not only when the weather turned wet, but almost all the time.

Having a chronic illness, Molly thought, was like being invaded. Her grandmother back in Michigan used to tell about the day one of their cows got loose and wandered into the parlor, and the awful time they had getting her out. That was exactly what Molly's arthritis was like: as if some big old cow had got into her house and wouldn't go away. It just sat there, taking up space in her life and making everything more difficult, mooing loudly from time to time and making cow pies, and all she could do really was edge around it and put up with it.

When other people first became aware of the cow, they expressed concern and anxiety. They suggested strategies for getting the animal out of Molly's parlor: remedies and doctors and procedures, some mainstream and some New Age. They related anecdotes of friends who had removed their own cows in one way or another. But after a while they had exhausted their suggestions. Then they usually began to pretend that the cow wasn't there, and they preferred for Molly to go along with the pretense.

Ahead of her now Molly could see Henry's Beach House, which was not a beach house but a famous restaurant. Its fame, however, was restricted to a select clientele. Though the place was often featured in expensive magazines, most Key West tourists never saw it. It was on an out-of-the way street of large private homes, and marked with the most discreet of signs. When Howard was alive he and Molly used to eat there two or three times a month, enjoying the excellent seafood and elegant camp decor: sea-green-and-white umbrellas, sea-green china, and linen napkins. The restaurant had also appeared in several of her watercolors, embellished with the Victorian gingerbread icing for which she was so well known.

Molly, somewhat against her own best judgment, was on her

way to Sunday lunch with Jacko's aunt, Myra Mumpson. Though she had dressed carefully for the occasion, in pale-pink flowered silk and a silk-flowered straw hat, she felt uneasy. According to Jacko, his aunt was a terror. It was true that this terror was not visible on the surface: rather, Myra's outer aspect was conventional, even reassuring. Knowing that she was Dorrie Jackson's elder sister, Molly had expected a fierce elderly lady. But Myra seemed at least a decade younger than her sister— more from across the room. She was a handsome, healthy-looking woman with expertly cut and rather too bright reddish-brown hair. Her skin was glossily tanned and tight, like expensive leather luggage packed to capacity (one face-lift at least, Molly decided).

"But why should your aunt ask me to lunch?" Molly had inquired when Jacko conveyed the invitation. "We've hardly met."

"Why not? Aunt Myra always wants to know the important people in town wherever she goes—"

"But I'm not—" Molly tried to interject.

"I told her you were a famous artist and a power on the local scene."

"Jacko, really! You know that's quite untrue."

"I talked all my friends up," he explained. "I don't want her to think I know only riffraff."

"Yes, but even so—"

"Maybe she wants something from you," Jacko suggested. "Aunt Myra always wants something."

Probably I should have said no, Molly thought. But curiosity, and her wish to get out of the house after days of total confinement, had overcome her suspicions. Anyhow I've got nothing Myra Mumpson could want, she thought, limping along the uneven sidewalk under the huge old sapodilla and mango trees. When Howard was alive he was on the Historic Preservation Board, and a lot of other boards having to do with history and literature and education, and people often wanted things from him, but that was years ago.

Four years now. Sometimes it seemed like yesterday: it seemed that at any moment Howard would come in from the garden, holding the *Times* with its white wings spread, smiling and reading out some item that had caught his attention. At other, darker moments it seemed as if their fifty-four years of marriage had been only a long happy dream—as if Molly were still a lonely, awkward art student, an excess person in any gathering of couples. Because now again she was a lonely awkward excess person. The only difference was that now she had no dreams of a brighter future.

As Molly followed the hostess through the restaurant and out onto the brilliantly sunny deck, she saw that Myra Mumpson had somehow secured a most desirable table, with an uninterrupted view of the shimmering turquoise sea. Perhaps the hostess had been impressed by her clothes: white sharkskin resort wear of the most obviously fashionable sort, and much gold jewelry.

"Lovely to see you," Myra cried, half rising from under

the green-and-white umbrella. Her manner was breezy and slightly gushing, with a touch of brisk down-home charm. "Now why don't you just sit right here by me, so we won't have to shout over all that noise." She gestured at the salty, foam-glazed waves sloshing against the piers below the railing.

Though the restaurant was crowded, something about Myra evidently attracted instant service. Almost at once a slight, handsome young Chinese man in a crisp white shirt and brief denim cutoffs appeared. "My name is Dennis," he announced, smiling winningly and offering menus the size of tabloid newspapers. "I'll be your waiter today."

Myra ordered a bottle of Asti Spumante, insisted that Molly join her, and began on the usual tourist topics: weather, travel, restaurants, and accommodations. She pronounced the Casa Marina, one of the most expensive hotels in town, "surprisingly comfortable."

"All I ever knew about Key West was that old film with Burt Lancaster, *The Rose Tattoo*," she confided. "Dirt streets and shacks and chickens running around. But it's not really like that." She gave a loud musical laugh.

"Oh no," Molly agreed.

"Only thing I can't understand is, why are there so many T-shirt shops?"

"Well, people say there aren't, not really," Molly lowered her voice and her wine glass, which to her surprise was nearly empty. "What I've heard is that some of them aren't real shops.

They're actually laundries, for laundering drug money, you know."

"Oh yeah?" Myra leaned forward with interest.

"The idea is, nobody can really tell how many hand-painted T-shirts they sell, or how much they mark them up. So the owners can claim hundreds or thousands of dollars more than they take in legitimately. That's what people say; I don't know if it's true. But rents on Duval Street have gone up incredibly over the last few years."

"Uh-huh." Myra nodded knowingly. "I've seen that sort of thing back home. It brings in a lot of cash for a while, but in the end it can't help but lower property values."

"They've ruined all that part of town, really. Most people I know never go there if they can help it."

"Yeah, that figures. But of course there's more than that to Key West, praise God," Myra said, brightening. "There are some very nice residential areas. Big lots, very attractive construction and landscaping. You have a beautiful home here, for instance. Of course I've only seen it from outside, but I really admired the tropical planting, and those elegant double verandas."

Was Myra angling for an invitation? Was that what she wanted? Molly resolved not to extend it; for one thing, she wasn't physically up to entertaining yet.

"And you certainly deserve a lovely home," Myra continued, raising her second—or was it her third?—glass of wine. "You know, I had no idea you were M. Hopkins until my nephew told me. Those wonderful, wonderful *New Yorker* covers, with the Victorian houses and gardens, and all those funny cats!" She gave her rippling laugh. "They were so much more attractive than the ugly cartoon covers they have now."

"Thank you." It was what Molly thought too, but would never have said.

Their waiter reappeared and began to recite the specials of the day. "Creole shrimp salad," Myra repeated, looking at him brightly. "That sounds real good. Or should I have conch fritters? I hear they're the Key West specialty. What's your opinion?"

"The shrimp is excellent today," he said with what struck Molly as an ambiguous Oriental smile.

"I get you." Myra laughed. "Okay, I'll have the shrimp."

"That's my kind of waiter," she said when he'd gone. "The conch fritters are terrible, I take it."

"Well, I think so." Molly heard herself giggle. Was it the wine? She never drank at lunch anymore, or on an empty stomach.

"I wanted to thank you," Myra said, pouring herself another glass. "For being so kind to my poor confused daughter."

"It wasn't—"

"Taking her in off the street, literally, when you hadn't even met her. Barbie told me all about it."

"It was only for one night." Maybe she doesn't want anything from me after all, Molly thought; maybe she's just paying me back.

"I don't know why she couldn't have gone to a motel; she has credit cards," Myra continued. "But that's how Barbie is. She's never really learned to take care of herself. Or how to manage a husband, poor child; I hear she told you all about that."

"Well, a little," Molly admitted.

"He's a congressman, you know, so he's awfully busy, working late a lot of the time. But Barbie got the idea he was playing around, so she ran home to Mother." She sighed. "You'd never think she was thirty-six years old."

"No," Molly agreed, wondering if Myra's version of the story were the correct one. After all, the events described were the same. It was like one of those modern sculptures, she thought: you turn the thing a few degrees and it looks wholly different.

"I figure you do always worry about your kids, though, no matter how old they get."

"Mm," Molly murmured noncommittally, for she no longer worried about her children, who were all in their fifties and well established in life. Instead, ever since Howard died, her children had worried about her.

"And now Barbie's got this idea in her head about some kind of endangered walrus, except in actual fact it's not endangered. I asked the concierge at the Casa Marina this morning." Myra gave her cheerful loud laugh.

"The manatee," Molly suggested. "But you know, even if it's not officially endangered, I think its numbers are declining in Florida."

"Exactly. It's not fitted for the modern world." Myra laughed again, then gave a little fizzing sigh. "Barbie's always been more comfortable with animals than with people ever since she was a little girl, you know. In college she was mad about whales. She was always playing records of the funny noises they make, like balloons popping and squeaking under-water, till I practically went out of my mind. And then she had to fly to Alaska and go out on a boat and look for them." Myra rolled her eyes upward, signifying baffled exasperation. "What I've never been able to understand is, why couldn't she get het-up about some animal or plant that's endangered in Okla-homa?"

"Perhaps there aren't any," Molly suggested.

"Aw, I'm sure there are. Or if not, those environmentalists will invent some. But it doesn't matter, because I gave her a talking-to, and she's going back to Washington with me in a couple of days. . . . Oh, thank you. That looks real lovely." This was to their waiter, Dennis, who had just set an elabo-rately decorated shrimp salad in front of her.

"You want to know the truth," Myra continued after the first few appreciative bites. "I'm glad to be getting Barbie out of here. There's an atmosphere about Key West I don't like. All those bars, and drunken bums and stray cats everywhere. It's a godless place."

"Oh, I don't really think that's true," Molly said, wondering if Myra was one of those Christian rightists they were supposed to have so many of in the Midwest. "Why, there's forty-four churches in Key West alone, I counted them once. And that's not including the Jewish temple and the Zen Buddhists."

"Where there is great need, there will be many temples," Myra said, as if quoting. "All you have to do is walk down the main street after dark and you'll see what I'm talking about. Well, you said you never go there, but let me tell you, it's disgusting. The drinking and fighting you see, and the expensive property defiled with excrement and vomit."

"That's just the tourists," Molly explained, slightly disgusted herself by Myra's description, which took no account of the conventions of mealtime discourse. "They do get a little wild sometimes, but after all they're on vacation."

"That's no excuse. I realize everyone needs a break once in a while. But there's a loose, perverse atmosphere here, like you never get in most American resorts. You know what I saw yesterday on the beach at the Casa Marina?" Myra leaned forward and lowered her voice. "I saw two men kissing each other, smooching right out in public. And they were both half naked. They wouldn't dare try that in Tulsa, let me tell you."

"I suppose not," said Molly, who had never been to Tulsa and now had even less desire to go.

"No. And honestly I don't care for the scenery," Myra confided. "Everything so damp and overgrown." She gave a little head-shake of distaste. "And there isn't even a good golf course."

"No," Molly agreed. She was reminded of a theory of her

husband's, that travelers were always drawn to landscapes that echoed the internal geography of their minds. Calm, even-tempered, slightly lazy people felt most comfortable in the plains or beside clear, placid lakes. Somewhat more active types were at home among rolling hills and sparkling streams; while the extremely adventurous and intense responded instinctively to alpine cliffs and crags and deep ravines and the pounding of towering cascades. Perhaps there were also people who preferred their scenery wet or, like Myra, dry.

While they ate Myra reverted to the topic of real estate. Once Molly would have joined in with interest, but she was past that now. Probably she would never rent, buy, or remodel a house again. She let her attention drift to the sun-bleached sky, the sea lit with sparks of light like bits of broken mirror, and the toasted triangles of her excellent turkey sandwich, each one pierced with a toothpick fizzed with red cellophane.

". . . So when I heard about poor Perry's condition, I realized I had to come," Myra was saying when she refocused. "I was real relieved to find that he'd inherited such a substantial piece of property, praise the Lord. Barbie's so vague, especially on the phone, and my baby sister was hysterical with anxiety. And God knows, when it comes to practical matters she's totally out to lunch, poor dear." Myra raised her glance to the underside of the canvas umbrella, as if calling upon the heavens to confirm this incapacity.

"Ah," Molly murmured. It occurred to her that it was Myra who was literally out to lunch, and not her sister. Where was Dorrie, and what was she doing all day?

"Of course if Perry needed it I'd try to help him out some-how," Myra continued. "Though frankly my resources are lim-ited. My husband passed away very suddenly about ten years ago, and he wasn't exactly a good provider." A shadow passed over her face, and a corresponding shadow over Molly's. She's a widow like me, Molly thought. I'd forgotten that.

"I'm sorry," she murmured, hoping Myra would realize that her regret was for the loss, not the lack of provision.

"As soon as I saw Perry's place, I knew I didn't have to worry about him—financially speaking, that is. He's sitting on a gold mine. There's already three good condo units in the compound, and space for at least two more, even with the ridic-ulous zoning laws they have here. Luxury area, big pool, mature landscaping, off-street parking; it's a natural. Of course the property needs some work, but I figure two million minimum at current prices."

"Really." Molly realized that she had never considered Jacko's situation from this angle.

"Someone must be doing an appraisal, to settle the estate. But Perry doesn't appear to know anything about it. Doesn't have any idea how to look out for his interests, and his family's interests too of course."

"I guess he has other things on his mind," said Molly.

"Oh, I know." Myra swallowed; her face lengthened. "Natu-rally I'm very concerned about his health; that's why I just dropped everything and came to Key West. And poor Sis is devastated. Well, it's a tragedy."

"Yes," Molly agreed, warming further. Myra was vulgar and

prejudiced; but she evidently had a good heart. Even though Jacko didn't like her, when she heard that he was ill she had rushed to be with him. Maybe I could get a small drinks party together for her after all, Molly thought. I do owe a great many people, and there's that new caterer Kenneth was talking about—

"When I think what Perry might have been," Myra was saying now. "He had the name and the looks and the personality: there was nothing he couldn't have accomplished in politics with the right kind of backing. I had big plans for him." She sighed. "But then he came to Key West and was hypnotized by that disgusting old man, and quit law school, and decided he was a pansy. I wouldn't have let him get away with that if he was my son, but Dorrie's always been soft. Still, it about broke my heart."

"Ah," Molly murmured. An alternative Perry Jackson appeared in her mind: equally charming, equally loved, but heterosexual, and a successful lawyer and politician. He would be married to some really nice woman and have delightful children, and would live to a normal old age. Wouldn't that have been better, after all?

"I don't like to ask you this, but for Dorrie's sake, I must," Myra continued, lowering her voice and at the same time leaning forward to block out the raucous yakety-yak of the people at the next table. "How much time does he have?"

"I don't know," Molly admitted. "I don't think anyone does." Maybe this is what Myra wanted, she thought, and tried to answer helpfully. "It could be ten years, if he's lucky. And perhaps by then they'll have found a cure."

"God willing," Myra said. "But has Perry had any of the symptoms yet? Those awful purple spots they get, or the pneumonia?"

"Not that I know of." As she lied, Molly winced with distaste: she had been brought up to believe that nice people do not mention the details of illness at mealtimes—or if possible, at any other time. But after all, Myra was his aunt; she had a right to know. "He's worried about something," she admitted. "His T-cell count, it's called."

"Yeah, I've heard of that. When the numbers start to go down, it's a bad sign. Well, we're all in the hand of the Lord." Myra rummaged in a white lizard handbag framed in gold. "Mind if I smoke?"

"Uh, well, if you could wait—" Molly began. Ever since Howard had been diagnosed with lung cancer she hated to see people smoking—sucking in and breathing out death.

But Myra already had a cigarette between her shiny red-painted lips, and was flicking a gold lighter. Soon a thin gray ectoplasm, like the wispy dirty-white substance exuded by spirits in Victorian séances, rose and circled her head. Keep that up, and you could be dead before Jacko is, Molly thought—maybe even before I am.

"Lissen, when I order something, you goddamn bring it, okay?" At the next table, the loud voices that she had been trying to ignore for some time were raised further. She glanced round at the occupants: two middle-aged couples in bright resort wear, navy and acid yellow predominating. The larger and more red-faced man, the one who was shouting, was obviously drunk.

"Now, Al!" "Take it easy, Al," cried the others.

"I'm sorry, sir, but I was just—" their waiter, Dennis, began.

"I don't give a shit what you were." The man's voice rose over Dennis's explanations and the remonstrances of his companions, attracting the attention of people at nearby tables. "I asked you for another beer fifteen minutes ago, it still isn't here. And these goddamn fritters, whatever you call 'em, they look and taste like turds."

"I'm very sorry, sir. If you'd like to order something else, I'll bring you the menu—" Dennis began edging away.

"Hey, you come back here!" the man shouted, even louder. Dennis continued to retreat. "Damnit, I'm speaking to you, you dumb little Chink!"

Understandably, Dennis did not obey. Instead, breaking into tears, he stumbled toward the kitchen. Many customers were now gawking at the scene, and a chorus of voices rose at Al's table, trying to subdue and reason with him.

Almost at once a tall, portly, well-dressed man, whom Molly recognized as the manager of Henry's Beach House, bustled up to the table, followed by two other waiters. "What seems to be the trouble?" he asked smoothly.

The chorus turned toward him, attempting to explain, but Al's voice drowned theirs.

"That dumb waiter of yours, he forgot my order. So I complained, and he insulted me."

"I'm very sorry that happened," the manager said soothingly.

"That's not true," a woman's voice insisted—Myra's voice, Molly realized with dismay. Though she rather enjoyed watching public scenes, she had a horror of being involved in one. But Myra, who was perhaps somewhat tipsy herself, continued to defend Dennis. "The waiter was very polite, and that's more than I can say for him—" With her smoking cigarette, she pointed directly at Al.

At another table, a couple of young preppies joined in on Myra's side. "Yes, that's right!" they cried. "He was out of line. He used a racial epithet—"

Al's face flushed even darker, and he seemed to swell to twice normal size. "You shut your trap, you interfering old bitch!" he told Myra, making a clumsy, threatening gesture that knocked over a glass on his table. The woman next to him grabbed for it, but missed, and it smashed on the deck between the two tables, splashing Coca-Cola.

"Now look what you've done, you big dope!" the woman cried, pointing at Molly's silk skirt, which had suddenly acquired an ugly brown stain.

A freezing change had come over the manager's countenance. Complaining of a waiter is one thing; insulting a patron and causing a public disturbance very much another.

"I'm sorry, sir," he said, but now in tones of threat rather than conciliation. "I'm afraid I'll have to ask you and your party to leave."

"Yeah, says who?" Al began to struggle to his feet, imperfectly restrained by the squeaks of his female companions and the growls of the other man. Maybe he's going to hit the manager or Myra, Molly thought, becoming frightened. Or even shoot them, who knows; this is South Florida after all. Should she try to hide under the table?

But Al only stood there, large and swaying, evidently registering that now, beside the manager, he was confronted with two muscular waiters.

"Okay, okay, we're going!" he shouted. "Glad to. Goddamn pansy place! Shitty food." Followed by the two women, he staggered between the umbrella-crowned tables toward the exit, continuing to curse as he went. The other man, lagging behind, nervously thrust a handful of bills and what sounded like an apology at one of the waiters.

"I'm very sorry for the disturbance," the manager told Myra and Molly. "Please try to forget it."

"Aw, that's all right," Myra said, smiling. "Happens." Her color was high, her eyes lit as if after a successful fight.

Molly's heart was still pounding. I'm too old for this kind of thing, she thought. She took a long breath and slowly released the sea-green napkin that she had been clutching as if it would somehow save her.

"You okay?" Myra asked.

"Uh, yes," she lied. "Well, I was a little worried. I thought that man was going to hit somebody."

"Aw, no chance. The guy was bluffing from the start. All talk and no action."

Yes, but that kind of talk is action, Molly thought.

"Hey, look at your dress." Myra pointed. "You should get that dry-cleaned right away, and send the bill to the restaurant."

"Well—"

"And if they give you any trouble, let me know."

"Mm-hm," Molly agreed, privately resolving not to do so. Myra had a good heart, she thought, and her defense of their waiter had been admirable. At the same time, she was someone whose public behavior could not be relied upon. Howard had always used to say that it was better not to get involved with noisy, combative people, if you could honorably avoid it, because there was a danger that they would be in your life forever. The same principle, he believed, applied to politics, and to noisy, combative countries; it was the thesis of one of his books.

Suppose that foul-mouthed, shouting, drunken man had had a gun, which was quite probable, and had shot Myra—or even Molly, by mistake. He would have become part of her life, however much more there was of it, and of her children's lives.

You can come to my house for drinks, she thought, gazing at Myra as she sat there by the warm, glittering sea, wreathed in smoke and self-satisfaction. But I'm not going out to lunch with you again.

Among the overgrown brick ruins of an old fort by the sea, on the same warm afternoon, Jacko and his mother and cousin Barbie were touring the Key West Orchid Society show. Jacko's interest in the event was professional: many of his customers had orchids, and the care and augmentation of their collections was one of his jobs. Today he needed new specimens for a woman who loved cattleyas of the sort she'd worn to long-ago debutante balls, and half a dozen showy hanging plants to decorate a new upmarket restaurant.

Dorrie, Jacko's mother, was in a daze of delight. Sheltered from the strong sun by a floppy leaf-green hat, she flitted from one exhibit to another with little cries of joy.

"Oh Perry, look! The most beautiful salmon-pink ascada! I've never seen one so large, it's as if it was covered with pink butterflies. And that big brown-and-gold oncidium there under the arch, like a cloud of wasps. Or hornets. You know, once when I was a real little girl there was a swarm of hornets in the summer kitchen on the ranch. Just like that—so golden and shining. I thought they were a crowd of tiny angels. I remember the zigzag way they flew, and the sound—as if the whole room was full of country fiddlers, and everyone was dancing."

"Yeah." Jacko smiled down at his mother.

"And all these orchids, they're doing this without any soil—just living and blooming. There must be something specially nourishing in the air here, don't you think?"

"Sure, probably," Jacko agreed, thinking that the Key West air had done something for his mother too. He hadn't seen her so happy and animated in years—not since his father died. But maybe it wasn't only Key West: maybe it was the suggestion he'd made last night that she should stay on another month or so, possibly longer.

A great idea: why hadn't he thought of it years ago? That was easy: before he'd inherited Alvin's property there was no place for Mumsie to stay. His cottage had only one room, and he couldn't afford a hotel. Neither could his mother, who hadn't been well off for years—and now, he'd gathered, was on the verge of becoming wholly dependent on her awful sister, Myra.

But that wouldn't happen, because now he could take care of her. Tomorrow he would start working on the pool house, make it really comfortable. He would repaint the bathroom—lavender blue, Mumsie's favorite color—and get a new refrigerator. She needed a better reading lamp too, and a rocking chair would be nice. Maybe they could go to some garage sales Saturday with Janice Stone, who always had good luck there.

"Oh, Perry darling, come see these lovely vandas!" Dorrie cried; and Jacko followed her to a bank of pale purple orchids, each petal checked in darker purple.

Several feet in the rear, Barbie Mumpson trailed behind her relatives, dragging her feet and looking sullen and sweaty in the damp heat. Wet, sticky patches had formed under the arms of her yellow-and-white-checked shirtwaist dress, and her hot, swollen feet hurt in their white pumps. She'd slept badly the night before, worn out by the effort of packing and by the knowledge that in a few days she would be in Washington with

Bob, unless she could get up the nerve to go down to the beach and drown herself first.

Barbie's mother claimed that everything was going to be fine back in Washington. "You won't have any more problems with Bob," she'd promised. "I gave him a good talking-to. Put the fear of God into him." The trouble was, Barbie didn't want Bob to be nice to her because he was afraid of God, or of her mother. That wasn't like love, she'd cried; it wasn't even like marriage, not the way she had imagined it when Bob proposed to her.

Mom had said Barbie's romantic ideas were irrelevant. For better, for worse, her place was with her husband; it was in the Bible. It was her job to be her husband's helpmate, especially in politics, where the wife was an important part of the public image. But probably she wouldn't be of any help to Bob's image anyhow, Barbie thought. She'd mess up again somehow, and make things worse for him, and everybody would be angry at her just like they always were.

"Hey, Barbie. If you've seen enough, why don't you go with Mumsie and get something to drink?" Jacko asked. "I've got to negotiate for some plants. There's soda and stuff over there, under that big banyan."

"Okay," she agreed listlessly; she had seen enough long ago. Like some lovers of animals (not including Wilkie Walker), Barbie had no particular love of plants. For her they were merely habitat and fodder; it was important that they be preserved to ensure the survival of mammals and birds, but they were without intrinsic interest. Many of the orchids on display looked kind of creepy to her, with their twisted and tasseled shapes, their quivering antennae, their thick, fleshy petals, their peculiar colors: neon purple, chartreuse, beefsteak.

"Oh, this is all so glorious, isn't it?" Aunt Dorrie murmured a few minutes later, sinking onto a bench with a paper cup of iced tea. The sun filtered through her green hat, giving her pretty, worn features a plantlike hue.

"Uh-huh," Barbie managed. She took a gulp of Coke.

"Glorious," Dorrie repeated. She gazed slowly round at the exotic foliage and the equally exotic clothes of several other visitors. "You know, dear, I've been so unhappy about Perry. But now I know he's going to be all right, whatever happens. I've been praying about it so hard, and finally last night I just put everything in the hands of Jesus and I told him, now it's up to you. And when I saw that beautiful big golden orchid back there, it was like a promise. It could even be that the doctors are going to find a cure in time for Perry."

"Um-hm," Barbie muttered. She had prayed a lot too, off and on, ever since she was a little kid, and a couple of times she had tried to put her life into the hands of Jesus, but it had never worked out. The nearest she came was once when she was fifteen, in the new Baptist church her friend Nancy went to. The organ was playing and the sun was shining through the pink and green windows. Everybody was praying and swaying, and the minister was calling them to come forward and accept the Lord.

Barbie tried, but she couldn't move into the aisle. She couldn't get past the idea that the Lord didn't want her life. "His eye is on the sparrow," they were singing, "and I know He watches me." But the way it always seemed to Barbie, it was like the Lord's eye might be on her, but he didn't care all that much for what he saw. He wouldn't give a hoot if she drowned tomorrow morning, because she wasn't any use in the world anyhow.

"I've got the plants, Mumsie," Jacko said, coming up to them. "I'm going to load up the truck now."

"I'll help, darling."

"No, you sit right here. Or look around some more, if you like. Barbie'll help me."

Outside in the sun it was hotter than ever. Because of the crowd, Jacko had had to park far down the beach road. By the time he and Barbie, heavily loaded with plants and pots and bags of orchid food, reached his truck, they were sweating and irritable.

"Hey, not that way!" he cried as she began to lift a heavy plastic tray of cuttings; but he spoke too late. Startled, Barbie let the plants slide sideways, and some fell onto the pavement and broke.

"Jesus, what a moron."

"I'm sorry," she gulped.

"Yeah." Jacko repacked the tray, lowered the tailgate, and slid it in. Then, breathing hard, he leaned against the truck.

"Gee, Perry, you look awful," Barbie told him tactlessly.

"You know what Mom says, she says the kind of work you do isn't good for a sick person, outside all the time in the hot sun, in this damp climate, that's what she says."

"Oh, does she," Jacko half-gasped.

"Um-hm. She thinks you ought to sell your property and move back to Tulsa."

"Yeah, that's what she told me. So what do you think?"

"I d'know," she replied, confused. "Mom says—"

"Oh, fuck it," Jacko interrupted. "You know what you are, Cousin Boobie, you're nothing but a mouthpiece."

"What?" Barbie said stupidly. She knew what a mouthpiece was, there was one on the trumpet she played in her high school band, when they marched onto the field at football games. She had a pretty red costume with gold braid and fringed epaulets, and most of the time she didn't even make any mistakes. For years afterward she kept her trumpet in its case lined with green plush on the top shelf in her closet, and sometimes when there was nobody else in the house she would take it down and blow a tune. "What d'you mean?"

"I mean Aunt Myra writes all your lines," Jacko said. "God. You don't know anything."

"Well, you don't know so much yourself," Barbie told him, choking back angry tears. His scornful expression, familiar since childhood, urged her on. "Like for instance you think Mom wants you to come to Tulsa so you can get well. She doesn't care anything about that, she just wants to get ahold of your property, so she can give it to the Republican party."

"Don't be stupid," Jacko said, ignoring Barbie's tears, which he had seen so often. "I'm not going to give Alvin's house to Aunt Myra."

"No," Barbie insisted, still sobbing. "But she figures that you'll die and leave everything to Aunt Dorrie, and Mom can get anything out of her. She always has."

"You don't know what you're talking about," Jacko said, but his expression was uneasy.

"I do too," Barbie gulped. "Like why do you think Aunt Dorrie traded in her house for that little nothing condo out by the mall? That was Mom's idea, when she needed money for Bob's campaign."

"Hold on." Jacko mopped his face with a green bandanna. "You're saying Myra made Mumsie sell our house?"

"Uh-huh."

"How come she didn't sell her own house?"

"Aw, she couldn't do that. She needs it for fund-raisers and receptions. Aunt Dorrie's place was no good for parties, it was too far out in the country."

For nearly a minute, Jacko said nothing. "Great," he finally managed. "Just great. Well, thanks for telling me." He slammed the tailgate shut, then frowned. "Hey, what happened to that other cattleya I just bought?"

"Huh?"

"That big white orchid with the orange center. The one I gave you to carry."

"I d'know." Barbie looked listlessly along the line of parked cars. "I guess I didn't bring it."

"Aw, shit," Jacko said. "You really are totally useless. Okay, you wait right here." Half running, half walking, he set off down the street.

For a moment Barbie followed his instructions; then, beginning to weep again, she stumbled slowly away along the beach road in the other direction, for no reason except the need to escape from Jacko's accusations and her continuing misery, and a vague idea of drowning herself and all her troubles in the sea.

The sun shone, the warm wind blew, the water shimmered deep violet and a clear, pale, liquid green, but Barbie saw none of this. She halted only when an obstacle appeared in her path, in the form of a folding table piled with books and pamphlets, and a hand-painted placard in large green letters:

SAVE THE MANATEE

Snuffing back tears, she stood and stared at this apparition, and then at the young man who sat behind the folding table on a folding chair, in the shade of a coconut palm. He had crimped yellow hair, a large sunburned nose, and dark sunglasses.

"Hey," she said finally, wiping her eyes on the back of her hand. "S'pose I wanted to save manatees, what would I do?"

"You'd sign this petition," he said, pushing forward a clipboard.

Slowly, Barbie took the pen he offered. "That's all?"

"Well, no. If you want, you could really help us." He removed his sunglasses to see her better, exposing watery blue eyes ringed with a rim of paler, untanned skin that gave him the look of a surfer or a raccoon.

"Like how?" she asked, inscribing her name and (after some thought) Jacko's address on the petition.

"Well, you could give us a few dollars," he suggested, evidently appraising Barbie as someone without extensive financial resources. "Or, you could address envelopes, hand out flyers at Mallory Dock, put up posters. Maybe sit at a table somewhere with this petition, like I'm doing now."

"Yeah?" she said thoughtfully.

"If you're really interested, you could come to the meeting next week with me."

"Yeah. I could do that," Barbie said slowly. "Sure. I'd like to save the manatee."

10

Later that day, as the sun grew even warmer, Jenny lay on the chaise longue beside the pool, protected by wire netting from the bugs that, since Mosquito Control, no longer existed. This afternoon the place looked neglected: Jacko was at work on other people's gardens and hadn't had time to sweep up the tropical debris that had fallen during the week of rain.

Jenny was tired of the pool and of the house that went with it. What she really wanted was to see Lee Weiss, even though she'd seen her on Friday and would see her again tomorrow. But she felt something almost like terror at the possibility that if she walked into Artemis Lodge unexpectedly Lee would look not only surprised, but a little bored.

Instead, she had thought, why shouldn't she go to the beach with Wilkie? After all, he was her husband, and couples who were married usually went to the beach together. She'd approached him to propose it as he descended from the study at the usual time.

"I thought I might come swimming with you," she'd said, touching his arm, smiling nervously.

Wilkie stopped cold. He stared strangely, fiercely at his wife, as if he were about to strike her. Then he said in the tight, controlled voice of a professor pointing out some obvious flaw in a student's argument, "But you're not ready."

"I'll get my suit on now; it won't take a minute," she'd promised.

"Sorry," her husband muttered. "I can't wait. Maybe another time." Then he pushed past her, across the sitting room, and out the door.

Jenny, stunned and faint, stood by the stairs, holding on to the ugly chrome banister so she wouldn't fall. Wilkie had been abrupt with her often lately—but never so harsh, so rude. Maybe he doesn't love me anymore, she thought. Maybe he hasn't loved me for a long time.

And maybe I don't love him either, she thought suddenly. Because how could anyone love a person who was so cold and unkind?

As she lay in the warm, dappled shade, a shudder went through her. Because if Wilkie didn't love her, and she didn't love him, everything was changed and wrong.

Perhaps he hadn't meant it the way it sounded, she told herself. Perhaps she was just touchy because she was physically frustrated. After all, it had been nearly two weeks since Wilkie had wanted to make love, and even longer before that.

Jenny wasn't used to being troubled by desire: for most of their marriage, Wilkie had always been the more passionate one, the one whose need was greater and more frequent. Then, about fifteen years ago, his demands had begun to slow down gradually, until at last they were perfectly matched at once a week. Those had been wonderful years, years of harmony during which Jenny never had the unkind thought (not that she'd ever expressed it, of course) Oh no, please, darling, not so soon.

But then, last autumn— It was because Wilkie was getting older, he claimed. One sad wet night he had mumbled those words, asking Jenny if she minded waiting a few days more. He had even asked if she'd like him to, as he put it, "stimulate her." "Would that be nice for you?" he had said.

"Oh no, thank you," she had replied with an embarrassed half-laugh, glad that Wilkie couldn't see her recoil and blush in the dark. No, that wouldn't be nice for me at all, she had thought. If he didn't want it too, it would be mechanical and horrible.

"Just asking," Wilkie had said, and he had laughed also, more freely. "I guess you're getting older too."

But she wasn't getting older, not the way he meant anyhow, Jenny thought. Especially not here in Key West where, as in most resorts, everything seemed designed to recommend and encourage sensual pleasure. In such a place, either you went along with it or, like Wilkie, you became more and more cross and tight and withdrawn.

Except for a few days last week, he's been even colder to me here in Key West, which was supposed to warm us up, Jenny thought. I wish we'd never come—

But she couldn't wish that, because if they hadn't come to Key West, she'd never have met Lee Weiss. And at the thought of Lee, she smiled in spite of her confused unhappiness.

When she couldn't see Lee it was nice just to think about her: Lee's deep laugh, Lee's smooth brown arms, Lee standing square on strong brown legs and feet below bleached cutoff jeans. Lee making salad in her big mahogany bowl: she never used a fork or spoon to mix greens, but tossed the lettuce and cucumber and tomato into a froth of green and white and red with her broad, tanned hands. Watching her, Jenny'd wanted to put her own hands into the salad with Lee's.

It was no use pretending, she said to herself, frowning now. It wasn't just Lee's intelligence and goodness and warmth she loved, it was the way she looked. She felt a sensual attraction to another person of her own sex.

And this wasn't anything new, not really. The only difference was that it was much stronger than ever before. Jenny had always thought that in general women were more beautiful than men. Most men, even good-looking ones like Wilkie, had scruffy hair in the wrong places—sometimes all over their backs, even—and coarse skin and rough hands and pale, knobby feet, and unaesthetic red dangling parts that ought to have been designed to be more private. Women were more graceful, more elegant, more delicately made.

She had always enjoyed looking at women's bodies, Jenny remembered. For instance, one of the best things about swimming at the college pool was watching people in the showers and dressing rooms: women of all shapes and colors, and all ages from toddler to grandmother. All so different, and most quite beautiful, really, even when they had tan lines or freckles or long strings of dark wet uncombed hair, big hanging breasts or almost none. They bent to pull on bathing suits, or twisted round to soap narrow knobby backs, or broad fleshy ones, or raised long-muscled legs to limber up before their laps.

Jenny had liked watching them for years without really thinking about it, or mentioning it to anyone. If Wilkie knew, he would be disgusted with her, even more than he probably was already. According to Wilkie, love of one's own sex was either a freak of nature, or a sign of immaturity, a selfish refusal to face up to adult responsibilities.

But that didn't make sense if you thought of Lee, who was more mature and responsible than practically anyone Jenny knew. And there were lots of mature responsible people like Lee, or like Jacko, one in ten, she'd read somewhere, and it wasn't their fault any more than it was anyone's fault for being tall or short or lame or blind.

When someone was handicapped in these other ways Wilkie was sympathetic, often generous. He gave money for the conversion of his books into Braille and tape, and he was kind to people with physical problems. A biologist friend of theirs at Williams had cerebral palsy, and at conferences and receptions Wilkie was always there to lift his wheelchair up steps or around obstacles, making a friendly joke of it.

About sexual abnormality, however, he had always been

rather unreasonable. This unreason had been socially inconvenient in the past, and it was even more inconvenient now here in Key West, where several of the most interesting winter residents were homosexual. "I don't really need to meet him," Wilkie had said of a famous elderly biographer and critic. "You know I don't get along well with fruits."

Fruits—that was a strange term, without any apparent referent in reality, Jenny thought as she drowsed in the sun—a term nobody else she knew used. According to Lee, Jacko was "gay," and the word made sense in his case, since he was usually cheerful. But nothing about him especially reminded her of fruit.

Though if Jacko were a fruit, she thought sleepily, it would probably be a peach, because of the warm tanned bloom of his skin, and the slight down on his arms and legs. Whereas if she, Jenny, were a fruit she'd be an apple: a McIntosh, or one of those white-fleshed Cortlands that were so good in salad. And Lee would be something more exotic: maybe a papaya, or a South American melon like the ones they sometimes had at the Waterfront Market. They smelled heavenly, and weighed heavy and warm in the hand; and when opened they showed firm, brilliant rose-orange flesh and exuded a rich sweetness. As Lee might if—

Half-asleep, Jenny smiled. Then she sat up, shocked at herself. No, that was awful, she mustn't think that way. Rising, she flung aside the thick flamingo-pink towel and plunged into the leaf-littered pool.

The first few inches, warmed by the sun, were pleasant; but

below that the water was icy from over a week of bad weather. Jenny shivered with the shock, but fought the impulse to climb out. Maybe it would do her good: after all, cold water was traditionally believed to be a cure for unwanted sexual desire. Setting her jaw, she splashed out in a fast crawl.

As she came up for air at the deep end of the pool, with dead leaves in her hair, and turned to start back, Jenny realized that there was someone else in the pool enclosure: a man in white pants and a red shirt. She blinked, resubmerged, and started swimming back more carefully.

"Hello there," he said, looking down from almost on top of her as she stood waist-deep in ice water, shivering and pushing sopping-wet hair and plant debris away from her face. It was Gerry Grass, holding some sort of large package.

"Oh, hi." Jenny's tone was flat. Wet, shivering, comparatively unclothed, and with her dripping hair on a level with Gerry's dry sandals, she felt at an unfair disadvantage. She waded toward the steps and climbed them. Now at least she was on his level; but though she was wearing a modestly cut green bathing suit from Land's End, she felt naked. It's the way he's looking at me, she thought, that overfriendly smile. Deliberately, she walked past him, wrapped the beach towel around herself, and sat down.

"I've brought you a present," Gerry said, following. "Happy Valentine's Day." He held out a large red heart-shaped box.

"Oh, really?" Jenny exclaimed. "I didn't realize it was—"

She laughed artificially. "Thank you." The box was heavily padded, and decorated with red satin ribbon. "I didn't expect— It's
years since—" Over ten years anyhow, she thought, since Billy
was young enough to give his mother a hand-made Valentine
cut from red construction paper and trimmed with sparkles. She
had five or six of them still in his folder, back home. Wilkie
had never given her anything on February 14; it was not one of
the holidays he recognized.

"It's because you were so good to me at lunch," Gerry said.
"Listening to all my troubles."

"Thanks, but it wasn't— You didn't have to—" Jenny
mumbled. In her view, Gerry's troubles were not of the first
magnitude. His laptop was acting up, his publisher had let one
of his books go out of print—the usual annoyances of the literary life, which even Wilkie sometimes suffered. It was also true
that Gerry's girlfriend had left him, but clearly that had been
coming on for a long time.

Gerry, now looking quite untroubled, pulled another chair
toward hers. "You can open it now, if you like," he suggested,
looking at the heart-shaped box.

"All right." She eased off the satin ribbon and lifted the
padded cover on a display of fancy chocolates in fluted dark-
brown wax-paper cups. "Oh, how nice," she said rather flatly.
"Please, have one."

Gerry reached, then retracted his hand. "Oh no; you first."

Jenny selected a small almond-shaped chocolate and put the
box on the footrest of her chair.

"Ah. Caramel," he said with satisfaction, smiling and chewing.

"Have another. Have as many as you like."

"I shouldn't."

"Oh, go ahead," she said, surprised at this wavering between greed and good manners in someone who after all was well over fifty and one of America's best-known poets.

"But it's your present," Gerry protested.

"One's supposed to share presents. That's what my mother always said."

"But it was hard, wasn't it?" Gerry grinned and shook back his thick, graying curls. "Especially when you didn't like all the other kids."

"Well, a little," Jenny admitted, smiling for the first time. It was restful lying here in the sun, having this totally childish conversation.

"That's the kind of sick society we were brought up in," Gerry announced. "Now what I believe is that you should share everything, but only with people you love and admire." He reached toward the chocolates again, giving her a sideways grin. Politely, she pushed them nearer.

"I hope that means you love and admire me," he said, plucking a cube wrapped in gold foil.

With difficulty Jenny restrained herself from moving the box away. "I never said I believed in your rule," she replied coolly. But Gerry only laughed, showing a gold filling that matched the foil.

Why, he's flirting, she thought; and he thinks I'm flirting back. Well, why shouldn't he think that? He knows he's an attractive man, with his broad-shouldered height and regular features. If I were to flirt with him, most people would think it natural, especially if they knew how strange Wilkie has been for months.

"You know what a friend of mine says," Gerry mused. "He says that even bad experiences, like what happened between me and Tiffany, can be productive for a writer. Because it's all fodder for poetry in the end."

"Mh," Jenny said, unconvinced and even a little repelled. The image of a large, fat workhorse appeared in her mind; he was standing in his stall, chomping greedily on the oats and hay of human unhappiness. She resolved even more strongly than before not to confide in Gerry, who might decide to feed her unhappiness, as well as his own, to that fat horse, whose name, according to him, was probably Pegasus.

". . . It's been good for me, being in Key West," Gerry was saying when she began to listen again. "Now that Tiff's gone I'm working really well. I was getting kind of stale back in California. Cynical, even. I hate that." He frowned, lowering his untidy gray eyebrows; then smiled at her, leaning nearer; she could see the thick growth of gray-blond hair sprouting from his fire-red shirt.

"Yes?" she said, smiling very slightly back.

"It was a bad atmosphere for me, L.A. Tiff and her friends were always talking about money. Sometimes they pretended to be concerned about art, or politics, or the environment, but what really interested them was the bottom line, you know?"

"Mm," Jenny uttered. One of the good things about Gerry was that he cared seriously about the environment. A few years ago he had published a book on nature and the contemporary men's movement called *Men of Oak,* which contained several quotations from Wilkie's works. Wilkie, in an exchange of civilities, had quoted from one of Gerry's poems in an article in the *Atlantic.*

"Fucking creeps, most of them, excuse me," Gerry muttered almost to himself, sitting back.

"That's all right," Jenny said pleasantly; but what she felt was annoyance and disappointment. Gerry had stopped flirting, if he ever had been flirting. But that was what she had intended, so why should it annoy her?

"Not all, though," he continued. "I met this really remarkable guy from Oregon last month. He's designing a wind-power system that's going to save God knows how much gas and coal. He was impressive. I get discouraged sometimes about the way the world is going, you know? Then I talk to someone like him, and I think we've got a chance. But Tiff and her friends— All they wanted to find out was, would his windmills make a profit, and if so how could they get in on the financial action, you know?"

"Yes; I've met people like that," Jenny said.

"It's good being out of that atmosphere. Being with someone like Wilkie. I've always admired him, even before we met. I was so damned pleased when he wanted to quote those lines from 'Voices of the Lost Woods' in his article. You know, people still come up to me, people who never read poetry, and say . . ."

He wasn't flirting, Jenny told herself. He was just being agreeable to me because I'm married to Wilkie, the way everyone is. Everyone except Lee.

"What he has is, he has integrity. He's never compromised, never done anything he could be ashamed of, or anybody could kid him about."

No, I suppose not, Jenny thought, tuning out again as Gerry's praise of Wilkie segued into regrets about the way the world was going, and his own guilty involvement in this deterioration.

". . . this ad for laptop computers; probably you saw it, it was in a lot of magazines last summer," Gerry was saying when she tuned back. "Some woman Tiff knew fixed it up for me. I didn't like the idea much, but I needed to pay Gaia's college tuition—that's my youngest daughter, she's at Stanford—and I agreed. So they put me in an ad with this football player. He was pushing seven feet and must have weighed well over two-fifty. The way we were photographed, he looked like a big healthy, happy jock, and I looked like some kind of loony aesthete. I got a check for five thousand and a new laptop, but I lost a lot of credibility. Tiff couldn't see it. She just kept saying, 'All publicity is good publicity.' "

"Mm." Jenny had often heard this dubious phrase; it was one of Wilkie's new agent's favorites.

"You ask me, that's like saying, all chocolates are good chocolates. The truth is, some might poison you." He gave a short unhappy laugh and helped himself to another, presumably nontoxic, piece of candy. "I bet Wilkie never did anything like that ad."

"Well, he— No, not like that," Jenny agreed, deciding not to mention the charity appeal in which a foolish unposed photograph of Wilkie had appeared. In this photograph Wilkie's mouth was open, showing his partial plate, and he was being presented, evidently much against his will, with a giant stuffed toy panda representing World Wildlife.

"But you know, people will forget that ad," she said. "I mean, if they ever saw it in the first place. I didn't, for instance." Automatically, she assumed the soothing, almost crooning tone she had perfected over the years for responding to any public insult or embarrassment to Wilkie. "Most people never remember ads."

"I hope so." Gerry stared down into the pool, then lifted his head. "You know that lost-looking white heron I was telling you about Friday, that I saw on the street?" he said. "I put him into a poem. I'd like you to look at it."

"That would be nice," Jenny said, aware that to refuse to look at a writer's work is always a deadly insult.

"Great." Gerry leaned toward her, put his warm hand on her cooler arm, and looked warmly into her eyes. "It's up in my study, if you don't mind climbing stairs— It's getting kind of hot here."

Yes, Jenny realized, it was hot—especially under Gerry's hand. Maybe she had been right after all.

"I'll give you a drink," he added, removing his hand but not his gaze.

"Oh— Thanks, but I don't need—" He's flirting again, she told herself; maybe more than flirting. Well, at least I'm not going up there half-naked. "I'll tell you what," she said. "I'll get some dry clothes on and be with you in ten minutes."

"Great," Gerry repeated. "Hey, don't forget your chocolates. They'll melt out here."

Carrying the oversized red heart-shaped box of candy, Jenny crossed the sitting room, glancing out the front window as she passed to see if Wilkie was on his way back from the beach.

There was someone by the gate, but it was only Jacko's cousin Barbie, a large, silly, blonde young woman, who had turned out to be one of Wilkie's fans, and "totally thrilled" to find herself staying in the same compound. Twice already she had informed Jenny that it must be wonderful to be married to a man like that. Yes, it used to be, Jenny had thought. Today Barbie, who was presumably waiting for her cousin Jacko, was wearing an especially silly getup: a pink ruffled off-the-shoulder blouse and short white shorts, like a female country-western singer.

Barbie's aunt, however, was a quiet, pleasant woman, Jenny thought as she climbed the stairs. She'd had an interesting conversation with her yesterday about plants. According to Dorrie Jackson, the luxuriant elephant-eared climbing vine by the gate was a common philodendron. In this tropical climate, when it found a suitable tree, it totally metamorphosed. Registering Jenny's polite but unconvinced expression, Mrs. Jackson had proved her point by showing her, on the ground by the tree, a shoot of the same plant in its smaller, northern form.

On the other hand, Jenny thought as she peeled off her bathing suit, Barbie's mother, Myra Mumpson, was a very annoying person. Yesterday, for instance, she had more or less forced her way into the house, saying that she wanted to "look it over" for Jacko, the future owner of the compound. "I'm a Realtor, you know," she had explained, pushing past Jenny into the hall. She then made a rapid tour of the place, letting fall at intervals phrases that might have come from a real estate brochure, phrases like "contemporary island kitchen" and "en suite luxury master bath."

Jenny had tried to keep Mrs. Mumpson out of Wilkie's study, but without success. "I just want a tiny peek, it won't take a minute," she had cried, opening the door. Wilkie, who was sitting in the rocker gazing out of the window, looked up, his expression of surprise quickly turning to rancor. "Who the hell was that awful woman?" he had asked Jenny angrily later, as she had known instantly that he would.

Opening the door of what Mrs. Mumpson had referred to as an "elegant built-in wardrobe," Jenny selected the clothes that seemed appropriate for a drink with Gerry Grass in his present state of mind: canvas shoes, tailored slacks, and a man's shirt in a dense weave that would neither suggest erotic advances, in case that was what he had in mind, nor make them easy.

Dressed, she descended the stairs, glancing out the window again. Wilkie was not on his way back from the beach now, she saw. He was here already, standing by the gate in his swim trunks, talking to Barbie Mumpson, who stood close to him, looking up with the worshipful expression common to Wilkie's fans.

But as Jenny began to turn away from this familiar sight, something unfamiliar happened. Barbie stood on tiptoe, flung her arms around Wilkie, and kissed him full on the mouth. Occasionally in the past Jenny had seen overeager women try to do this, and her husband's reaction had always been a speedy though polite flinch of withdrawal. But now Wilkie did not withdraw; he might even have joined in, though it was hard to be sure. He just went on standing there.

And maybe nothing unfamiliar has happened, Jenny thought as Barbie finally let go of her husband: nothing that hasn't happened before. Maybe that's why Wilkie's been so strange lately, so distant. Maybe when he said last year that they were getting older, it was her age he was speaking of, not his own. He meant that Jenny no longer interested him romantically, that he wanted someone younger. Well, I'm not interested in you either, Jenny thought. I hate you.

Meanwhile Wilkie was still standing close to Barbie Mump-son, gazing dumbly at her. But soon probably he would come into the house and pass Jenny with the same quick, chilly, distant glance he had thrown in her direction when he left for his swim.

She couldn't bear that, not now. Turning away, Jenny ran across the room, out through the sliding glass doors, toward Gerry's apartment.

An hour earlier, fleeing his wife and his house, Wilkie Walker had hastened along the cracked sidewalk toward the ocean. He breathed heavily, and his heart thudded as if he had narrowly escaped some disaster. No, two disasters. When Jenny'd looked at him and laid her soft hand on his arm and said, so lightly but so longingly, that she'd like to come swimming with him, Wilkie had been shaken by two almost uncontrollable, irreconcilable impulses: first, to embrace her and cry "Save me!" and then to shove her away, shouting "Leave me alone, get your hands off me!" Just barely, he had resisted and escaped.

He kept twisting round, looking back every few moments to see if by some dark chance Jenny had scrambled into her bathing suit and was following him. That would be fatal—no, anti-fatal—because even if he was in the water first he wouldn't be able to carry out his plan. He couldn't disappear with his wife gazing after him, swimming after him, calling him to come back, crying aloud that he was out too far— But that's just what Jenny would do if he refused to hear and plunged on. It would probably end with his having to save her, because though graceful in the water, she was not a strong swimmer.

Again Wilkie glanced over his shoulder. The street, blood-spattered with the wet crimson petals of bougainvillea, was still empty. Perhaps Jenny wasn't coming. Perhaps this time he would make it. He hurried on.

Now the ocean opened up ahead. The sun was low in the sky, a flat, pale orange; it wouldn't be long to sunset. Conditions were ideal: a strong wind blew from the south, the tide was high, and the sea was streaked with irregular, rocking clumps of creamy camouflaging foam.

Wilkie passed—for the last time, he hoped—the list of Higgs Beach Regulations. Deliberately he strode across the rough sand to the pier, ignoring the people gathered there. At the far end he dropped his sandals, shirt, and towel onto the boards. He descended the wet stairs, holding tightly to the salt-slimed wooden railing as the waves sloshed against him. He must not slip now and merely injure himself.

The sea, after a week of rain, was cool, almost cold. Wilkie stroked strongly away from the pier, then paused, treading water and watching the sun slide into its slot between sky and sea, waiting for the sunset-gawkers to disperse, for the air to flush from gold to gray for the last time. The horizon, almost to the zenith, was piled with thunderclouds, possibly signaling imminent rain. That was good; a sudden storm would make his drowning more plausible.

Soon only five people remained on the pier: a teenager down near the beach, plugged into a Walkman; a late-middle-aged couple near him; and at the far end a man in an electric-powered wheelchair and his slight, black-haired Chinese (or possibly Japanese) attendant. Wilkie had seen this pair before: almost every day, before the weather changed, they had been here at sunset. The invalid was young, painfully thin, and breathed through a tube. According to Molly Hopkins, he was probably one of the many AIDS victims who came to die in Key West. At the end of their lives they returned to the place where they had once been happiest—and where, quite possibly, they had been infected and infected others.

As Wilkie waited, fending off the small, choppy waves, the Asian attendant came round in front of the chair and leaned over the invalid. They gazed steadily at each other and appeared to speak. Then the attendant bent down, moved the breathing tube aside, put his hands on the other's shoulders, and kissed him passionately. At last he replaced the tube, stood up, and started back down the pier toward the van in which they always traveled, stumbling once or twice as if blinded.

Wilkie, embarrassed by this scene, turned away. For a moment he continued to tread water, watching the fading red light on the outer sea, resenting the delay, resenting the presence of the dying man. The sun was gone, the rose-colored clouds were fading; why the hell didn't they leave? Wilkie frowned: though no one would ever know, it displeased him to realize that the last strong emotions of his life had been irritation and distaste. Shaking his head, he struck out for the darkening horizon.

Almost at once there was a loud, heavy, explosive splash in

the water behind him. Wilkie stopped swimming and looked round. The pier was empty except for the three tourists near shore. The sick man in the wheelchair had disappeared as if wiped off the sunset with a sponge.

The tourists had heard the splash too: they were scrambling to their feet, shouting, running out along the pier, then huddling together and staring into the water on the far side. One of them waved and screamed something unintelligible at Wilkie.

His first reaction was pure black rage. Goddamn it, why did that have to happen now? Then, automatically, he started swimming hard toward the pier.

That wasn't an accident, he thought suddenly as he clung to the soggy railing and began to haul himself up. That was a suicide, deliberately and courageously planned. It was high tide, and a heavy wheelchair with a man strapped into it would go— had gone—straight to the rocky bottom in ten or twelve feet of sea water. Four minutes, that was the longest anyone could live without air, and this fellow wasn't anyone, he was fatally ill.

Down by the beach the invalid's Asian attendant—no, lover, Wilkie realized—began to run toward them, shouting. I saw them say good-bye, he thought. I saw their last kiss. He clung to the slimy steps, above which the tourists stood now, jabbering and pointing. Witnesses, he thought, on hand to prove that the other fellow—the lover—wasn't physically involved in this death. And I also am a witness.

We won't be able to get him up, and it's not what he wanted; but we have to seem to try, Wilkie told himself as the teenager and the Asian descended the wet stairs. And it'll be a nasty, hopeless business. Meanwhile, the two middle-aged tourists pounded back along the wooden walkway, probably to call the police.

The next fifteen minutes, as Wilkie had foreseen, were highly disagreeable. With great difficulty, he and the other two men splashed and forced their way through the rusted, barnacle-encrusted supports of the pier. The wet, rubbery, floating seaweed, and the high surf, made it hard for them to reach the heavy wheelchair; the fading light prevented them from seeing it clearly. The third time Wilkie dove, he half grasped something bony and limp that must have been an arm, then lost it. Soon he had a pain in his hip and a long bleeding scrape on his shoulder.

Now the police and an ambulance had arrived; followed by a tow truck with a winch attached. Already a little crowd of those human ghouls who are attracted as if by magnetism to disaster had begun to gather. Men with heavy equipment ran out along the pier, shaking the boards.

Obeying their shouted instructions, Wilkie and the other amateur rescuers swam and squeezed their way back under the pier. He dragged himself out of the water into a cold wind, realizing that he was exhausted and shivering. His arm was bleeding, but there was nothing to staunch the blood with: his towel, his shirt, and one of his sandals were gone, no doubt knocked into the water by some fool in the confusion.

Wearily, he tramped back up the pier. One of the policemen

stopped him, asking stupid repetitive questions and clumsily recording his name, address, and phone number.

"Okay, Dad, you better get on home now, warm up," the cop told him officiously. "We'll be in touch with you later to take a statement."

Exhausted, furious, Wilkie limped across the beach in his remaining sandal, and started along Reynolds Street in the windy dusk. It was beyond reason, beyond justice, that he should be balked this way, over and over again. It was as if there were some invisible but vicious force that wanted to thwart him; that had already thwarted him again and again. Something that wanted him to die slowly, humiliatingly, in agony.

Halfway up the first block he stopped. What the hell am I doing? he thought. I could go back now and finish the job. He turned. The tow truck and ambulance were still there, their red and white lights flashing off-sync. He'd have to wait till they left, and he was now shivering almost continually, but what did that matter? He'd be dead before he could come down with anything.

But if he died tonight, his death would be arbitrarily but inexorably linked with that of the man in the wheelchair. Wilkie could imagine the headline in the *Key West Citizen:* TWO DROWN AT HIGGS BEACH. Worse, the *Times* would probably mention it in his obit. Forever and ever after, his life of respectability and achievement would be associated with that other pathetic death.

Yes, and some might even wonder if there was an actual link between them. The human mind is confused by coincidence into suspecting connection; it formulates false explanations. Synchronicity, it had been called by Jung (a thinker for whom Wilkie had little use). Was Professor Walker's death at the same time also a suicide? That was the kind of question that would occur to the sort of critics and biographers who are always sniffing out scandal where it doesn't exist.

He'd seen it happen to others, friends who were gone now. Bill Lumkin, for instance, killed in a fire trying to rescue his neighbor's old tomcat. Afterward people started wondering why the cat was in the Lumkin's barn anyhow, what did that mean? When the answer of course was, it was there to catch mice.

Maybe Wilkie Walker knew the man in the wheelchair, the scandal-hounds would speculate. Maybe they had once been intimate.

No. That must not be. He must postpone his accident until there was clearly no connection between it and the one he had just witnessed. He must wait a day—probably, to be safe, two. Two days of pretending to eat. Sleep. Talk. Of more promises to lecture and write that would never be kept, but would prove he planned a future and was a good and generous person. Wilkie felt the weight of those days crushing him like stones falling from the darkening sky. Chilled to the bone, almost dizzy with despair and exhaustion, and becoming increasingly conscious of a full bladder, he turned and limped on through the cold evening.

He would have to tell Jenny what he'd just seen, to prepare her for the arrival of the police. But not just yet. First he needed a hot shower and a shot of bourbon. The windows of their house were unlit: maybe nobody was home.

No such luck. There was a female figure by the gate, half illuminated by the outdoor lights that went on routinely at dusk. Not Jenny, but the friend of the manatee, Barbie Mumpson.

"Oh! Professor Walker!" she cried in a rush, grabbing his sore arm. "I've been waiting for you, I've got so much to tell you! I met this really nice man on the beach this afternoon, and he says there's a lot of wonderful people in the Keys that are working to save the manatee. And I told him you might be interested, and they were absolutely thrilled. They're having a big meeting here next week, and I said I'd ask you to speak. So please, please, say you will, because I promised I'd try as hard as I could—"

The girl stood close to Wilkie, clutching his injured arm, looking up at him with her round, stupid baby face, panting at him, blocking his way into the house. Get rid of her, he thought.

"Yes, all right," he growled, because in two weeks he would no longer exist. Exhausted, he tried to put her aside, but Barbie wouldn't let go.

"Oh thank you, thank you!" she whined; and then suddenly she bounced up and planted a long wet, sloppy, warm kiss on his mouth. "Oh, that's so wonderful. They'll be thrilled, I know they will. I just hope I'm still here to hear you, that would be so great!"

"Yes, well, excuse me," Wilkie said, detaching himself finally, rather roughly. "I need to—"

"Oh, gee, of course, I'm sorry—" Finally, she got the hell out of the way. "I didn't realize, I was just thinking—" But the rest of her gush of words was lost, amputated by the slam of the front door.

11

On Tuesday morning, as Lee Weiss sat on her veranda fringing some handwoven napkins, Jacko's pickup truck swung into the driveway. He leapt out, carrying a great armload of white hothouse flowers, followed by his fluffy white cat, Marlene.

"Hey," Lee called. "What've you got there?"

"They're from Dennis," he said, mounting the steps. "People keep sending them, and he wanted them out of the house."

"Out of the house?" She contemplated the mass of foliage: lacy ferns, sprays of daisies, waxy trumpet lilies, ruffled carnations, tall gladioli, and roses in every shade of white from snowflake to heavy cream. "But the funeral's tomorrow. They'll keep until then."

"He doesn't like the white ones. For Chinese people, white is the color of death."

"Yeah, I read that somewhere, but— Well, hell, after all, Tommy is dead."

"Dennis says they spook him. Anyhow, the service is supposed to be a celebration of Tommy's life. So I thought maybe you could use them."

"Well— Sure I can, I'm not Chinese. Thanks, that's great." She removed her bare brown feet from the battered wicker coffee table and stood. "Bring them into the kitchen; I'll find some vases.

"So how's Dennis doing?" Lee asked as she filled her deep sink with cool water and immersed the mass of flowers.

"Kind of strange." Jacko sat on the creaky wicker sofa and took Marlene onto his lap. "I think he's still in shock."

"That figures." Lee began to cut the stiff, woody stems of the carnations under water.

"He phoned me late last night, asked me to come over. He didn't sound too bad, but by the time I got there he was really down. He started in again about how his life was over, and he'd never love anyone the way he loved Tommy. Then he said he might as well be dead too, and if he hadn't promised Tommy to go on living he'd probably kill himself sooner or later."

"Tommy made Dennis promise to go on living? That was smart of him." Lee started to fill a glazed blue jug from White Street Pottery with white carnations.

"Oh, yeah. Tommy told him that because he was HIV-negative it would be his job from now on to enjoy all the things Tommy used to enjoy, twice as much. Drink Dubonnet and lime, and play their Callas records, and have artichokes with home-made hollandaise at least once a month. He said he'd be watching, and if he looked down and saw that Dennis wasn't having a good time he'd be very cross."

"Down from where?"

Jacko pointed toward the ceiling.

"So he was sure he was going to heaven." Lee took a breath. Indoors, the scent of the hothouse flowers, especially the lilies, was almost oppressive.

"Yeah. You know Tommy. Always the optimist, right to the end."

"So Dennis is supposed to enjoy food and drink and music," Lee said. "But not sex." She moved the carnations aside and started on some ivory roses with dark red, thorn-studded stems.

"Oh no. Sex too. Tommy told Dennis he had until Easter to get laid."

Lee laughed. "He was a sweet guy, you know, Tommy, even if he had a lot of dumb political opinions. Most people might not want to think about how their partner was going to go on screwing after they were dead."

"Yeah," Jacko said after a pause. He wiped a curl of thick, dark hair out of his eyes.

"You think Dennis will meet the deadline?" Lee asked, setting aside a battered but elegant silver coffeepot full of white roses.

Jacko raised his shoulders, dropped them. "Who can say? He's such a romantic. Always wants to be 'in love.'" He crooked the fingers of both hands, placing imaginary quote marks around the phrase. "Wants to 'really know someone deeply.' "

"That makes it harder," Lee agreed, contemplating a rose so thick and perfect that it seemed to be shaped of white suede.

"I don't get it, you know," Jacko said. "The way people have to clutter up sex. When I see somebody I think is hot, it can ruin everything to know too much about him."

"I know what you mean," Lee said. "I can't tell you how many times I've lost interest when I found out some really attractive woman was a right-wing Republican, or believed in previous lives."

"Right. You want them to stay strangers. The best thing is if I don't know where somebody comes from or even what his last name is. Just that he's strong and beautiful and sexy, like those flowers." He gestured at the tall copper vase of lilies with their almost pulsating golden stamens.

"But there has to be more to it than that," Lee said, frowning.

"Not for me. What I really like is, I look at some guy, he looks back, that's it. Fast and hard. The first time is always the best. Then if I don't get away soon enough, he starts to tell me how he has migraine headaches or he was unhappy at work that day. I want to say, Look, would you please shut up? You're ruining everything. Only if I do, the guy will either get hurt feelings or try to kill me. So I hang around awhile to be polite, and he starts explaining how he grew up in New Jersey and didn't get on with his father, or how he's training to be a computer programmer, or he has a terrier named Oscar with a flea problem, whatever."

"But hell, that's part of the fun." Smiling, Lee began to add lacy maidenhair ferns to the roses. "It is for me anyhow. Getting to know somebody, who she really is and where she comes from, feeling more and more comfortable with her, knowing she'll be around awhile, that's all part of it. Don't you ever want that?"

"You're like my mother, you want me to meet a nice man," Jacko said, smiling. "My trouble is, I've met too many nice men. The better I know somebody, the less he excites me. Pretty soon he isn't a great fuck anymore, he's just some guy I know."

"Yeah, but—"

"The last thing I want anyhow is a permanent live-in relationship; that'd be like prison. You don't want it either, or you'd have one by now."

"It's not as easy as all that," Lee said. "Not if you're stuck with love." A troubled expression appeared on her face.

Jenny Walker loved her, she was almost sure of that. What she feared was that Jenny loved her only as a friend. When they met Jenny smiled with pleasure. Lee could hug her then, even kiss her quickly, and Jenny would reciprocate, but no more. Sometimes when they were together, sitting close, leaning over the loom or a book or a pot of lime marmalade, Lee couldn't help touching Jenny as if by accident.

Jenny never startled or drew back; usually she smiled, but also she never moved nearer.

A dozen times Lee had psyched herself up to make a serious move, and then chickened out. What if she shocked Jenny, drove her away? Then it would all be over, and she would have nothing. Jenny would never sit in this kitchen again, looking so slim and beautiful, never stand next to her at the stove, laughing as they made pumpkin soup and licked each other's fingers.

"So how's it going with Mrs. Walker?" Jacko asked, demonstrating again his intermittent ability to read minds.

"Okay," Lee answered repressively.

"You mean you still haven't leveled with her."

Lee shrugged and said nothing. Jacko was silent too; he sat there slowly stroking Marlene, causing her to purr even louder and blink her pale-green eyes. But Lee knew what he was thinking: he was thinking, if love is so great, how come it's making you miserable? I'm not miserable, she told herself. Whenever I see Jenny I'm wonderfully happy.

"I don't get it," Jacko said. "I mean, hell. The way she's over here all the time. And the way she looks at you. I bet she's just waiting for you to make a move."

Again, Lee said nothing, but she could not prevent the expression that came over her face. To conceal it, she looked away from Jacko toward the mass of creamy roses, the darkest of them almost the same shade as the skin on Jenny's neck when she lifted her hair.

"Well, I better get on home," he said finally. "See how Mumsie's holding up."

"Isn't she well?"

"She was fine when I left. But she's been having lunch with Aunt Myra; that's enough to get anyone down." He laughed shortly. "You want to know something? Now that Myra knows I'm sick, she won't touch me. Won't even shake my hand, in case she should catch something."

"That's disgusting. Stupid, too."

"I had this sudden idea yesterday to grab Myra's hand like I was going to kiss it, except then I'd bite it, really give her a scare. Only I'd probably get blood poisoning, she's so mean."

Lee laughed.

"Y'know, it's weird, having this disease. It's like I'm carrying a concealed weapon. Been carrying it for years, probably, only I didn't know it. Didn't want to find out."

"Uh-huh." Lee frowned.

"The thing is, at first you tell yourself, it's not true, it's just something they have in Haiti. You think, it can't happen to me, I'm so young, so beautiful, so healthy and strong— But all the time I was sort of walking around in my sleep, killing people without knowing it, like some zombie in an old horror flick."

"But you don't know that," Lee insisted. "You don't know that you gave it to anybody."

"No. But the odds are pretty damn good I gave it to somebody, just like somebody gave it to me. Sometimes I get really down. I tell myself, for a few years you were a murderer. You'll burn in hell." He laughed uneasily.

"Not if you're sincerely repentant," Lee said. "Isn't that the rule for Christians?"

"I don't know," Jacko said. "Even now, when I think of some of the fantastic times I've had, I can't make myself wish they'd never happened. Sometimes I think it was worth it, those years. That I was lucky to have been born when I was. The younger guys now, they're all scared shitless, or else they're really crazy and self-destructive." He shook his head. "Well." He stood up. "You'll be there tomorrow," he added with a slight upward inflection.

"Oh, sure," Lee said. "Tommy made me furious sometimes, he was so opinionated and bossy. But he was a smart guy, and a damn good real estate agent. He found me this place; he helped me get a loan and start the business. If it wasn't for him, I don't know if I'd have had the nerve."

"You always had the nerve," Jacko said. "All you needed was a little push. Come on, Marlene. Time for some lovely kibbles."

Her back stiff under the white pique sundress, her hands hot and wet on the wheel, Jenny Walker drove toward Artemis Lodge. It was Tuesday afternoon, and she wasn't supposed to be there until Wednesday morning, but she couldn't wait any longer: she had to talk to Lee. Anyhow, she had to talk to someone, and Lee—so warm, so lovely, so unjudging—was the only possible person.

Since Sunday afternoon, when she saw her husband kissing Barbie Mumpson, Jenny had been in a state of confused misery, gradually deepening to despair. She'd planned to tell Lee about it the next day, but that had been impossible. When she got there Monday morning the place was crowded with people mourning and exclaiming over the death of a local real estate agent called Tommy Lewis, which was featured on the front page of the *Key West Citizen*. Even Jenny had been drawn into the conversation when she realized that he was the man in the wheelchair whom Wilkie had seen drown at Higgs Beach the day before.

According to Lee's friends, it hadn't been an accident at all. Tommy, who was terminally ill with AIDS and in constant pain, had deliberately released the brake on his wheelchair and steered it off the pier into ten feet of water. He was strapped in, so he couldn't rise to the surface, and by the time the police and the ambulance arrived he was dead. Tommy's friend Dennis had known what was coming, and just before it happened he went back to the car, pretending to be getting Tommy a sweater, so that nobody would suspect him of murder afterward.

If Wilkie were still Jenny's trusted and beloved husband, she would have tried to remember all the details in order to relate them when she got home. But he hadn't really spoken to her in weeks; and since she'd seen him kissing Barbie Mumpson, she was afraid to have him speak to her; afraid of what he might say.

For over twenty-five years, whenever she had a serious problem, Jenny had taken it to Wilkie. He would listen patiently, console her, advise her. After a while, what had seemed "really heavy," as their son Billy put it, would begin to weigh less. Under Wilkie's steady gaze the problem would lose substance, like a block of ice gradually melting into water and mist. What helped tremendously was that Wilkie looked at everything in a long-term perspective. Compared to global warming or the destruction of animal species, even awful things like the fatal illness of Jenny's favorite aunt, or Billy's flunking chemistry at Cornell, began to diminish and dissolve. Such events, Wilkie's response suggested, were a natural part of life. They would pass; or they would not pass, but would be survived.

Now, though, Jenny couldn't go to Wilkie with her pain and her problem; he was the problem. What she'd seen on Sunday had proved to her something she'd dreaded for months, but hadn't wanted to know: that her marriage was probably over.

And now an unpleasant, long-forgotten incident from the early years of her marriage surfaced in Jenny's mind, like an ugly catfish rising to the surface of a clear forest pool. It had occurred in Manhattan, when she was making conversation at a literary party with a nervous, goggle-eyed woman who claimed to be a close friend of Wilkie's first wife. "I'm sorry for you," this woman had whispered, or rather hissed. "You look like a nice girl. But you'd better watch out. He won't stay with you either."

After all these years of happiness the prediction, or curse, of the catfish woman was about to come true, Jenny thought. It was clear that Wilkie didn't love her any longer—maybe didn't even like her. She wasn't sure yet that he loved Barbie Mump-son instead, because he had started being strange and cold and distant long before he'd met Barbie. Besides, how could some-one as brilliant and serious as Wilkie love a ninny like Barbie?

But a lot of men did love women like that, Jenny thought. Sometimes even brilliant, famous men. She knew several who had left their wives for girls half their age, often silly blondes like Barbie—who was, Jenny recalled now, thirty-six, about half Wilkie's age.

Of course not all men were that way. Jenny's father, as far as she knew, had never run after stupid blondes. And Gerry Grass had said outright yesterday that girls like Barbie bored him. He knew the type: "art groupies," he called them. In the sixties and seventies, he said, when he started appearing at political demonstrations and writers' festivals, there were a lot of girls like that around. Most of them were totally uninteresting; they couldn't tell one poem or one poet from another, and they had no real depth. They weren't "grounded."

Jenny had been glad to hear this, even if it possibly wasn't relevant to her situation. She had felt grateful and warm toward Gerry, but she didn't even want to see him now, because shortly after that he had become part of her problem.

At first, talking to Gerry in his disorderly apartment over the garage—or rather, listening to him, which was what men always wanted and needed—had been a relief and a diversion. She hadn't of course told him what she'd just seen. Instead she had listened while Gerry read his poem about the heron, in which he imagined himself becoming the bird and soaring over the "blood-pulsing" ocean. She continued to listen when he went on to deplore the current condition of poetry and its audience. Even ten years ago, he said, he had real hopes for the literacy of our civilization. But now, though he tried to keep up his courage, telling himself that there must be readers out there somewhere, often his energy flagged.

"I keep fighting, keep writing. I hang in there," he had said. "But it's damned hard sometimes."

"Mm," Jenny replied, with a sympathetic, automatic smile.

"We're in a bad piece of history." Gerry took another gulp of vodka and tonic.

"Mm."

What made it harder, he continued, was not having support at home—having what, when you got right down to it, was an enemy in your own house. Yeah, he meant Tiffany.

"Oh, surely, she . . ." Jenny began, but then her voice trailed off. Why should she defend Tiff, whom she didn't like or approve of—who was really just another Barbie Mumpson, with more self-confidence and a degree in accounting. After all, Gerry too was one of those famous men who had left a very nice wife for what in his case had turned out to be a series of younger women.

"The goddamned truth is," Gerry went on, "women these days, most of them, aren't on your side."

"Mm," Jenny said, thinking of Cynthia, Gerry's ex-wife, who had certainly been on his side and also very sweet, though not much of a cook and a bit spacey—Wilkie once said she was the kind of person who should stay off all drugs, even marijuana. So why did you leave her? she thought.

"They're all suspicious of men; they have a chip on their shoulders— Sometimes I think their shoulders are covered with chips," Gerry said, producing in Jenny's mind an image of Tiff and Cynthia, both looking suspicious and sprinkled with wood chips and sawdust. "When you ask for a little help, a little warmth or sympathy, they think you're trying to exploit them or denigrate them. You want to know what Tiff said before she cut out?"

No, not particularly, Jenny thought, but Gerry did not wait for an answer.

"She told me, 'If you need your proofs read, you can hire a professional proofreader. I want to relax when I'm on vacation.' "

"Really," Jenny said, without surprise.

"I have to tell you, I envy Wilkie," Gerry continued. "There aren't many women around like you these days, so understanding, so beautifully supportive—and so beautiful too," he added, giving her an appreciative, romantic look. "I just hope he knows how lucky he is. I hope he's grateful."

"Well, that's— Thank you," Jenny said, smiling nervously and looking down, suppressing the impulse to tell Gerry how grateful Wilkie had recently been.

"I mean it." Gerry reached out, not for his drink this time, but for her hand. Partly out of politeness, she did not pull it away. After all, he was very good looking; and (though irrationally) she valued compliments more when they came from good-looking men.

"That's what I need: someone like you. I know it now." He fixed her with his long-lashed dark eyes.

"Oh, I don't really . . ." Jenny murmured. Men had often said such things to her before, and she had always gently, firmly, almost automatically discouraged them, putting on what someone had once described (though not to her) as "Jenny's go-thither look." But today her response was slower; something sore and lonely in her wanted to savor the moment.

"If you'd like me to look over your proofs, I could," she said, gently but firmly withdrawing her hand.

"Thanks." Not discouraged, Gerry leaned closer and shifted his grip to Jenny's bare arm just above the wrist. "I couldn't ask you to do that. But it means a lot to me, that you should offer."

"No, really. I'd be glad to help."

"You're a wonderful woman."

"Not at all, it's nothing," Jenny stammered, both warmed and embarrassed by the current of feeling directed at her. "Wilkie doesn't need me all the time right now." She swallowed painfully, thinking, He doesn't need me, doesn't want me, any of the time. "I mean, I'm sure he'd be glad to share me," she added with an awkward light laugh.

"Yeah?" Gerry put his other hand on her arm, further up. "That wouldn't be my reaction," he said. "If you were mine, I wouldn't want to share you with anyone."

"Oh, I don't know . . ." she heard herself reply inanely. You see, she said in her mind to Wilkie. Some people still want me and think I'm wonderful. "Wilkie says—" She didn't know how to complete the sentence: she only knew she must mention his name again, to remind both of them again that she was married.

But it was Wilkie, really, who should be reminded of this, Jenny thought. He was the one who had forgotten. And if he had forgotten, why shouldn't she? She liked Gerry: his enthusiasm, his seriousness, his thick, curly, graying hair. And he was a famous American poet. Her mother always said, two wrongs don't make a right. But why shouldn't they? Wouldn't that be fair?

"I'm sure you don't mean—" she said distractedly.

Gerry, paying no attention to these fragments of speech, began to move his hands up Jenny's arm, like a boy eagerly climbing a soft white rope. "You're the woman I've looked for all my life," he said. "You know that?"

"No I'm not—" Jenny began, but the rest of the sentence was smothered in an enthusiastic embrace. Still clutching her arm, Gerry launched himself toward her. He smudged a warm, damp kiss on her mouth—as might have been expected, it tasted of vodka and tonic. Then he browsed sideways, finally burying his face in her hair, while Jenny, stunned by the suddenness of it, did nothing.

"Jenny, my sweet Jenny," he mumbled. "I love you so much."

Jenny gasped. For the first time in months someone was holding her and kissing her and saying fond romantic things. But it was all wrong, because she didn't love him.

"Please, don't!" she choked out, pushing the heavy warm arms and face away, almost weeping with the effort and the disappointment. "I can't— I mean, I love my husband and he loves me." It was something she had said before; something she regularly had to say now and then when some acquaintance tried to push a flirtation or a friendship too far.

Always in the past, as these words were uttered, they had magically formed themselves into a delicate but impenetrable thorny hedge. Now, though, they fell to the ground and lay there like the plant debris round the pool outside, broken and faded, because they were a lie.

But Gerry didn't know this. He moved back, gazing at her, blinking his long eyelashes. "Oh, Jenny. God, I'm sorry. I couldn't help—"

"That's all right," she said weakly, trying to catch her breath.

"I had to give it a try, I guess." He grinned. "I mean, well, the way I figure it, when you really want something, you go for it."

"Mm," Jenny uttered, though in fact this had never been true for her.

"I suppose you're furious with me."

"No. Of course not." Jenny smiled gently.

"God, you're wonderful." Gerry spread his arms, as if to

embrace her again, this time theoretically. "Most women these days, they'd set the PC police onto me."

Breathing more normally now, she managed a smile. "Oh, I'd never do that."

"And you won't say anything to Wilkie," he added uneasily.

"Of course not," agreed Jenny, who had never revealed such incidents in the past. "I wouldn't want to worry him."

That's not true, she thought. I would like to worry Wilkie. I would like him to know that another famous gifted man is romantically interested in me.

Gerry sighed. "It makes me desperately unhappy, your loyalty to him," he said. "Don't get me wrong. I respect it; I honor it. Only, goddamn it, I think it's a mistake." Again, he leaned toward Jenny and put his hand on hers.

"Please, don't—"

"Wilkie doesn't need you anymore, not the way I do. You have to realize that. He hasn't published anything important for, I don't know, maybe ten years. His career is pretty much over. Anyone can take care of him now."

"That's not true," Jenny exclaimed, her voice trembling. "He's just finishing an important new book—"

"And he's not all that considerate of you, either. I've noticed— Anyone can see it. The other evening at dinner, cutting you off when you were talking, and complaining because the coffee wasn't already on the table—"

Again, Jenny suppressed the impulse to confide in Gerry. "That was nothing," she said. "And Wilkie does need me," she added. "Anyhow he will, as soon as his book is finished."

"But I need you more." Gerry smiled. "I've got so many projects— Besides, I need you as a woman."

"Wilkie has lots of projects too," Jenny said, refusing to hear the implication. "As soon as he finishes this book, there's so much to do— There's so many speeches and articles he's promised— It's only now, while he's still writing, that I could possibly have time for your proofs."

"You mean the offer still holds?" Gerry looked at her with the expression of a large hungry dog.

"Yes, why not?"

"That's great." He smiled broadly. "God, you are a wonderful woman," he added for the third time; and Jenny did not protest the repetition.

But the warming trend caused by Gerry's romantic enthusiasm had been short-lived. That evening, going through the proofs of his collected essays and reviews of poetry, *Walking on Fire,* a reaction had hit Jenny, followed by a depression that was with her still. A very well-known and attractive American poet had embraced and kissed her, and though briefly amused and flattered, she hadn't cared really, because she didn't love him.

She didn't love Wilkie either, Jenny thought now. Maybe she even hated him. The only person in Key West she really loved and wanted to see was Lee Weiss.

As she pulled into the driveway, Jenny saw that Lee was on the front porch, framed by the orange and gold of her trumpet vine and—thank goodness—alone. She wore a scarlet mumu, and her lap was full of crimson cloth; but in the brilliant sunlight these usually clashing colors were somehow beautiful, like a flock of tropical birds.

"Well, hello there," she called as Jenny climbed the steps. "How's everything?"

"It's—it's awful." To her embarrassment, Jenny's voice began to shake. "I have to talk to you," she said in a rush. "I've been wanting to for days, but then your friend died, and I couldn't— There were so many people here yesterday, it didn't seem right." She swallowed.

"Oh, Jenny. I'm sorry, I didn't know— What is it?" Lee rose and came close, putting one warm hand on Jenny's bare shoulder.

"It's, uh, Wilkie. Sunday afternoon— He was late coming home from the beach, and then I looked out the window and saw him, by the gate—" She sobbed and swallowed. "He was just standing there, where anybody could see him, kissing Barbie Mumpson."

"Sunday afternoon? You mean, when Tommy drowned? But your husband was there, he was one of the people who tried to save Tommy."

"I guess so. Yes." You're missing the point, she thought. But maybe that was part of the point, too, that Wilkie should do such a horrible thing right after he'd seen someone die.

"Jesus, what a creep," Lee exclaimed. "I'm sorry," she added in a different voice. "I didn't mean— Hey, don't cry." She sat beside Jenny and put one arm around her. "I mean, what the hell, go ahead and cry if you feel like it." Pulling Jenny strongly against her, she kissed her wet cheek.

"I don't— I can't—" Jenny began to weep in earnest. It was a relief to sob openly, a relief and a pleasure to lie close against Lee's warmth and strength. "The thing is," she said finally, still clinging to her friend, "I never thought Wilkie could be like all those men who get tired of their wives after a while and just throw them away. I thought he was different."

"Has he said he's going to throw you away?"

"No," Jenny said, raising her head. "Not yet."

"Maybe this thing with Barbie is just a kind of temporary insanity," Lee suggested.

"Maybe." Jenny smiled weakly.

"It could be. Hell, she's going back to Tulsa in a couple of days anyhow. Besides, anybody'd have to be crazy to even look at an airhead like her if they had you." Lee clasped Jenny gently but closely now, stroking her back through her thin cotton dress.

"But it's not just Barbie. Like I told you before, Wilkie's been so strange for months, and when I try to ask him about it he won't listen, he gets all cold and angry and frightening, and then he goes into the study or the bathroom and shuts the door. I think he hasn't liked me for a long time really."

"That's hateful. There must be something wrong with him."

"I thought it was me," Jenny sobbed.

"Of course not." Lee laughed. "There's nothing in the world wrong with you."

"So what do you think is wrong with Wilkie?"

Lee shrugged. "Who knows? Men get like that sometimes. They see time running out, and something in their hormones starts telling them to chase after younger women, and they get kind of mean and crazy and boring for a while."

"So you think he'll get over it?"

"I don't know," Lee said. "Sure, he might."

"But what if I don't get over it?" Jenny wailed. "I mean, right now, I'm not sure I love Wilkie either. I think I might sort of hate him, actually." She gulped tears.

"Well, that sounds natural." Lee smiled. "Anybody might feel that way." She pushed a long, slightly damp strand of Jenny's pale hair back from her face.

"But it's me too. I'm so confused; I don't know what I'm doing at all. And Gerry Grass, you know, that poet I told you was living over the garage?"

"Uh-huh," Lee agreed.

"I agreed to read the proofs of his new book, and now he keeps coming around and telling me I should leave Wilkie and go to Los Angeles with him and help him with his work. He says Wilkie doesn't appreciate me, and he's in love with me and we'll be very happy together."

"Really?" Lee scowled and sat back, gazing at Jenny. "And are you in love with him?"

"No, of course not." Jenny laughed shakily. "But I was thinking at first, maybe that's what I should do, because that way I would be of some use in the world. But then I decided that was silly, because Gerry's book won't make any difference to the world anyhow, it's just all about him and what he thinks of other poets."

"I see." Lee smiled slightly. "Well, that makes sense," she said, gathering Jenny back to her again. "I wouldn't want you to go to Los Angeles with somebody you didn't love. Especially since I know you hated the place when you lived there."

"Oh, Lee." Jenny gave a final gulp, drew away a little, and looked up at her friend. "It's such a relief to talk to someone. I'm so happy I know you—"

"I'm happy I know you, too." Lee kissed Jenny again, but this time, as if by accident, the kiss fell on her mouth. It was a soft, gentle kiss, and Jenny met it equally and gratefully.

"You're so kind," she said, smiling. "Listening to me go on this way."

"And you're so lovely." Lee kissed Jenny again, but this time it was deeper and longer than the kiss of a friend.

"Oh!" Jenny murmured, when she could speak. She felt dizzy, as if she were inside of a snowball globe that had suddenly been turned upside down, showering her with sparkling flakes. She blinked and put one hand to her head, trying to focus.

"You don't know how long I've been wanting to do that," Lee said.

"N-oh," Jenny admitted.

"Ever since I met you on the beach, practically."

"Really? I didn't think—" Jenny smiled unevenly. "I mean,

I only thought—" The air still seemed full of sequined snow-flakes, whirling in some substance thicker than air: fine, transparent oil, or a heady, gold-tinged solution of perfume. "I wanted to too," she admitted. "But I never thought—"

"I love you, you know," Lee said, taking a step back to look into her face. Jenny, still faint, could only stare and smile.

"Oh, hell," Lee added in a very different voice, looking past Jenny toward the street, where a pink Key West taxi had just pulled up. "That's got to be the woman who's rented the tower room; she was supposed to be here at five."

"Oh." Slowly, dizzily, Jenny moved away. "I should go home anyhow," she said. "There's all these people coming for dinner, and I haven't even started to cook. I wish I'd never asked them."

"But you'll be back tomorrow," Lee reminded her.

"Oh, yes."

Lee moved closer and kissed her again; and Jenny, out of love and gratitude and desire, kissed her back.

"Call me when you get home, all right?" Lee said.

"All right," Jenny whispered. "I'll try."

12

In the house on Hibiscus Street, the following day, Wilkie Walker was killing time until the time came to kill himself. The act, he had realized by now, would be relatively easy; what would be hard was making it seem accidental. Already he had been balked three times: by Gerry Grass, by the weather, and by the death of the man in the wheelchair. Fate, he was beginning to believe, wanted to thwart him. But the imaginary goddess (whom he pictured as an elderly, ugly version of classical statues of Justice, in a bunchy chiton) would not succeed. He would die today; all he had to do now was live through the next six hours.

He had already made what preparations he could without betraying his purpose, and taken all possible actions that would tend to conceal it. He had opened today's mail and set the bills

aside for Jenny to pay as usual. He had scribbled notes of acceptance for her to type up and send to two publishers who wanted
him to read and recommend books. He had even agreed to
speak without remuneration on "Life Below the Surface" at a
Key West Conference on The Writer and Nature—an event
that under normal circumstances he might have declined to
attend, let alone participate in. Now, however, he could agree,
with no consequences except an enhanced posthumous reputation for generosity and goodwill.

But all this had taken only an hour or so, and the rest of the
day still extended before him like the barren, endless salt flats of
the southwest, where he had made some of his most difficult
excursions as a naturalist. To maintain an appearance of normality he had walked to Valadarez's newsstand on Duval Street as
usual and purchased the *Times*. He had spoken as usual to the
proprietor: the last words he would utter in his life, the lie:
"Fine, thank you."

Back home, he had methodically unfolded and refolded the
newspaper page by page—another lie, a lie of commission—so
that it would not seem to have been unread. There was no point
in reading it. He would never know how the vote on taxes went
in Congress tomorrow, nor pay these taxes; he would not view
the new plays or films recommended by the critics.

When about to die, some men overindulge, since there will
be no consequence to their health. "The condemned man ate a
hearty meal." But the idea of such a senseless binge—indeed of
any sort of food or drink—now repelled Wilkie. He was not
hungry; he had not really been hungry for a long while. If he

were to create the illusion of normality, however, he would have to eat, or at least appear to have eaten, the sandwich his wife had left for him.

Facing this necessity, he opened the fridge and slowly removed the sandwich, which rested on an orange Fiestaware plate in company with a frill of Boston lettuce, a sliced tomato, and a dill pickle, the whole covered by plastic wrap. His impulse was to shove everything in the trash. But if he did so Jenny might find it later and wonder about his health or state of mind. It would be better to conceal the food in the garbage can outside.

Wilkie glanced toward the kitchen window. Barbie Mumpson was still reading in a lounge chair by the overheated communal pool, with her legs wrapped in a pink towel and another towel over her head and shoulders. This struck Wilkie as wholly idiotic. If she didn't want a sunburn, why didn't she stay indoors?

But the answer was simple: Barbie hadn't stayed indoors because she was lying in wait for him, just as she had often done before. If he were to start for the garbage bins she would call out to him; she would want to talk about the endangered manatee. And if he didn't reply calmly and cordially, later she would report to Jenny and everyone else that his behavior had been strange.

Wilkie had nothing against manatees per se, or even against Barbie—who, he thought now, somewhat resembled one. Like her the aquatic mammal was a little heavy, a little fleshy, a little slow; not too well adapted to the modern world. The manatee, however, caused no trouble to anyone: it rested in shallow warm waters eating water weeds. As he watched, Barbie's large-breasted, towel-wrapped (and thus apparently neckless and one-legged) form blurred in his nearsighted vision into that of a female manatee of the sort that sex-starved eighteenth-century sailors on long voyages mistook for mermaids. And of course Barbie herself belonged to a declining species: the fans of Wilkie Walker.

Right now Wilkie did not have the energy to converse with or about a manatee, or risk reaching the garbage bins without the creature spotting him. Also, it occurred to him, it would be best that his stomach contain the remains of a normal lunch in case of an autopsy. He opened the fridge again, poured himself a glass of seltzer, placed the plate containing the sandwich (chicken, apparently) on the kitchen counter, sat on a chrome-and-plastic kitchen stool, and attempted to eat. In his mouth the bread and meat tasted like chilled cardboard.

He got the first bite down, then another. The third, though, seemed to stick somewhere in his esophagus, causing sudden acute pain. Wilkie tried to swallow, but in vain. Instead of easing, the pain increased and spread.

A gulp of seltzer, rather than relieving the situation, worsened it. In growing distress he pushed the plate away and stumbled to the fridge, where he remembered seeing an open box of baking soda. Breathing hard, he mixed himself a dose and choked it down.

There was no relief. Instead the pain grew worse each moment, spreading inside his chest, modulating rapidly into agony. Not indigestion, he thought, gasping for air. This is a heart attack.

Shakily, Wilkie clutched at a chair and lowered himself onto it. Yes, he thought. Fate, having denied him his chosen exit from life three times, had now awarded him an ugly, painful death of her own choice: a death that presumably had been hanging over him for years, though that stupid doctor back in Convers had said his heart was fine, would last him to ninety.

Still the pain worsened, becoming agonizing. It was as if he had been shot or, as had actually happened when he was in fifth grade, been hit in the chest with a baseball bat. Then, though, the effect had gradually diminished; now it continued to increase, so that it was hard to sit upright. Clumsily, he collapsed onto the tiled kitchen floor, and though he tried to stop it, a shameful noise, half-groan and half-scream, forced its way out of his mouth. I don't want to die this way, Wilkie thought. That's too bad, Fate said to him unpleasantly, rattling her scales.

Hang on, he told himself, lying in a fetal position on the cold floor and breathing with difficulty. It can't be long now. Soon it will all be over, soon I'll be dead in this ugly rented house, where Jenny, when she returns from her stupid part-time job, will find me—

But that will be horrible. His beloved wife will walk into the kitchen and see him lying on the cold, ugly green-and-white marbled floor—a floor composed of genuine antique Cuban tiles, Kenneth Foster had told them with admiration, though to Wilkie they resembled some disgusting dish made of boiled cabbage and whipped cream. Jenny will find him lying dead here, his face distorted, in a puddle of urine and feces. A disgusting, terrible sight; a disgusting, terrible memory for the rest of her life.

No, no. Somehow he must get out of here, go somewhere else to die. Slowly Wilkie struggled to his hands and knees, then to his feet, gasping with pain. Dragging himself along the kitchen counter, he reached the back door, got it open, and shouted to the towel-wrapped manatee by the side of the pool.

In the front room of Artemis Lodge, Jenny Walker moved restlessly between the desk, the sofa, and the wide window-seat, where she perched on the handwoven red and purple cushions and stared out at the street, waiting for Lee to return, waiting to be alone with her again. When she'd arrived that morning other people were already there, preparing to accompany Lee to Tommy's funeral and the reception afterward.

Though the house was quiet now—all the guests were out too—Jenny's thoughts were loud and stormy. Lee had said she loved her, but what did that mean? Did it mean as much as it meant to Jenny? She might know if she'd been able to call Lee as she'd promised, but when she got home Wilkie was there, and if she called he might pick up the phone, as he sometimes did, and overhear her. Was Lee angry that she hadn't called, was that why she'd hardly spoken to Jenny this morning?

Though the guests had seemed to enjoy it, to Jenny her dinner party last night had been almost unbearable—simultaneously boring and tense. She had been thinking of Lee the whole time, wanting to be with her. Wilkie had drunk rather a lot, and had been alternatively almost wildly talkative, and silent. At the end he had suddenly announced to everyone that *The Copper Beech* was finished, something he hadn't yet told Jenny.

Though upset and insulted, she had managed to conceal her surprise. And after the guests had congratulated him and left she had said only that she was glad the book was done, and she looked forward to going over the final chapter with him.

"Yes," Wilkie had said repressively. "We'll talk about it tomorrow. I'm too tired now." He had glanced at her in a blurred, peculiar way, and opened his mouth as if about to say something more.

"Yes?" Jenny had murmured finally. But Wilkie had shut his mouth and fallen into a morose, stubborn silence.

It was wonderful that the book, their book, was finished. But why hadn't he told her? What if he wasn't planning to let her help him with it? What if he were going to ask Barbie Mumpson to help him instead from now on?

That would be disastrous. Barbie would make a complete mess of the job. She wouldn't realize how much editing and revision Wilkie's work always needed: she probably wouldn't be able to read his handwriting—few people besides Jenny could. Possibly she couldn't even spell. She wouldn't know how and where to find illustrations, or check the statistics and quotations, things that Wilkie, because he could rely on Jenny, was rather careless about.

When the book appeared it would be full of errors, and the reviewers would point this out. That would serve Wilkie right, but it mustn't be allowed to happen, because *The Copper Beech* was too important, because it was her book too. She must speak to him, must persuade him to give her the manuscript.

But what if, when she spoke, Wilkie were to say, No thanks. What if he were to say, I'm sorry, but I've found someone else to help me. I don't love you anymore.

All right, she could say back. I don't love you either. I've found someone else too.

Outside somebody was turning in at the gate, coming up the walk under the palms; but it was only Perry Jackson. At first Jenny hardly recognized him because he was dressed formally in black slacks, a gray sports jacket, a white shirt, and a formal unsmiling expression.

"Hi," he said, leaning against the door frame. "Lee asked me to tell you, she'll be a little late. If you want to leave now I can hang around till she comes."

"No, that's all right," Jenny said, determined to hold her ground. "I don't have to go anywhere."

"It won't be long. She just stayed on to be with Tommy's parents."

"That's fine," Jenny assured him, thinking again how kind Lee was, how warm-hearted and generous. "Was it a nice memorial service?"

"Yeah, I guess so," Jacko said flatly. "The music was good, and there was a big crowd. Your husband didn't come, though."

"Oh, no," said Jenny, surprised. "Did you expect him?"

"Well. Sort of. Most of the other people who tried to save Tommy were there. The cop and both the paramedics, and a couple of tourists."

"Really?" Remembering the detached, exhausted way Wilkie had spoken of the incident, Jenny knew that it would never have occurred to him to attend. She looked down, embarrassed.

"Hey, don't worry about it." Jacko smiled briefly. "Listen," he added. "I'd like to ask you a favor."

"Yes?" Jenny said politely, but in a manner that withheld assent. People often asked her favors in that tone of voice; usually what they wanted was some sort of access to Wilkie, something she couldn't always promise, and soon would never be able to promise.

"I'd like you and your husband to witness my will."

"Oh. Yes, of course," Jenny said, surprised.

"It's because you're not mentioned in it, and everyone else I know is, more or less." He smiled, shrugged.

"But you're not—" Jenny swallowed the rest of the sentence, recalling that in spite of appearances Jacko was ill; was perhaps even dying.

"You'll have to come to the lawyer's office. Maybe sometime this week, if you can make it."

"Yes, of course— I mean, I'll ask my husband and let you know," Jenny said, wondering if Wilkie would in fact agree to witness Jacko's will—if he would ever again agree to do any-thing she suggested.

"Thanks. Well, see you around."

Fifteen tense minutes later, Jenny looked up and saw Lee climbing the front steps, crossing the porch. She was also dressed formally, in a black dress, black espadrilles, a black and purple handwoven chenille shawl, and a black, brooding expression.

"Hi, sorry I'm late," she said, hardly glancing at Jenny. "How's everything?"

"Oh, fine," Jenny replied in a thin voice. "Vicki and Sara checked out of Room Three, and the woman who's arriving today phoned to say she'll be here around six. There were a couple of calls about rates and vacancies for March, and Marie-Claire wants to come back in April. I wrote down everything and said you'd be in touch. How was the memorial service?"

"I guess it was good. If anything like that can be good." Lee did not look at Jenny but at the blank wall next to her. "The church was full, and they played a Maria Callas tape, and Allen Ingram read a poem. People who didn't know Tommy or Dennis very well probably felt better." Her voice broke.

"Oh, Lee." Jenny went toward her. "I'm so sorry."

"I want everyone to stop dying. I can't take it anymore." Lee began to sob. Unlike Jenny, she did not cry easily and grace-fully, but in a loud, wrenching manner. "Dennis is devastated. Tommy was his life, more or less. Now he doesn't know what the hell to do with himself."

Like me, Jenny thought.

"And Tommy's parents," Lee went on, gulping back angry tears. "That was so awful."

"I guess even if you know it's coming—" Jenny suggested.

"It wasn't like that. They were upset all right, but they were mostly sorry for themselves. They didn't do anything for Tommy when he was sick except send money. They came down maybe twice for a couple of days. They were embarrassed by the whole scene today, Tommy's friends crying and one of the waiters at Henry's Beach House coming to the church in full drag and sobbing out loud, with tears running down his makeup."

"Mm," Jenny murmured, thinking that she too might have been embarrassed by this.

"And now his parents want Tommy's ashes, so they can put them in the family plot in Raleigh. They think that'll make up for everything, show they accept him. They don't grasp why everyone is enraged and Dennis won't even speak to them."

"What's going to happen?"

Lee shrugged. "We're working on it. Tommy wanted to be buried in the Key West cemetery, he bought a plot there with room for both of them. But now his lawyer thinks Dennis should forget about that and scatter the ashes before the parents get a lawyer of their own. The whole thing is moronic, fighting over a cardboard box full of grit and flakes. I said to Dennis, what do you care, if Tommy's around anywhere he's here with you. But he's not rational right now."

Neither am I, Jenny thought. Look at me, she thought, not letting go of her friend. Speak to me. And finally Lee did.

"So, how's everything with you?" she said.

"Oh, all right, I guess. And I think Wilkie's better. Anyhow he's agreed to be in this conference here next month on The Writer and Nature, you know?"

"Yeah, I heard about it. My cousin Lennie Zimmern's going to be there too."

"The one from New York who criticizes everything."

"Uh-huh." Lee smiled. "Hey, I'm glad you're here," she said in a different voice. "Last night, when you didn't call, I thought—"

"I couldn't, I didn't dare."

"Never mind. You're here now." From a distance of only a few inches, Jenny and Lee looked at each other with the searching, fearful expressions of people about to jump into a dark, fast-running river. "Tell me something," Lee asked. "Did you mean what you said yesterday?"

"Yes. Oh, yes." They were so close now that Jenny could see the separate springy dark hairs of Lee's heavy baroque eyebrows, the faint scatter of freckles over the strong bridge of her nose. "Did you?"

"Yeah." Lee moved closer, and first offered, then received, a long, soft kiss. "You can stay for lunch, can't you?" she asked finally, moving back.

"Oh, yes," Jenny repeated.

"That's great. There might not be much to eat though, except bread and cheese. I didn't have time to shop."

"It doesn't matter. I love bread and cheese." Jenny smiled, and lifted her hand to stroke Lee's thick, dark hair. I can touch her now, she thought. I can touch her whenever I want.

"There might be some tomatoes. Let's go see." Lee started for the kitchen, then turned back abruptly, almost banging into Jenny.

"What is it?"

"Nothing, I'm just going to put on the answering machine." Lee smiled. "We don't want to be interrupted."

"Nobody's answering either number," Barbie reported, coming into the hospital room where Wilkie lay—no longer in acute pain but blurred, bruised, and exhausted by this pain, and by the many shots and tests and procedures he had endured over the past several hours, including one in which he had had to drink a glass full of thick, sickly-sweet, nauseating liquid chalk. It was the fourth or fifth time Barbie had tried to phone his wife, first at the lodge and then at home.

"I don't understand it," he said, sounding as if he were speaking from the bottom of a cold, foggy well. "Jenny should have been home hours ago."

"How're you feeling?"

"Better," he managed. Physically, this was true. Mentally, however, Wilkie was frustrated and enraged. Why was he still alive? What was the point of such agony, if it wasn't the prologue to a speedy death?

"It doesn't look like a heart attack to me," the doctor on call (a small, skinny, probably incompetent young man) had said.

"But I'd like to keep you under observation overnight, do some more tests, right?"

"Awright," Wilkie had agreed, confused by pain and thinking, You'll find out you were wrong. A mistake. If he wasn't going to die today, he had better get out of here as soon as possible, before they turned him into one of those half-corpses that are kept half-alive in intensive-care units for weeks and months producing profits for a hospital. Hooked up to tubes, and a machine to monitor his heart.

And even if I do get out today, Wilkie thought wearily, it'll be too late to swim. That means another entire day to drag through before it's over. Again, as often in the past weeks, he saw Death retreating from him along the shore. He visualized him as a classical Ingmar Bergmanesque figure: tall, pale, stern-faced, skeletally thin, wearing a black, hooded cape and carrying a scythe and an hourglass full of dark sand. But that was wrong, he thought. Death was not retreating any longer, but turning to look over his shoulder, waiting for Wilkie to catch up.

"Is there anything I can get you?" Barbie interrupted.

"No," Wilkie muttered. "Thank you," he added, not managing to smile at Barbie, though he was, or should be, grateful to her. After she understood what was happening she had been reasonably competent. She had called a taxi, remembered that he would need his wallet and insurance cards, helped him into the cab, and accompanied him to the hospital. And once there, she had insisted on immediate treatment.

"This is Professor Wilkie Walker, he's a very important, famous person. You've got to take care of him right now, right now!" she had more or less screamed at the emergency-room staff, while Wilkie, half-fainting from pain, almost unable to speak, slumped in a plastic chair. "If you let him die it'll be on TV and in the newspapers. I'll tell them all about it, and everybody in America who cares about animals will hate you forever." And almost immediately someone had located a doctor.

If I wasn't going to die, Wilkie thought, I'd do something for her, something for the manatee. (In his drug-blurred mind they were still merged.) A moving but scientifically sound essay in the *Atlantic,* say. Something that would counteract the public disregard for ugly endangered species—nonphotogenic, noncuddly.

". . . Or maybe Mrs. Walker went to the grocery," Barbie's voice said; apparently she had been speaking for some time.

"Possibly," Wilkie agreed faintly, opening his eyes halfway. Again he felt irritation at his wife's foolish, low-status job. It was clear that she was being exploited, paid not much more than their cleaning woman back home. Normally he would have strongly discouraged Jenny from working at any guest house. But, wanting her to form local connections, he had decided not to interfere.

"I'll try Mrs. Walker again in fifteen minutes, okay?"

"Thank you," he repeated. It occurred to him that seen from below and to the side, as he was seeing her now, Barbie Mumpson, like the manatee of whom she had reminded him, was what many people would call "cute" or "cuddly" rather than childish and overweight. The manatee of course was not overweight; it only seemed so because of its streamlined, fat-insulated shape. But so did seals and penguins, whose images were all over the museum and nature shops. With proper handling, and the right sort of illustrations—drawings, not photos—the manatee could probably be made to seem cute, even cuddly.

"I appreciate your help," he added, realizing that something of the sort was called for.

"Gosh, that's all right," Barbie gushed. "It's a privilege. I mean, really, it's great for me to be some use to somebody, especially somebody like you." She swallowed audibly.

"Mm," Wilkie said, his attention beginning to drift again. A children's picture book, with a preface for their parents; that might be a good idea, he thought. He could probably get something down tomorrow morning, leave it for Jenny. Manny the manatee. Or did that sound too Jewish? And you had to think of the PC angle these days too. Maybe Manny and Annie. He could already imagine the stuffed toys, though, thank God, he wouldn't be around to see them. Jenny and his agent would find the right artist and the right publisher, and the profits could go to Save the Manatee.

". . . And I guess my husband had an excuse, in a way," Barbie was droning. "I just kept messing up with reporters, and I couldn't even give him a baby."

Irritated by the interference with his thoughts, Wilkie gave Barbie an impatient glance that she missed because she was staring at the floor. "Maybe he couldn't give you a baby; did you ever think of that?" he said.

"No, I—" She shrugged helplessly. "We were going to go

for tests in D.C., but then everything got bad and I left. But it was probably my fault. I mean, everything usually is." Her voice wavered. "So I was really low when I got here. But Mom says I'm just being selfish."

"Selfish?"

"Well, yeah. Thinking only about myself, and not about Bob and how he needs me to support him and be there for him. A wife belongs with her husband, Mom says."

Though in general Wilkie agreed with this statement, he said nothing. Why was Barbie telling him all this? he thought. Why did she imagine he was interested? If she would go away he might get some rest.

"Anyhow, Mom said if I didn't go back it could ruin him, was that what I wanted? Didn't I love him, like I promised in First United Methodist?" She gave a wet sigh.

"Mh."

"So I said, I didn't know if I loved Bob now, not really. But she said that didn't matter, and it was my Christian duty to forgive his sins and cleave only unto him."

"Uh-huh." Wilkie's frown deepened. He despised religious cant and managing women, and in their only meeting he had formed an aversion to Myra Mumpson, who had asked if he were the author of "that sweet little old book about the mouse."

"Only the thing is, when I think of going back to Washington, I just can't bear it. But if I don't, it's like I'm no use to anybody in the world, and I should just go down to Higgs Beach and drown myself, you know?"

"For Christ's sake," Wilkie said. Was everyone in Key West

planning to imitate him in this farcical way? He gave Barbie Mumpson a look of great irritation, which she missed because she was staring out the window into the hot, pale sky.

"It'd be easy," she went on, "because there's no lifeguard. So I thought I'd go real early some morning, like five or six, when it's still pretty dark and nobody's around."

"I hope you've given up that stupid idea," Wilkie said as strongly as he could. "You're a healthy young woman; you have your entire life ahead of you."

"Yeah, well, you can have my life. All it is is one big mess."

"So? You can change it."

"I d'know," Barbie replied vaguely, not admitting this. "Anyhow I'm sorta glad I didn't drown myself yet, or I wouldn't have been home today."

"No," Wilkie agreed.

"I mean, that kinda made me feel like there was something I could do, you know? Usually I just think, I'm alive, but what for?"

Wilkie turned his head on the stiff hospital pillow to look at Barbie. Her thick untidy yellow hair, her plump shoulders slumped in the pink T-shirt, her expression of confused despondency. It would be just like her to go and drown herself at Higgs Beach before he could do it. Then when he did, he would be part of a trend.

"There are plenty of things you could do," he muttered crossly, casting about for examples.

"I d'know," Barbie muttered, raising her head a little.

"For example, you could stay in Key West and get some kind of useful job."

"Like what?" She snuffled up tears and stared hopefully at Wilkie. Feeling exhausted and incapable of further encouragement, he shut his eyes.

"Maybe I should try Mrs. Walker again?" Barbie said finally. Wilkie, feigning sleep, did not answer; and after a while he could hear her leaving the room.

The sooner I get out of here the better, Wilkie thought as he lay there. He had a long-standing hatred and distrust of hospitals. Under a pretense of public service, the system was infantilizing and commercial. When you were too weak and frightened and in too much pain to protest, they took away your clothes and forced you into a wrapper that reminded him of the baby clothes his children had worn in the first months of their life: flimsy limp cotton garments tied with tapes. And the hospital bottom line was money. Though he was obviously in agony when he arrived, possibly dying, before anyone would even speak to him they had to see his insurance card.

"Well-well, Professor Walker." Halfway to sleep, Wilkie opened his eyes again reluctantly. The sissy little doctor stood looking down at him. "How are you doing?"

"Not bad," Wilkie admitted.

"Well-well. You know, I was absolutely correct. There's no cardiac trouble. No sign of anything of the sort. In fact, your heart should be good for another twenty years."

"Really," he mumbled skeptically.

"My guess is, you've had a gallstone attack. That's what the tests suggest."

"Really?" Wilkie frowned, unconvinced. "But the pain—"

"Oh, that's standard. Gallstones can be really nasty. Famous for it." The doctor smiled, showing small, even, yellowish teeth. "But nobody ever died of them."

"Ah?"

"You've never had an attack like this before?"

"No. I told you that already."

"Well-well. If you're lucky, you might never have another. And incidentally, Professor Walker, you'll be glad to know that the barium X ray shows a very healthy digestive system."

"How do you mean?" In spite of himself, Wilkie's voice rose.

"All clear. No sign of any obstruction." The doctor paused, checking Wilkie's face for comprehension and apparently not finding it. "No sign of a malignancy, for instance," he added, lowering his voice as he pronounced the dreaded word. "We were a little concerned, naturally, because of the rectal bleeding."

"Bleeding?" Wilkie bleated. I have been found out, he thought.

"You hadn't noticed it?"

"No," he lied. "You mean, you're telling me," he said slowly, trying to clear his head, "that I have rectal bleeding, but in your opinion I don't have, for instance—" He took a breath "—cancer of the bowel or colon?"

"That's correct." The little doctor positively smirked. "But it wouldn't hurt to do something about those hemorrhoids when you get home, especially if you see any more blood in your stools. You should be checking for that regularly at your age."

"Ah," Wilkie muttered, trying to evaluate the information he had just received. Keys Memorial was a nowhere provincial hospital, and this doctor was a wimp and an asshole. Possibly he was too dumb to read test results correctly and realize that Wilkie was terminally ill with heart disease or cancer of the bowel or probably both. "So I can go home now, right?" he asked.

"Well-well, no, I wouldn't recommend that. I would strongly recommend that you stay here overnight and get a good rest."

"Hmph," Wilkie said, marveling again at the belief of the medical profession that anyone could get a good rest in a hospital. But he did not waste time on the paradox. What he had to consider was that possibly he was not going to die of a heart condition, at least not immediately. He could get on with his life; that is, with his death. But not today. It was already late afternoon, and after what he had been through he doubted that he had the stamina to swim out far enough. There was no hurry, after all.

"So I'll look in again early tomorrow morning," the little doctor was saying. "Oh, and before I forget, Professor Walker. Could I have an autograph? My nurse is a great fan of yours, it seems."

"What? Uh, certainly."

"Great." The doctor produced a pen and a prescription pad. "Her name is Bessie."

Awkwardly, Wilkie raised himself on one elbow, causing his head to spin. He scribbled the name as he had done so many times before, and now perhaps for the last time, adding the usual meaningless phrase, "With best wishes" and his signature.

"Thank you," the little doctor told him, removing the pad and pen. "She'll be thrilled."

13

At Artemis Lodge, the following day, Lee Weiss sat behind the desk trying to match guests and rooms for the months of April and May. Ordinarily this was easy, since by then the rush of refugees from winter began to slacken, and after mid-April it was mostly only Canadians who still wanted to come.

Now, though, Lee was finding it hard to concentrate. Every few minutes she raised her eyes from the schedule to stare out the window into the green jungle beyond, and think of Jenny. Sometimes, remembering her cool, soft voice, her cool, soft skin and the sudden warmth of her last kiss, she smiled. Then she frowned, recalling Jenny's panic on the phone when she'd called an hour ago.

"I should have been there with him," she had kept on saying, just as she had when she called from the hospital last night, "and I wasn't."

"No," Lee told her. "You were with me. Are you saying that makes it worse? Would it be better if you'd been at the grocery?"

"No—yes—I don't know." Jenny laughed nervously.

"That's magical thinking. If you go on that way, you'll be telling me next that when you said you loved me, it gave your husband a pain in the chest."

"I know it's silly," Jenny admitted. "But I feel so awful. I wish I could see you."

"Then come over, why don't you?"

"I can't, not yet," Jenny had half wailed, half whispered. "I have to stay here, in case Wilkie wakes up and wants me."

Why should he want you now, he hasn't wanted you in months, Lee had thought but not said.

She knew she had to be patient. Apparently whatever had been the matter with Wilkie Walker wasn't serious. A gallstone, Jenny had said: that made sense—from what she'd heard, he was probably full of gall and bile. He had been released from the hospital that morning, and soon enough he would be back to his usual disagreeable normality.

Suppose it had been serious, Lee thought. Suppose Wilkie Walker were really ill; suppose he got worse and worse, suppose he died. That would be no loss, because what use was he anyhow? All he'd ever done was to write pompous articles and give poisonous advice and make the woman she loved deeply unhappy.

But whether he was ill or not, soon Jenny would be here; Lee would hold her again, comfort her, kiss her, feel her softening and warming.

Right now, though, she had to stop fantasizing and get back to the schedule for April and May. Lee bent over her desk again, but almost immediately she was distracted, not by internal clamor now but by an external one: the sound of Myra Mumpson and her daughter quarreling on the front porch, where they were waiting for Jacko and his mother. Some of this quarrel was inaudible, but the tone was familiar: Lee had heard it often in couples who came to stay at her guest house in a last-ditch effort to repair a long-term relationship.

"You're making a big mistake," Myra said in a voice that had some of the characteristics of a leaf-shredder. "If you really want to save manatees you can do it much more effectively in Washington."

"There are no manatees in Washington," Barbie said weakly but stubbornly.

"Don't be stupid, darling. If you're sincere about helping those peculiar animals you're so interested in, you have to be where the power is. In Washington. You could accomplish something there, God willing. It could even become your specialty, endangered species, why not?" Her tone modulated from leaf-shredder to lawn mower and became speculative. "I could get you the help of experts. Trained lobbyists, and a good publicist. Bob might even sponsor a little bill in Congress eventually."

There was a reply from Barbie, inaudible except for the words "spotted owl."

"Of course he wouldn't support anything that interferes with productivity and threatens jobs. But there must be lots of other endangered animals. You could do so much for them in Washington, with your connections." Myra's voice was now almost a purr. "But in this backwater, one inexperienced girl, what can you accomplish? Nothing really."

Her daughter muttered a few words.

"They sound like a bunch of amateur crackpots to me. Besides, if you were here I'd worry about you all the time. Key West looks like a pretty resort town, but underneath it's a corrupt, godless place. Streets full of bums and drunks and perverts; anyone can see it. And how would you support yourself, have you thought about that, honey? You're used to a very comfortable life. You've never had to think about money for one single second."

Again, Barbie's reply was inaudible, but the mulish tone of it was clear.

"That's ridiculous," Myra declared, turning on the leaf-shredder again. "You have no retail experience, and you can't even type. You've got to come to your senses, darling."

A second of silence; then Lee heard Barbie cry, "No, I don't!" and the sound of a porch chair scraped back and falling over.

"Where in God's name do you think you're going?" There was no answer, only the thump of feet descending the front steps.

"My poor hysterical daughter's run off," Myra announced a

few moments later, letting the screen door crash behind her. "She went to some meeting last night, and now she's suddenly got this dumb idea in her head about staying in Key West."

"Oh, yeah?" said Lee neutrally.

"Yeah." Myra began to pace back and forth. "And what I say is, let her try it. She'll come running home soon enough. This is an expensive town. Barbie won't be able to pay her way here for a week. And I don't think Perry will feel like paying for her."

You're right about that, Lee thought, but she made no comment.

Myra positioned herself on the edge of a rattan rocker and set it lurching noisily back and forth. She was wearing an outfit suitable for first-class air travel: an expensive lime-green polyester blazer and tailored pants, matching lace-up shoes, and a shiny silk shirt hung with gold chains. She looked extremely out of place among Lee's handwoven fabrics, Haitian paintings, and disheveled tropical plants.

"Spoiled," she told Lee, rocking. "Her father spoiled her rotten. Spoiled both of them really. Not like my pa, he was the other way. Couldn't hardly please him whatever you did."

"Mh." Lee raised her head only briefly.

"He was weak," Myra continued, undiscouraged. "A pushover for anyone with a sob story, not just his own kids. If something in the house wasn't nailed down, he'd give it away; you know the type."

"Mf," muttered Lee, who had been accused of being this type herself.

"I made a big mistake when I married him. I told myself he was bound to succeed in politics, because he was smart, and everybody liked him. He was the best-looking man I'd ever seen, too, and the sweetest, underneath. Too sweet for real life. You have to look soft and be hard, right?"

"Mh," Lee said. If she didn't look directly at Myra, and spoke only in monosyllables, maybe the woman would shut up and go away.

"Trouble was, he didn't have the God-given ambition you need in politics. Didn't have much ambition for anything, if you want to know the truth. Or sense. Couldn't see ahead. Last thing he ever did in his life, he went on this real strenuous tour of England, looking for his ancestors, even though he knew he had a bad heart. Not thinking once of his Christian duty to his family, what would happen to us if he passed on. Selfish it was, really."

"Mm." Lee frowned. Her attempts to discourage Myra were having the opposite effect: her muttered interjections, like the neutral murmurs of the therapist she had once been, invited confidences.

"Course, it takes a special kind of gift to make it in politics," Myra continued, almost to herself. "You have to have the personality, and you have to have the know-how. Now my son, Gary, he's smart enough, but he doesn't have the personality. He isn't likable. Sometimes I don't even like him myself." She rocked even faster, shaking her head in time with the swings.

"Gary's good with money, up to a point," she added. "But

he takes bad risks. Some shyster lawyer he met at the gym got him to go in on this funny-sounding land purchase. Gary should've smelled a rat. Lord God, the signs were there—the deal was full of rats. I could have told him that, if he'd had the sense to ask. But the money was too good and he got greedy."

"Yeah?" Lee said, becoming interested in spite of herself. "So what happened?"

"Aw, not much in the end, thank the Lord. Most of the charges were dismissed, and they settled out of court. Except Gary was finished as far as public life went. I could see that right away, though it about broke my heart. But you have to be a realist, right?"

"I guess so," said Lee, who considered herself one.

"Like with Barbie's husband, Bob Hickock. Potentially, he's a winner, but he's got a wild streak. Impulsive. He doesn't care anything about money; he's not going to get into that kind of trouble. But he's a hot-blooded bastard, excuse the language. Back when he was in the statehouse I realized what the score was. I told him straight out. Listen here, boy, I said, if you feel like fooling around behind my daughter's back again, you go out of state. And you pay for it up front; none of this messing around with party workers that could fall for you and make a scandal, or get themselves pregnant and blab to the media. Go to Dallas, I told him. Ask somebody you can trust for a phone number." Myra sighed.

"Acourse Bob didn't take my advice," she added. "So pretty soon this over-the-hill ex–Vegas showgirl got her claws into

him. I figured it'd run its course, but he's still nuts about her.
Out of his mind. I phoned him day before yesterday, said would
he please call my poor Barbie, and ask her real sweet to come
back. She's just waiting to hear from you, I said. Tell her you've
given up what's-her-name. Laverna, yeah. I told him, listen,
buddy, Laverna is professional suicide. Her history and some of
her old photos get in the papers, you'll be dead politically."

"And what'd he say?"

"Aw, he was totally unreasonable. He said maybe that'd be
better than the way he was living now. Told me he wished to
God he'd stayed in North Gulch and just practiced law. Maybe
he'd resign his seat and go back there, he said. They were decent people, they'd like Laverna, they'd accept her. In a pig's
eye." Myra laughed sourly. "I know those small towns.

"Course, Bob was just bluffing," she added. "He'll calm
down in a while, see reason. If he wants to stay in Congress he'll
do what I tell him in the end, 'cause I've got too much dirt on
him. But there's no use talking to him again until Barbie comes
to her senses."

"Mh," Lee uttered.

"Lord God, the whole thing makes me sick sometimes."
Myra stopped rocking and stared out the window at the pale-
green palms blowing in the warm green wind. "I look back over
my life, y'know, and I see what I did wrong so clear. All that
time I wasted trying to get some man elected. Standing behind
some dope who couldn't learn what we had to teach him, didn't
appreciate the time and, Holy Jesus, the money we put into his

campaign. If I'd seen the light sooner, I would have run for office myself years ago. I figure I could have made it to the state senate at least. Maybe further."

"Maybe you still could," Lee suggested.

"Naw. It's too late. I might not look it, but I'm sixty-five."

"Really?" Lee reexamined Myra's appearance: the upright posture, square jaw, tight skin, helmet of reddish-brown hair. She had estimated Jacko's aunt as at least ten years younger.

"I should've gone to law school, but nice Christian girls didn't do that back in the fifties. The Fudd women mostly got married right from college. Before graduation sometimes, like I did. After that they didn't work outside the home, that was the idea, though my aunt Sophie ran a two-thousand-acre ranch. I was brainwashed, like those crazy feminists say. They're not so dumb sometimes."

"No," Lee said. Again she felt some sympathy, and had to remind herself that if Myra Mumpson had gone into politics she would have been against everything Lee was for. She would have been anti-gay, anti-choice, anti–affirmative action. It was one of the things that had made Lee give up therapy: the realization that half the time she was helping people she didn't like to become strong and confident enough to do things she didn't like, such as write deceptive advertising and sell jerry-built condos.

"I have to plan my schedule for the next couple of months now," she announced, assuming that Myra would take this broad hint and shut up.

But apparently the hint was not broad enough. "Never a letup in the hotel business," Myra said. "I know. I have a friend back home, she runs a B and B too. You wouldn't believe the thefts, the damage, the last-minute cancellations— Well, I guess you would. Except you've probably got it easier. That was a smart notion of yours, only renting to women. Cuts down on wear and tear, I bet."

"Mm," Lee agreed, bending over a full-page calendar for the third week of April.

"I guess you get some homosexual couples, too," Myra continued.

"Yeah," Lee almost growled. You give people the wrong impression, she told herself; you look too straight. But what the hell was she supposed to do about that? Should she wear overalls and heavy leather boots, and get a crew cut? But an outfit like that would be intolerably hot in Key West; besides, Lee liked her long, thick, near-black gypsy hair, and so did other women. For instance, Jenny—

"Don't get me wrong, I'm not saying you should turn them away," Myra said, apparently registering Lee's angry inward expression. "After all, it's good business. And just between ourselves, I don't see the harm." She rocked more slowly. "Not like with the men. The things they get up to, I don't even want to think about. Disgusting." She gave a little shudder.

"Women, that's different," Myra continued. "My aunt Sophie Fudd, that I mentioned to you before, she never married. Lived most all her life in a big bungalow out on the ranch with her best friend, Rose, who taught fifth grade in town. There was some talk now and then, jokes about old maids. But they were respected. And the way I see it, if they did cuddle a little and make each other happy, what was the harm, right?"

"Yeah," Lee agreed, recognizing what Jacko had meant when he described his aunt as "steamrollering you with her opinions." With a conscious sense of resisting heavy road machinery, she added: "Matter of fact, I'm that way myself."

"That so?" Myra gave Lee a long, interested look that made her wonder if she was about to make a similar declaration. "Well, live and let live is what I say." She rocked back and forth, then consulted an expensive watch. "What's the matter with Perry and Sis? They should've been here half an hour ago. Didn't you hear me tell him we have to catch a five-thirty plane?"

"I heard you," Lee admitted.

Myra stopped rocking. "Well, I'm not going to hang around waiting any longer," she announced. "I'm going back to the hotel. You tell Perry when he gets here, I expect him to be there at four o'clock. Sharp. And the same for Barbie, if she turns up."

For ten minutes, Lee worked on her schedule uninterrupted. Then, far more quietly than her sister had left, Dorrie Jackson drifted up the steps. She was wearing a faded oversized white shirt that had belonged to Jacko, and her floppy green hat.

"Perry's dropping off some orchids," she explained. "He'll be back soon. Where's Myra and Barbie?"

"They left." Lee decided not to go into details. "Myra got tired of waiting."

"Oh, dear," Dorrie squeaked, apparently not deceived by Lee's softening of this message. "Was Myra awfully cross?"

"No, not really. She said he was supposed to meet them at the hotel at four."

"Oh, Perry knows that. Is it all right if I wait for him here?"

"Yeah, of course."

Like her sister, Dorrie chose the rocker; but she settled back fully onto the handwoven purple cushion, and the motion and sound she produced were minimal.

"You've been a real good friend to Perry; he told me so," she murmured presently. "I'm so glad of that. And acourse you don't hold it against him that he's the way he is."

"No, of course not," Lee said, realizing that Dorrie Jackson, unlike her sister, did not assume that she was straight.

"He's a good boy," Dorrie continued. "I don't believe it's a judgment, his sickness, the way Myra does. God isn't like that. Back home, you know, I stopped going to First Methodist after the minister said all these mean things about boys like Perry. I got really cross. I told him, God knows our hearts, and he knows Perry's heart is good."

"Mm-hm," Lee remarked, thinking that if there was a God, he presumably did know this.

"Acourse everyone starts out good," Dorrie said several moments later. "We're all born innocent; only we're weak, so we go wrong. The wrong sorts of people and things come into our lives, and we can't fight them off."

"Yeah." Lee thought of some of the wrong people and things she had known.

"Like with Barbie's husband, Bob Hickock. He was just a poor hometown boy with a law degree from State, working in the district attorney's office. But Sis saw his potential. She started asking him to events and having him over to the house. Then after he and Barbie were engaged she got behind him in a big way. And acourse now he's real successful, even kinda famous. But I liked him better when he first came into the family. He was a real sweet boy then, with such nice shy manners. Only you could see he was always going to draw the girls like molasses draws flies."

Dorrie rocked quietly for a few minutes. Then she asked, "Did Barbie go back to the hotel with Sis?"

"Uh, no," Lee said. "I don't think so."

"No? Where is she, then?"

"I don't know. But I guess if she doesn't turn up pretty soon she'll miss that plane."

"Oh, I just hope to the Lord she does miss it," Dorrie said.

Surprised, Lee looked up. But though the chair was still rocking slightly, Jacko's mother had closed her eyes.

14

In the shadowy sitting room of the house on Hibiscus Street, Jenny sat on a slippery orange leather sofa, nervously knitting a gray cotton chenille sweater for her husband, and waiting for him to wake. He was upstairs now, sleeping off the events of the last twenty-four hours. On the drive home this morning he had been silent except for some irritable comments about the routine of the ward and the stupidity of nurses. Though more alert than he'd been last night, Wilkie was no more friendly or communicative. But he hadn't been that for months, she thought: he had been changing, rejecting her, choosing someone else all along.

And she was different too, Jenny thought. Especially since yesterday, when everything in her life had turned upside down.

She had lain in Lee's arms and been warmly, deeply happy. Then she had gone home and found the house strangely empty, with a half-eaten sandwich on the kitchen counter and two kitchen stools overturned. Before she could figure out what it meant, there was that awful phone call from Barbie Mumpson. Finally she had seen the cold, withdrawn person who used to be Wilkie Walker, her loving husband, in the hospital on Stock Island.

As if her unconscious knew what was coming, Jenny had been apprehensive as she walked the hospital corridors, clutching an L. L. Bean canvas bag to her chest. In the bag were Wilkie Walker's pajamas and bathrobe and toothbrush, and the library books he had demanded that she bring. Three of them, though the doctor had assured her over the phone that he was recovering well and could go home tomorrow. The request hadn't surprised her: it was typical of Wilkie to fortify himself with reading matter even on a trip to the dentist.

What Jenny had feared as she followed the corridor was not the distressing sight of her husband in a hospital bed, but an interrogation. Why hadn't she been there when he was taken ill? Why had she got home so late?

By the time she reached Wilkie's room Jenny was breathing hard and trembling slightly. She looked at the hospital-green metal door and imagined her husband behind it, sitting stiffly up in bed as he always did when not sleeping, fixing her with a scowl as if she were a bad specimen. Jenny had almost never seen Wilkie direct that look at her—but she had seen it di-

rected at others. In her mind she heard the words that would
come out of his mouth if he knew what she'd been doing when
she should have been with him: how she had broken down and
sobbed in Lee's arms, accusing him of adultery and revealing
things that should always remain private between a married
couple. If he knew about that, Jenny thought as she stood in
the wide corridor, which smelled strongly of disinfectant,
Wilkie would use words like "disloyal" and "hysterical." "I am
disappointed in you," he would say, as he used to say sometimes
to the children.

She pushed open the heavy door. There was a hospital bed in
the bare room, and someone lying in it with the sheet pulled up
over his face, as if he had died. Her heart gave a great lurch.
Then she realized that the person in the bed was breathing,
with a kind of half-snore that she recognized.

"Hello?" she uttered.

The figure in the bed turned over heavily, pulled the sheet
down, and became a heavy elderly man with strong features,
thinning hair, and a sour expression. He looked at her without
apparent enthusiasm, blinking, not speaking.

"How are you?" she squeaked.

"Jenny," the man said in a slurred version of Wilkie's voice.
His tone was neutral, as if identifying some object of no particular interest or attraction.

"I brought the things you wanted," she said.

Wilkie did not speak.

"I'm so sorry I wasn't home when you got sick," she babbled

on. "Lee was late getting back from the funeral, and then I had
to drive to Searstown, to the supermarket—"

"It doesn't matter," Wilkie interrupted. "It wasn't anything.
I never was seriously ill, I only thought—"

"I know, Barbie Mumpson told me, you thought you were
having a heart attack. That must have been awful." Moved by
duty and habit and good manners, Jenny approached the bed,
leaned down, and with closed lips brushed the dry, puffy cheek
of the man who lay there: an irritable, cold-hearted man who
deceived his wife with silly young women.

"Yeah— No. I actually thought—" Wilkie swallowed. "It
doesn't matter now. I'm all right, just kind of knocked out by
all those drugs they gave me." He closed his eyes, then opened
them again. "Did you bring the books I asked for?"

"Yes, they're right here, on the table."

"You're a good woman."

This was a statement Jenny had often heard from Wilkie
before, though not for many months. Once she had acknowl-
edged it with a glad private smile, and sometimes with the
matching phrase: "And you're a good man." But now this
phrase would be a lie. "Is there anything else I can do for you?"
she asked instead.

"No thanks. That idiot doctor insists I have to spend the
night. So he can charge our insurance for another day, I assume.
Can you come tomorrow morning at nine and pick me up?"

"Yes, of course."

"Right. You go on home now, get some rest. I might as well

try to sleep some more. Have to take every chance you get in a hospital—wake you up every couple hours to take your temperature or some other damned nonsense."

"I'll come back this evening, after supper."

"Don't bother." Wilkie gave his wife a weary, neutral look, then turned onto his other side, away from her.

If she were really a good woman, Jenny would have done what Wilkie told her and gone home. Instead, she'd driven straight to Artemis Lodge.

Lee had welcomed her, listened to her, comforted her; she had opened a bottle of Italian chianti, made fettuccine with tomato pesto and roasted peppers, followed by key lime sherbet.

Jenny's guilt was wholly irrational, Lee had declared when her friend paused for breath. It wasn't her fault that Barbie Mumpson had been there and she hadn't. After all, hadn't she said that Wilkie had continually told her to get out of the house and meet people? Evidently he hadn't wanted her around.

Yes; it felt like that, Jenny said miserably.

And while she was out of the house, presumably, Lee went on, Wilkie Walker must have been sleeping with Barbie Mumpson. He didn't care who knew it, either, or he wouldn't have kissed her right out on the street where anyone, including Jenny, could see. Wilkie was the one who should feel guilty, Lee said. And it could be that he was already being punished too. His attack, gallstone or heart or whatever it was, might have been the result of what was sometimes called "overexertion" with Barbie; you often read of such things in the newspapers.

As Lee spoke, angry, hopeless tears rose behind Jenny's eyes, and overflowed into her bowl of lime sherbet. Lee rose and came round the table: she held her, kissed her gently, and stroked her hair. It was hard, she said. She knew that. But it was best to face these things. Jenny had to accept that her marriage was probably over.

"But that's—" Jenny sobbed. "But I tried so hard. I did everything I should, for so many years."

"Of course you did," Lee agreed. "It's not your fault, not in any way. Here, have some more wine."

"But I've always done everything for him. Not just keeping house, but typing and researching his books, and writing parts of them, and the articles, and the lectures— I mean, that's my job," Jenny continued between bursts of sobbing. "If I'm not working with Wilkie, what am I supposed to do? I won't know what to do. I won't even know who I am."

"Sure you will," Lee told her, stroking her back and shoulders as she began crying again. "It just takes time. It's hard to break these old habit patterns, these old guilt patterns, after so many years."

In the end, Jenny hadn't gone home till nearly midnight, and then only because she was afraid that Wilkie or a doctor or a nurse might call. When she proposed leaving after supper, Lee had pointed out, quite correctly, that she was in no shape to drive. Then, somehow, she had ended up, exhausted and blurred with wine and tears, in Lee's bedroom.

Wilkie had probably not slept much last night either, Jenny thought now, coming to the lumpy end of a row of knitting and starting back. But while he was lying uncomfortably awake on a hard hospital bed, his sleep broken by noises and interruptions, she had been on another wider and softer bed, under an orange Indian spread patterned with huge pink and red flowers, fading in and out of tears and sleep, letting Lee hold her and stroke her and kiss her.

It had felt familiar and comfortable, but strange too, because the things Lee began to do after a while were things Wilkie had never done—or if they were the same, Lee did them so much slower and softer that Jenny, when she wasn't drifted away into unconsciousness, felt as if she were dreaming.

But she wasn't always dreaming, Jenny thought. Sometimes, now and then, she had been aware of everything: the way the wind pressed the leaves against the screen outside Lee's window, pressing them together, and the colored-glass chimes on the porch glittering and tinkling in the porch light. The softness of Lee's sun-browned skin, and her dark, springy hair thick on the sheets, like raveled raw silk— She had wanted everything that happened, because Lee was so kind, because Lee loved her, and she loved Lee. And because Wilkie had turned into a person she wasn't sure she even liked, who didn't like her.

It was true what Lee had said: she had to get used to the idea that her marriage was over, and that probably, as soon as he was well again, Wilkie would tell her so. She had to get used to the idea that he loved Barbie Mumpson, absurd as that seemed, because how could anyone love someone as silly as that?

But those things weren't logical; Lee had said that last night. "After all," she had said, "when you look at it rationally, it's improbable that any two people in the world should care so much for each other. Only sometimes it happens."

"But isn't it sometimes, I don't know, sort of ridiculous?" Jenny had asked. "I mean, take us. Two middle-aged women."

"Love is sort of ridiculous, sure," Lee said, "but also it's not ridiculous. The way I see it, anyone has the right to be in love. It's just a dumb convention that they have to be the same age and race and religion and class, and they can't be the same sex. You're just goddamn lucky if you love anyone and they love you back."

Jenny turned her knitting again and saw that the last dozen rows were distorted and uneven, as if she had been alternately pulling the yarn too tight and letting it fall slack. Now the sweater looked the way she felt, full of lumps and no use to anybody.

"Jenny!" a voice called from above.

"Coming!" She dropped her work to the tile floor and began to climb the stairs.

Wilkie did not smile as she came in. He lay there with a pale, inward expression, under a painting of a sunset with pink flamingoes flying across it. "Did you get the *Times*?" he asked.

"Yes, here it is."

"You might read some of it to me. Just run through the headlines, I'll tell you what I want to hear."

"All right," Jenny said. It wasn't a new request—Wilkie had made it sometimes in the past when his eyes were tired—but not for many months. "DEMOCRATS TEST STRENGTH," she read in a flat voice. "U.S.-CANADA RIFTS GROW OVER TRADE. NEW PLAN FOR AILING BANKS. DOLPHIN COURTSHIP."

"Yes, read that one."

" 'As much as puppies or pandas or even children, dolphins are universally beloved,' " Jenny read. " 'They seem to cavort and frolic at the least provocation.' " It's like when the children were small and he was working so hard on *Whispers in the Dark,* she thought, up all night so many nights watching the creatures that never come out till the sun goes down, straining his eyes through special binoculars. At dawn he'd come home and I'd have his breakfast ready, oatmeal with cream and brown sugar, or bacon and scrambled eggs, and after he'd told me how the night had gone I'd read to him from the *Times.* We were happy then.

" '. . . Their mouths are fixed in what looks like a state of perpetual merriment,' " she continued in a monotone, not trying to take in any meaning, but noticing that Wilkie too was smiling very slightly. We're doing the same things, she thought, but we're not the same. It's over between us: all that has to happen is for you to say so. From now on Barbie Mumpson will read the *Times* to you.

Wilkie's eyes were half-shut. " 'Their behavior and enormous

brains suggest an intelligence approaching that of humans—' "
Jenny continued, lowering her voice to a hum. " '—or even,
some might argue, surpassing it.' "

"The usual guff," Wilkie muttered. "Thanks, that's enough.
Think I'll try to sleep a bit more now."

"That sounds like a good idea. Oh, I forgot to tell you.
Gerry Grass stopped by a while ago."

"Mrh," Wilkie said, without interest.

"He asked me to say he was very sorry you'd been sick, and
hoped you'd be better soon," Jenny said, reporting Gerry's
words but not his gestures or the subtext of his message.

Gerry had held her hand in both his large warm hands,
stared into her eyes with his large warm eyes, and assured her
that if she needed him for anything at all, he was right there.
Even in her preoccupied condition, it had been clear to Jenny
that he was repeating his offer. Well, she had thought dimly
and rather dismally, maybe that's what I'm supposed to do with
my life next.

The trouble was, she liked Gerry Grass, but she couldn't
love him. For one thing, she couldn't believe he was a good
poet. Jenny had often been moved by poetry: Wordsworth and
Robert Frost and Emily Dickinson, especially. "The soul selects
her own society. . . ." She had begun quoting those lines to
Lee yesterday, and Lee had joined in, so that they finished the
poem in a soft, close chorus. Gerry's poems didn't rhyme or
scan, and the collection of essays whose proofs she had been
reading for him was even worse, being wholly concerned with

himself and his impressions and opinions of other poets. It wasn't the sort of book that would ever make a real difference in the world.

What Lee did, though, had made a difference and would continue to make a difference. She listened for hours to women who stayed in the guest house, like the therapist she had been, but she didn't charge them anything. And quite often, when someone was in trouble or couldn't pay, she let them stay there for almost nothing or even absolutely free.

"Is there anything else I can do for you?" she asked Wilkie, lowering her voice in case he was already asleep.

"No thanks. Wait— There is one thing. You can keep that silly girl out of here."

"Girl?"

"You know. My new fan. She called my room twice this morning, before you got to the hospital."

Jenny sat silent, her mouth half-open.

"You know who I mean. Came to the hospital with me. Wants to save manatees."

"Barbie? You don't want to see Barbie?"

"No. Certainly not now."

"I thought you—" Jenny heard her own voice, a kind of hysterical gulp, and swallowed the rest of the sentence.

"What?" her husband murmured drowsily.

"I thought you liked her."

"Well, I suppose I'm grateful to her. Ought to be anyhow. But she exhausts me. Bores me too. I can't be bothered with fans now."

Jenny swallowed again. Liar, liar, she thought. "Barbie's not just a fan," she said, her voice shaking. "I know all about it. I saw you kissing her on Sunday."

"What!" Wilkie repeated, but this time the syllable was a firecracker.

"I saw you. Right out in front of this house. On Valentine's Day." Jenny laid out the facts in a tone that wavered but made each word an accusation: of adultery; of cold-blooded hypocrisy; of blatant public exposure.

"Nothing of the sort," her husband said, raising himself on one elbow, frowning heavily.

"I saw you, from the living room window."

"That's ridiculous, I never— Wait a second." Wilkie pulled himself up into a sitting position. "Was this the day that poor fellow in the wheelchair drowned at the beach?"

"I guess so. Yes."

"I remember." He stared past Jenny, the frown between his bushy piebald eyebrows deepening. "Yeah. She stopped me at the gate, tried to give me some pamphlets. I was exhausted after all the fuss over the accident. Shaking with cold. All I wanted was to get inside, have a hot shower. So I took her handouts, I figured that was fastest, and she jumped on me and gave me a big sloppy kiss."

"I-uh," Jenny stuttered. Maybe he's not lying, she thought. Or else he's lying awfully well.

"You didn't think, darling— You couldn't—"

"Yes, I did," Jenny said. "Anyhow I wondered— I mean, you've been so strange, you've hardly spoken to me for months.

I thought you were angry with me about something. But then after Sunday I assumed you were probably involved with Barbie Mumpson."

"That is totally insane," Wilkie said with force. "I had no idea— You must know, Jenny, I could never seriously care for any other woman. You should have realized that. After all these years— And a goop like, what's her name, Bobbie. How could you possibly believe that?"

"Barbie," Jenny corrected. Suppose he's telling the truth, she thought. Suppose he does still care for me, in some sort of way. But if that's so he's not guilty of adultery. He's not guilty of anything except being unpleasant for months. I'm the one who's guilty.

"Whatever. I'm very sorry you got that impression. I admit I've probably seemed preoccupied. I've seemed— I've been—" He frowned and looked away, out of the window, as if the words he was searching for might fly past like birds; then he looked back.

"Strange," Jenny supplied, when he did not continue. "Very strange and cold and unfriendly."

"I'm sorry," Wilkie said for the second time, rather haltingly; it was not his usual habit to apologize. "It's true, Jenny, I've had things on my mind. I didn't want to burden you with them."

"What things?" she demanded.

"Different things. How to finish the book, and I thought—" Wilkie paused for almost a minute. Jenny, waiting, did not speak. "I thought I was sick," he said finally.

"You *were* sick, yesterday," Jenny said, worried now. Was her husband losing touch with reality? Had he had a stroke, a memory loss?

"Not that," Wilkie said slowly and gratingly, as if he were drawing the words up from an old well, with long pauses between the sentences while the bucket went down again. "I mean before yesterday. I thought I was seriously ill. For quite a while. Since last fall. I thought I had—" he paused again, swallowed "—cancer, actually."

"Oh, that's awful— You really thought— But Dr. Felch said—"

"Yeah, I know. It was a mistake." He gave a weak half-smile. "At least I hope so. The head doctor at the hospital who came in this morning says the same as Felch. Says I'm in good shape."

"But all this time, since last fall, you thought—"

"Well. Yeah. That's probably why I've seemed— What was it you said? Strange. Unfriendly." Wilkie's eyes began to close, then opened again. "I suppose that's why you had those absurd ideas about that girl," he said. He gave a thin, wheezing sigh, and shut his eyes.

Still holding the *Times,* Jenny stared at her husband. It wasn't like him to say what he'd just said, to apologize, to worry about his health. It was like another person, a wholly different sort of person. And as she thought this, Wilkie began to change while she watched, from a strong, handsome, healthy, but cold and unfaithful husband into a heavy, slack, elderly person with gray chenille hair and irrational fears.

She looked at his hand, fallen slack against the pink sheet printed with pinker flamingoes: the square-cut nails, the faded-red scar shaped like a quarter moon, the underwater watch. That was Wilkie's watch; and the scar on the veiny hand was the one Wilkie had got fighting a brush fire in Canada while researching an article about wolves for the *Smithsonian*. The man in the bed was her husband, Wilkie Walker; but at the same time he wasn't.

It was like in Convers last fall, she thought, only worse, because when after a minute or so Wilkie half opened his eyes again and looked at Jenny the illusion didn't end. His expression remained unfocused, weak, even confused. And she wasn't the same either, she too was weak and confused.

"Jenny?" Wilkie said, opening his eyes again. "Come over here." He smiled and indicated a place beside him on the shiny pink bedspread.

"I—" She hesitated, then automatically moved to sit in the designated spot. Wilkie, levering himself up from the pillow, put one heavy arm around her, and gave her half a hug.

"That's better, isn't it, darling?" he said.

"Mm," Jenny lied. Slowly, because it was so clearly expected of her, she leaned forward to touch the shoulder and kiss the dry, ruddy cheek of the person who used to be Wilkie Walker.

"All right now?" he asked.

"All right," she repeated. But it wasn't all right, she thought. Everything had changed.

"Why don't you try to sleep a little more?" she suggested in the gentle, controlled tone of voice she would have used to a fretful child. "I'm going out now, I have some errands."

"Yeah. I might," Wilkie agreed, subsiding against the flamingo pink pillows.

"I'll be back soon," she lied.

This time there was no answer. Jenny left the bedroom, descended the stairs, got into the car, and drove to Artemis Lodge.

Alone in the house, Wilkie Walker did not sleep, but rather fell in and out of a restless doze. He was no longer in pain, but he felt heavy and waterlogged, like something washed up on a beach. Last night, still aching all over in spite of the drugs, he had rejected the little doctor's diagnosis. In the morning, though, after speaking to the senior physician, he had had to consider that they might both be right. If so, he had not had a heart attack, but had passed a painful but non-life-threatening gallstone. Also, if the doctors were correct, he did not have cancer of the colon and was therefore not going to die agonizingly and shamefully in a few months, unless he killed himself first.

After the doctor had left a cold wave of rage and depression had washed over him. For years more, if the man was right, he would not only live, he would have to go on playing the worn-out part of Wilkie Walker, formerly famous naturalist and environmentalist. He would have to continue writing and speaking: shouting about all that was going wrong in the world. Greed, stupidity, waste, the exploitation and extermination of species, the destruction of the environment, it's happening now, you've got to do something about it! he had shouted for nearly fifty years, his voice growing weaker every year. Most people who heard him didn't give a damn. The few who seemed to care were mostly either lying or incompetent. Now he could go on shouting for years more, while the world continued to spiral downward, into the dark and muck.

But I don't have to go on, Wilkie thought. I know the way out: it's located just off Higgs Beach. I can still swim away from life whenever I want, and no one will ever know it wasn't an accident. Or maybe they'll think it was a heart attack, proving the doctors wrong. And they could be wrong, after all. He didn't have the strength for it today, but tomorrow, or the next day—

It wouldn't be the same, though. If you're terminally ill, killing yourself is an act of courage and generosity to your survivors; if you're healthy, it's cowardice. Of course if he was successful nobody would know. But he would know, though not for very long. Lying in bed, with the warm wind blowing the elegant shadows of palm fronds across the flamingo pink wall opposite, Wilkie heard his own breath come shallow and fast; his head spun.

If I'm not terminally ill, I probably should hang around for a while, he thought, so as to get *The Copper Beech* into final shape, get all the graphs and tables and illustrations right. That could take a month, maybe two months. . . .

To his own surprise, at this idea Wilkie felt not a darker wave of depression, but a kind of dizzy euphoria, like that of a prisoner temporarily reprieved from execution. He was going to live, to survive for a little while at least: he would be here tomorrow and the day after tomorrow and next week and probably next month. He glanced out the window, where two bright green palms tossed against a bright blue sky. They were alive, and so was he.

Maybe it's like Elisabeth Kübler-Ross's stages of dying, he thought. If death was what you'd expected and sought for months, the news that you weren't necessarily going to die soon produced the same series of emotions: first denial, then rage, then bargaining. After that there was nothing left but stage four, acceptance.

If he didn't drown himself, he would have to go on living, with all that implied. In fact the next month or two would be hell, because of all the stupid and unnecessary jobs he'd taken on in the belief that he'd never have to perform them: the lectures, the meetings, the articles and letters of recommendation and book blurbs he'd promised to compose, the conferences he'd promised to attend. Some of them Jenny could write and cancel, giving some excuse (what?), but each excuse, each withdrawal, would create resentment and ill will somewhere in America or, in a couple of cases, abroad.

And there were jobs too immediate for cancellation. He had,

for example, promised to appear on a panel at a symposium here in Key West a few weeks from today on The Writer and Nature. A younger and more fashionable naturalist from out of town had opted out, and Wilkie had agreed to fill in, thinking at the time that when the day came the only thing he would be filling was a watery grave.

There was also Jenny to consider: his wife, his one true love. For months he'd been trying to shield her from his illness and his rage and his despair, and from what he planned to do about them. With great difficulty, he had been avoiding her so as not to break down in front of her. As a result he had seemed—how had she put it, with her usual gentle tact?—"very strange and unfriendly." And also, as a result—Wilkie groaned and turned over in the hot, rumpled bed—Jenny had come to believe that he no longer loved her and was screwing that ninny Barbie Whatshername.

And it was not, Wilkie realized, completely irrational for Jenny to believe this, considering the way he had been behaving. And considering how the world went today. Statistically, genetically, he was aware, a man of his age was supposed to wish to discard his aging wife and impregnate younger and presumably more fertile females. His selfish genes were said to be urging him constantly to produce more and more children, so that they, the genes, could be sure of survival. The results of this for established marriages were reported all the time in the media, and he had observed it frequently among his acquaintances. If a man was well known and well off and successful, it was almost expected of him.

But Wilkie Walker was not interested in the survival of his genes. It was the survival of his work that he cared about, not some random, rather unsatisfactory collection of DNA like the two he and Jenny had already produced. Besides, in his opinion there were far too many human beings on the planet already.

Jenny didn't believe that he was involved with Barbie anymore, of course. She would forgive him for being difficult and distant, she would understand why he had behaved that way. No, she already understood. It was all right now, she had said so, with her usual wonderful generosity and kindness. She would realize that it had been irrational of her to suspect him; probably she would never mention it again.

But he had had a very narrow escape, Wilkie realized. If he hadn't been taken ill, yesterday afternoon he would have put on his swim trunks and bathrobe and sandals and walked down to the sea and done his best to drown himself. Probably he would have succeeded. And Jenny would have gone on thinking that he no longer loved her and had become sexually involved with some sappy, bubbleheaded fan.

For the rest of her life, maybe thirty or forty more years, his beloved wife would have believed that lie. Maybe, if the pain were great enough, she would eventually have told someone; perhaps more than one person. Gradually, whispering and sniggering talk would have started to circulate; the story would have reached one or more of his biographers. Finally this plausible lie would have been recorded as truth: a sordid, shaming blot on his otherwise reasonably creditable life.

"Jesus Christ," Wilkie said aloud, contemplating these possibilities; but he did not hear himself speak. Instead, inside his head, he heard another voice, that of his beloved grandfather, dead now nearly sixty years. "Willie-boy," it said in a strong Kentucky accent, "you've been a goddamned fool."

15

At the Arts Center on Stock Island a panel discussion titled "Naming the Natural World" was moving toward its end. On stage, at a long table under bright overhead lights, the four speakers (including Wilkie Walker and Gerry Grass) were more or less patiently listening and responding to questions from the floor. Gerry had opened the session with his new poem, "White Crane Woman," which made a dramatic and moving, but fortunately obscure, comparison between his love for and loss of Jenny Walker, and the decline of various equally picturesque Florida bird species. Though it did not rhyme or scan, the poem was given shape and form by the alternation of two refrains:

> *It is going, it is gone.*
> and
> *She is going, she is gone.*

Wilkie, like most of the people present, had not made the connection. He had spoken with polite appreciation of Gerry's work, and gone on to recommend the conservation not only of Florida's birds, but of its aquatic mammals—thus, he hoped, paying his debt to Barbie Mumpson for once and all. Not that he owed her a great deal: true, she had driven him to the hospital at the time of his gallstone attack, but she had also flung herself on him in public in a way that had caused his wife days of suspicion and misery.

For Jenny, however, the reference point of Gerry's poem was all too obvious, especially as during the reading he had several times sent a burning glance in her direction. She also thought it quite likely that many members of the audience—at least those who knew her—had made the connection. But she couldn't worry about that now: there was heavier freight on her mind.

This morning at breakfast, breaking off a low-key discussion of the relative merit of two brands of marmalade, Wilkie had suddenly brought up the subject of Lee Weiss.

"This woman you've been working for, that I met last night at the reception," he had remarked, setting down a section of English muffin.

"Yes," Jenny said, her voice almost trembling. From his tone, it was instantly clear to her that he hadn't taken to Lee— and indeed, when they were introduced she had suspected as much. Lee was not the sort of woman Wilkie usually liked: she was too outspoken, too abrupt. She had looked beautiful last night, but too flamboyant, Jenny knew, for her husband's taste. The party had been a grand affair, held outdoors under the palms at one of the big motels, and Lee had worn a kind of gypsy costume, all swishing sequinned silk and gold beads. Also, though Lee's manner had been friendly, she hadn't shown any particular awe of Wilkie or expressed any admiration for his books.

"I really didn't care much for her. I know she was helpful to you while I was so preoccupied." This was the term Wilkie had settled on to describe the weeks and months of his fear of death and resulting cold and unkind behavior to his wife. "But I think it would be better if you were to let the relationship cool off now."

"I can't do that," Jenny said. Though internally panicked, she managed to match his casual, affectionate tone. "Lee's my friend."

"But you must see that she's not an appropriate friend for you, darling." Wilkie smiled and took another bite of English muffin thickly spread with Oxford-cut English marmalade. For the last two weeks, ever since he left the hospital, Wilkie had been amazingly considerate and agreeable to Jenny. He had asked her advice constantly about the manuscript of *The Copper Beech,* and accepted her suggestion (Lee's suggestion, originally) that each chapter should be headed with a drawing by Molly Hopkins. He had deferred to her wishes about times and menus for meals; he had assured her often of his affection, and also demonstrated it, though never passionately. All that, he seemed to imply, was over.

"No, I don't see it," Jenny declared shakily but loudly. "She practically saved my life, that time I was stung by the jellyfish.

I mean, it could have been serious—I could have gone into shock, maybe even drowned—"

"I appreciate that, darling. But you've got to admit that Lee Weiss isn't the kind of person we usually know." Wilkie smiled in a conciliatory manner. "The manager of a bed and breakfast."

Not trusting herself to speak calmly, Jenny remained silent.

"And what troubles me more, I understand she rents rooms only to women, many of them lesbians."

"I told you it was a women's guest house," Jenny said. "And I suppose some of the people who stay there— But what difference does that make?"

"I've heard on good authority that your friend may be homosexual herself, even though she's been married. Or at least she's had some homosexual relationships." Wilkie held out his coffee cup for a refill.

"I don't know," Jenny lied, breathing hard but managing to keep her hand steady as she poured the coffee. "But even if that's true, why is it so terrible?"

"I didn't say it was terrible, darling. But it does suggest that she's not the sort of person I'd like to think was a close friend of yours." Wilkie smiled and put his hand on Jenny's for a moment, then moved it back to his coffee cup.

"I don't—I don't understand, really," she said, trying to turn the subject, to avoid direct confrontation. "I mean, if homosexuality is unnatural, why are there so many of them? Why doesn't it just die out, by natural selection?"

Wilkie smiled. "Well, of course it is a genetic anomaly, darling," he said. "But it probably had survival value in the past, among primitive people." He leaned back in his chair and assumed his lecturing voice, deeper and slower and more confident. "A tribe or a family that included extra adult men, men who didn't reproduce, had a competitive advantage. There would be fewer children to care for, and more adult males to hunt and fight for them. If some of these males were sexually attracted to each other, they would be less likely to fight over the women, or to leave the group and form families of their own."

"Yes, I see that," Jenny murmured, falling into her own customary role of student. She thought of Jacko, who seemed to have made no effort to hunt or fight for his family. But he was planning to set up a trust fund for his mother; it was in the will she and Wilkie had witnessed.

"The same might be true of the females, of course," Wilkie continued. "If some of them were genetically programmed to be sexually attracted to each other, they would remain available to care for the children of their brothers and sisters. Naturally this would give the family, or the tribe, a better chance for survival. Whereas a family or a tribe with no excess adults would be less able to protect and feed its children."

"Yes, I see," Jenny repeated.

"Even today, in some societies, you find this pattern. It can occur without actual homosexuality, of course. Late marriages, the economic responsibility of unmarried siblings for their nephews and nieces. But it's unusual in our society. Most homosexuals in America today are pretty useless. They don't take any responsibility for their families, in fact many of them break with their families. They devote their resources entirely to lavish, unproductive spending on themselves, and they're often drawn to a kind of depraved extravagance. I mean, for example, look at this house. Gold faucets in the shape of fish that never existed, and that table you hate so much." Wilkie smiled broadly, gesturing at the glass coffee table in the next room, with its supporting plaster monkeys, and Jenny managed a matching though weaker smile.

"Homosexuality isn't as useful to the species as it once was," her husband continued. "It may even die out eventually, but genetic change is slow. Still, the numbers are declining even now. Partly as the result of AIDS and other diseases, of course. Nature can seem cruel, but she balances her books." He leaned back, the lecture concluded.

"But Lee Weiss is perfectly healthy," Jenny burst out in spite of her resolve. "And she's not useless or selfish. She's very close to her daughter, she's putting her through graduate school in Boston right now. And she does lots of other good things, she lets women come and stay in the guest house free if they need to and can't pay."

"Darling," Wilkie said, leaning forward and putting his hand on her arm. "I didn't mean to upset you; I was speaking in general terms. I know you think of this woman as a friend, and I'm sure she's quite admirable in her own way."

"She is admirable," Jenny insisted. Amazed by her own

boldness, she gazed directly at Wilkie. In the past, he would have become visibly impatient or even angry by this time; but today he only sighed slightly.

"Maybe it would be easiest if you didn't try to end the relationship right now," he conceded. "Just let it lapse while we're away, and then if we do come back to Key West next winter, you don't have to take it up again."

Oh yes I do, Jenny thought.

"But it might be best if you were to stop working at her bed and breakfast. All you have to say is that you're going to be busy now with my book. I'm sure she can find someone else."

"No, she can't," Jenny said, surprising herself again. "And I can't let her down now. Besides, it's only three mornings a week."

"Well," Wilkie sighed again. "If you feel you must."

"Yes; I do," she said.

As she sat in the auditorium on Stock Island, recalling this exchange, a peculiar feeling came over Jenny. It was as if for most of her adult life she had been leaning against a heavy stone wall that both imprisoned and supported her. Suddenly, almost by accident, she had given the wall a shove, and the stones had crumbled and fallen, leaving a gaping hole. Had the wall been that weak all along? Or was it only recently that it had become vulnerable—only since Wilkie had come back from the hospital as a different, weaker person?

Maybe it was true what Lee had said, when Jenny told her how strange she felt, how frightened even, by the way Wilkie had stopped being in charge and knowing what was right. "I worry," Jenny had said. "I mean, suppose he gets sick again, and can't make up his mind about anything, or starts forgetting things, what will I do?"

"You'll take care of him," Lee had said. "It's what you've been doing all along anyhow, isn't it?"

After a final word from the moderator, the four hundred members of the audience burst into applause; some even rose to their feet, still clapping. Then, rather slowly, for many of them were past retirement age, they began to make their way to the exits.

One of the first to emerge into the wide sunny lobby was Barbie Mumpson, in new pink denim jeans and a T-shirt bearing the idealized image of a smiling manatee. Dodging other members of the audience, she made a rush for a table piled with identical T-shirts and related pro-manatee and pro-dolphin propaganda and merchandise.

"Everything okay, Liz?" she said to a woman at the adjoining display of books.

"Sure. Here's your cash box."

"Hey, thanks. It was great of you to watch my stuff. I would've just died if I couldn't hear this session."

"How'd it go?"

"Oh, they were wonderful." Barbie gave a gasp of enthusiasm that caused the manatee on her T-shirt to rise and fall as if slowly swimming across her breasts. "Specially Professor Walker."

．　．　．

The lobby was filling fast; customers began to approach Barbie's table, inquiring about sizes and prices. Meanwhile the speakers were taking their places at another table, preparing to sign copies of books purchased from Liz. Lines were already forming, the longest one in front of Wilkie Walker.

Among the crowd pressing toward the exit, Molly Hopkins stood out by reason of her lean height and a new white straw hat trimmed with white silk gardenias. Limping slightly, she moved toward the doors, greeting and being greeted by friends and acquaintances. One of them was Barbie's aunt Dorrie, to whom Molly offered a ride back to Key West.

"No, thank you." Dorrie smiled. "Perry's picking me up." Blinking as they emerged into the midday sun, she put on her own new hat. It was green like the old one, but stiff instead of floppy, having been constructed from strips of palm leaf by a sidewalk merchant. "But maybe Barbie would like a lift."

"No; she and the other manatee people will be here all day," Molly said. "I believe they're bringing in sandwiches."

"That's nice."

"And are you still enjoying Key West?"

"Oh, yes. It's such a beautiful place. And I feel so good here, so full of energy, I hardly ever need a nap even. I'm so happy I can't believe it, really. Happier than I ever thought I'd be again in this world, thank God." Dorrie gazed gratefully up into the pale, hot sky.

"I've found this wonderful church," she continued. "They're so understanding and accepting, not like back home. You know what the minister there said Sunday? He said that sometimes God doesn't seem to take very good care of boys like Perry in this world, but he's always watching over them, and when it's time he welcomes them into heaven. Wasn't that nice?"

"Very nice," Molly agreed, adding silently, If you believe it. "And are you planning to stay for a while?"

"Oh yes," Dorrie said. "As long as Perry needs me. Though we're thinking of going to Europe in May or June; I've never been, you know. We might sign up for this tour of English gardens Perry read about; it sounds really exciting. Oh, there he is now." Dorrie waved, then scampered toward the Greenfire truck.

Much more slowly, for in spite of the warm weather her knee was stiff and sore today, Molly limped toward her car. She would drive straight home, she decided. Then she'd take two pain tablets, lie down, and skip this afternoon's session, "Ecology and Economy," which didn't sound like much fun anyhow.

If she felt up to it when she woke from her nap, she would go back to the drawing of two squirrels she'd started yesterday—one of the two dozen she'd promised for Wilkie Walker's new book. It was exactly the sort of job Molly liked; the only problem was that she never knew how long she would be able to work before her hand and arm began to hurt too much, or her head to throb from eyestrain.

The real question was, would she be able to finish the assignment and get it right, or was she too old, too ill, too near death? She remembered what Jacko had said on a very hot day last week when together they had dug up a shade-blighted vermillion and pink bougainvillea and replanted it in a sunnier spot. Afterward both of them were sweaty and exhausted. "It was awful there in the sun," she had remarked as they drank seltzer under the shade of her gumbo limbo tree. "I felt so dizzy and weak, as if I was dying. Well, of course in a way I am dying." She laughed unhappily.

"Yeah," Jacko had said suddenly. "If you look at it that way, you're dying and I'm dying. But at the moment, we're alive. So are we living or are we dying, or both?"

"I don't know," Molly had confessed.

"The way I figure it, everyone is living, everyone is dying."

That was true, she thought. But at least they had moved the bougainvillea. It would flourish and flower splendidly this year, and for years to come, long after she and Jacko were gone.

In fact Molly was less often exhausted now, because two weeks ago Barbie Mumpson had moved into her spare bedroom, and in exchange for room and board she was now doing much of Molly's cleaning, laundry, and shopping. Barbie had also repaired two broken screens, fixed the downstairs toilet, and replaced the burned-out bulbs in the outdoor lights. Watching her carry the stepladder across the deck, Molly remembered how once that sort of thing had been easy for her too; how she had wondered why old people moved so slowly.

When she agreed to take Barbie in, Molly had assumed that

she'd have to hear more about her unhappy marriage and help-less self-doubt. But in fact Glory Green and the other dolphin and manatee people seemed to have taken over most of this task. They had also provided a lawyer to handle Barbie's divorce from her husband, Wild Bob Hickock.

"I felt just awful about it at first," Barbie had declared. "But Glory and Stewart, that's my lawyer, think it's for the best really. I mean Bob and I weren't ever exactly suited to each other. For instance he never really liked animals, except his own dogs."

As might have been expected, Barbie's mother was vehe-mently opposed to the divorce. For several days she'd as-saulted Molly's house with phone calls, some of which had reduced her daughter to noisy tears. But presently, on the ad-vice of the manatee people, Barbie had refused to speak to Myra Mumpson.

"Glory says, when Mom calls, I should ask you to please just tell her I'm not here. She says talking to angry people is counterproductive and bad for the soul. And she says they've all noticed that after I've been on the phone with Mom I'm too upset for hours to be any use to anybody or any-thing."

As a result of this policy, for the next few days Molly had found herself having daily conversations with Myra Mumpson. At first these conversations had been very unpleasant. Myra had accused her (sometimes with justice) of lying about Barbie's whereabouts. She had dwelt upon the thanklessness of all her relatives, on the ditsiness of her sister Dorrie, and on Barbie's immaturity and incapacity for success in what Myra referred to as "the real world."

The last time she phoned, though, Myra had been more concerned with her own situation. She had confided to Molly that she'd decided to run for state representative in the Republican primary. "At my age, can you believe that?" Myra gave a hoarse giggle. "But the other candidate is a complete washout as a speaker, plus he's pro-choice. He hasn't a chance in this district. So I thought, why not? I feel it's what God's directing me to do now. And besides it'll get my mind off the mess my poor silly daughter is making of her life, right?"

But she's not, Molly had thought but not said. As far as I can tell, her life is less of a mess now, and so is mine.

Recently, now that Barbie was apparently planning to be in Key West indefinitely, Molly had begun to think seriously of staying on longer here this year: through June, and perhaps even into July. She might be lonely after the other winter residents had left; but she was lonely everywhere these days. Everywhere the world had been gradually emptied of her friends, by death. And one day, perhaps quite soon, she too would go. But even death, Molly imagined, would be different here, easier—a kind of slow dissolving into the almost perpetual heat and moisture of Key West.

With a somewhat fixed, but essentially satisfied smile, Wilkie Walker signed the last of the many books presented to him, and stood up. A handful of fans still lingered, hoping for a handful of personal words, repeating their praise of what he had said or written, and offering to take him to lunch. But Wilkie excused himself, saying truthfully that he had promised to eat with the other seminar members, and that he had to go now (gesturing vaguely toward the washroom). His fans, many of whom had prostate trouble, or were related to someone with this ailment, moved out of his way with apologies.

Though he had agreed to participate in this conference only in the belief that he would be dead when it took place, Wilkie thought as he crossed the lobby, it hadn't been bad so far. The younger people on the panel, unlike some of those he had encountered in the past, had been pleasant and even deferential. Wilkie understood what that meant: it meant that he had ceased to be a competitor, and become a kind of elder statesman. Having been out of circulation for a while had been an advantage. He and his books were too out-of-date now to be attacked: instead they were patronized or even acclaimed as historical documents.

As a result, for the first time in years he was experiencing the rush and crush of popularity, the long lines, the ache in his wrist from signing books—all the phenomena of celebrity that had once surrounded him. What had caused this? Wilkie wondered as he stood in the washroom. Was it something he'd said? It had been a good speech, but no better than many others he'd given in the past.

Or was it some characteristic of the audience? By definition, the conference participants were people who were willing and able to pay several hundred dollars in order to sit indoors and listen to other people talking for two days, on a sunny Florida weekend. Not ordinary tourists, therefore; not students or working men and women on holiday. This audience would have to be well off, and middle-aged or elderly—often retired. In fact, it was largely composed of old people, who had preserved their old enthusiasms, among which were Wilkie Walker and his books.

And these people, of course, were also an endangered species—endangered by age and illness and irrelevance—but most obviously and immediately by death. When Wilkie declared that an aquatic mammal, though not productive or attractive or well adapted to its present environment, was still very valuable, interesting, and worth preserving, they naturally felt better. Because by analogy, so were they.

As retirees, most members of this audience were by definition unattractive and unproductive. But they might in fact not be entirely useless, Wilkie thought as he zipped up his pants. Many of them were wealthy, and most of them meant well. If anything could be done for the manatee and the dolphin and the other declining species of South Florida, it might be done here.

It wouldn't be easy, because rich old people, as Wilkie knew from observation of himself and others, were reluctant to part with their money. Consciously or unconsciously, they often realized that only this wealth made most of them attractive—though a few, like him, might have kept a certain amount of power and influence. And there were so many competing causes: other animals and birds and plants, the arts, diseases, universities. . . . Not to mention, of course, the forces of agribusiness and commercial and sport fishing. It would be an uphill fight.

But Wilkie had always liked a good fight. Some of his most agreeable memories were of arguing down smug representatives of commercial interests, or (at the other end of the political spectrum) noisy Luddites and vegetarians. If he were quick on his feet, he could often get these competing fanatics to turn on each other, while he sat calmly between them, representing the voice of reason.

It would be interesting to see how Barbie Mumpson and her new friends got on with their campaign. He might give them the names of some of the well-to-do local fans who had crowded round him just now, pressing business cards and telephone numbers on him. He was also seriously turning over in his mind a possible article for the *Atlantic* about the manatee— perhaps eventually even a book.

If he decided not to leave week after next, if he stayed through March, or perhaps even longer, Jenny could start the research now. And after all, why shouldn't they stay on? The house was available, and according to reports the weather back in Convers was still cold, gray, and icy. And since he'd got out of the hospital he was sleeping well at night, even heavily: nine or ten hours sometimes.

Jenny would like it if they stayed on, she'd said so only the other day. She hated cold weather, and she had made friends

here, though not always wisely. And with modern technology—
fax and E-mail and an Internet connection—she could do most
of the necessary editing and checking for *The Copper Beech* right
here in Key West. Besides, it would make up to her for that
stupid misunderstanding over Barbie Mumpson.

Possibly they could return to Key West every winter from
now on, Wilkie decided. Jenny would like that too. With
enough advance notice, she could probably find a house she'd
prefer to this one. Or they might buy a place, as many of their
acquaintances had. It was a good investment, everyone said so.
They might even become Florida residents the way Howard and
Molly Hopkins, and the Fosters, had done, staying at least six
months and a day every year in a state with no income tax.
Why not, after all? His editor was almost exhaustingly enthusiastic about *The Copper Beech,* and the balance of his advance
would cover a substantial down payment on a substantial vacation house. If the first serial rights deal his agent was now
negotiating went through, they probably wouldn't even need a
mortgage.

The ending of the book was better now, Wilkie thought.
Instead of actually describing the melodramatic death of the
Copper Beech in a great storm, he had cast the last chapter in
the future conditional, and posited several possible futures. As a
result, he had been able to include all the good passages of
writing he would have otherwise regretfully had to discard.

Beeches are long-lived, he had written: some existing specimens are known to be well over three hundred years old. Yet

one day the Copper Beech, like all trees and all men, will die. It might perish prematurely: struck by disease, demolished by human stupidity, or toppled in a great storm. But if we cared for it, and were vigilant, the Copper Beech might adorn and enrich the world and us for many more years—and so might all the other endangered flora and fauna on the earth. It was probably too optimistic an ending; but if you weren't optimistic, in his experience, there was no chance of getting people to do anything at all.

Though only a few weeks had passed, it was hard now for Wilkie fully to recall the depressed, desperate, almost demented state he had been in before his gallstone attack—a state in which it had seemed clear that the only way out was one that would have destroyed not only his own life, but Jenny's and possibly those of his children.

Three times Wilkie had done his best to accomplish this destruction, and each time Fate had thwarted him. He pictured her still as he had in his deranged state of mind: as a dumpy, elderly version of Justice. But now, instead of sneering spitefully at his failure to do away with himself, Fate was smiling, even perhaps rather smugly.

Later that same hot day L. D. Zimmern, the New York professor and literary critic, settled into a creaking wicker chair on the front porch of Artemis Lodge and extended his long thin legs. As usual, he was wearing an old denim work shirt and a skeptical, penetrating expression.

"Well, Cousin Lelia," he said. "It's fun to see you again. What has it been, five years?"

"I guess so," Lee agreed.

"You look like a real native Key Wester. One of those, what is it they call them? Some kind of clam."

Lee did not reply. Years ago, as a teenager, she had resolved that Lennie Zimmern would never again get a rise out of her. She pulled down her crimson embroidered mumu, wishing as she did so that she had followed her earlier impulse to change into jeans and a T-shirt before he arrived.

"A Conch, that's it. Yeah." He reached for the bottle of imported beer he had brought with him. "Quite a change from Dr. Weiss, Ph.D., with her briefcase and box of Kleenex for weepy clients."

Again, Lee said nothing, though she thought that Lennie, on the other hand, was unchanged: still thin, dark, clever, and sour. His thick hair and close-cropped beard were grayer, his face more sardonically creased; that was all.

"So the place suits you?"

"I like it," she admitted, gathering her forces. "I never expected to see you here, though."

"Why not? I had two perfectly good motives: curiosity and cash. Besides, it was a chance to visit my favorite little cousin Merilee in her new natural habitat."

In spite of her resolution, Lee winced visibly at the first utterance in many years of her silly adolescent nickname.

"Sorry. I should have said Lelia Weissfrau." Lennie grinned

as he made this old joke, which dated from the time when Lee, on becoming a feminist, had altered her original surname from Weissmann to Weiss. With difficulty, she did not react.

"Seriously," he added. "When you get to be my age, you start thinking about your family. Like that Gauguin painting. Where do we come from, Who are we, Where are we going? I even have occasional embarrassing impulses to show people photographs of my grandchildren."

"Oh yeah? Do you have them with you?" Lee asked.

"I must admit I do. All three."

"Okay. Hand them over."

For the next ten minutes Lennie and Lee exchanged photographs and family news. It was in a more relaxed manner that, as he put the snapshots away, she remarked "You know, I'm surprised you should come to a conference on The Writer and Nature. I thought you didn't care for nature."

"You're right, I've never been a great fan. Seems to me it's what civilization was invented to get away from. But there's not too much of the stuff around here."

"Come on." Lee nodded at her trumpet vine, still thick with red and gold blossoms, and the leafy street beyond. "What do you call that?"

"Aw, that's just pretty scenery. I have nothing against scenery, as long as it stays in its place." Lennie raised his glass to the trumpet vine, and drank.

"And what really surprises me is that they invited you."

"That's easy. I'm here as the bad guy." He set down the

glass, pulled his still thick, coarse gray-black hair into two horns, and gave his cousin a devilish grin. "They need someone like me to rile them, make them rush to the defense of their favorite useless plant or animal, get the energy level up. Otherwise it's all too nicey-nice. That's why they've called my panel 'Nature and Anti-Nature.' I'm Anti-Nature. When I go on tomorrow, it'll liven things up, you'll see."

"So what will you say?"

Lennie shrugged. "I haven't decided yet. Maybe I'll start in on one of their heroes, say for instance Thoreau. You know he was a mama's boy, like so many naturalists? Used to send his laundry home from Walden like some kid at summer camp."

"Really?"

"God's truth. Or should I say, Goddess's truth?" Lee did not reply. "You still into all that?"

The answer was, Yes, in some ways, but Lee did not supply it. "But it'll be three to one," she said instead.

"So what?" He shrugged. "It'll be easy going up against those famous softheads. Kind of fun, really. There won't be any surprises; I know most of them already." Lennie smiled. Altogether, there were fifteen speakers at the conference, and it was safe to say that in the past he had insulted or annoyed every one of them in some way, either in person or in print—though in many cases Lennie (unlike his victims) had forgotten this.

"Really."

"Listen, I've known Gerry Grass since we were both at an arts colony thirty years ago. He's not a bad guy, but he's still stuck back there in the sixties, trying to get in touch with Nature. Wandering about the world looking for her like Bo-Peep's poor lost sheep."

"I thought he was a famous American poet."

"Sure, why not? You don't have to be intellectually brilliant to be a famous American poet. It's a handicap, sometimes. Innocent egotism, good looks, romantic sensibility, a thrilling speaking voice, and a nice little lyric gift, that's what makes it with the reviewers and the public. You met him yet?"

"Just yesterday, at the opening reception."

"I hear he's split with his girlfriend, what's her name, Huff or Tiff or Spat, something like that. Poor dope. He should have been warned the moment they were introduced; he's supposed to be sensitive to language."

Lee laughed. "So who else is on the panel with you?"

"Well, there's Wilkie Walker, the Friend of the Salt Marsh Mouse, and all our other little furry friends." (Lee opened her mouth to make some equally negative comment, then closed it.) "And Dilly Acker, of course, author of *Whale Music,* the most famous nature writer of her generation, according to the brochure."

"It sounds as if you don't care for her," Lee said.

"Not all that much, no. I don't like beautiful women who prefer fish to me. If I get lucky, I can make her cry. I'm looking forward to that."

Lee laughed again. "If you make Dilly Acker cry, that audience will lynch you."

"You think so?" Lennie raised his heavy eyebrows. "But you'll protect me, won't you, Lelia? You'll charge onto the stage and fight the assailants off with your umbrella, like you used to when you and Cousin Roger were playing Robin Hood and the Dragons, or whatever it was."

Below the porch a car pulled into Lee's driveway. Jenny Walker got out, slammed the door ineffectively, and ran up the steps. Her long pale hair was loose over a gray cotton dress printed with paler gray bamboo leaves, and she looked flushed, anxious, and very pretty.

"Oh, Lee!" she cried in a tremulous rush. "I'm so glad you're here. I just can't make it tonight, Wilkie's changed his mind, he says we have to go to the art opening, and the dinner tomorrow too. I can't possibly see you until Sunday. I know that's awful. But I've got good news too: we're going to stay through April, and we're probably coming back in October. So you'll forgive me, won't you?"

"Don't worry about it," Lee said awkwardly. "Jenny, this is my cousin Lennie Zimmern, that I've told you about. Jenny Walker."

"What?" Jenny gasped. "Oh, hello, I didn't see you." She took a breath and shifted with evident strain into a social manner. "I mean of course I knew you were coming, I saw your name in the program. But you weren't at the lunch today at the Rusty Anchor."

"No," Lennie agreed. "I make a point of never eating at restaurants with cute names."

"And are you enjoying Key West?"

"I can't say yet."

"Oh, you'll like it, I'm sure. Everyone does. Well, I must dash." With a brief helpless glance at Lee, she ran down the steps.

"Well," Lennie said, as Jenny's car pulled out of the driveway. "What was all that about? No, on second thought, don't tell me, let me guess. You're in love."

"Don't be stupid," Lee said rather tensely. "Jenny's just a little frantic and overextended now, because of the conference. She gets like that sometimes."

"Come on, Lelia. I've seen Jenny Walker for years at Academy dinners, and I've never seen her like that. She's always been the perfect lady. Calm and cool and collected."

"That doesn't prove—" Lee, who detested lies, lied with difficulty. "It's not what you think."

Lennie looked at her, frowning a little, then smiled. "Come on, Lelia," he repeated. "You ought to realize by now that I won't tell on you. Shit, it's been nearly fifty years, and I'm still the only person that knows who broke the bathroom window in your aunt's house in Queens.

"I should congratulate you," he added, when Lee said nothing. "She's a very attractive woman. Beautiful, even. Maybe a little flavorless for my taste."

"Jenny is not flavorless," Lee heard herself protest against her better judgment, in a voice that, she realized too late, gave everything away.

"No? Well, you know best." Lennie allowed himself an aggravating smile. "I've never tasted her myself."

"She's too good, that's all," Lee said, ignoring this smile and trying to speak casually. "The trouble is, she wants to make everyone happy, including her husband, who's a complete egotist and MCP."

"Really."

"He thinks he loves her, but he has no consideration for her. Treats her as if she were his secretary, even though he couldn't write his books without her. But she won't leave him."

"No, I can understand that. After all, who would she be if she weren't Mrs. Wilkie Walker?"

Lee sighed, but managed to say nothing, though she couldn't help remembering what Jenny had whispered to her only yesterday: Yes, of course I love you. But Wilkie's work is my life. Anyhow, it's what I can do for the world, you know?

"She seems to be a popular item," Lennie remarked. "I have the impression that Gerry Grass has a crush on her too. When he was reading this rather obvious poem about lost white birds and lost white-skinned women at the symposium this morning he kept gawking at her."

"He hasn't got a chance," Lee said.

"Glad to hear it." Lennie smiled. "But you know, Wilkie Walker might not be around forever. Gerry told me last night that he was in the hospital here a couple of weeks ago."

"Yeah. But it wasn't anything. He had some sort of intestinal attack. Nerves I think it was."

"Could be. I have to say that he still puts up a good show in public, though. Father Nature, all wise and kind. You should go and hear him sometime this weekend, see what you're up against."

"No thanks," Lee said. Last night, at the opening reception of the conference, she had met Wilkie Walker for the first, and she hoped the last, time. As she'd expected, he had been both polite and patronizing, recognizing her as Jenny's friend, but showing no wish to know her better himself.

What had surprised Lee was Wilkie's appearance. Nothing that Jenny had said, and none of the magazine or book-jacket photographs, had prepared her for his being so heavy, gray, worn, and slow-moving. Why, he's an old man, she had thought, and an inconvenient flood of compassion had sloshed over her. No wonder he'd believed he was ill, dying even.

Lennie's right, she thought now. Wilkie won't be around forever. But whether or not he was around, Jenny would be determined to get his book into publishable shape. There was no point in trying to fight that, because in Jenny's mind it was her book too. When he and the manuscript went north she would go with them. And though she and Lee might manage to meet somehow, somewhere, this summer, she would be gone for the next half-year.

But that wasn't going to happen just yet. Lee remembered something she had read once, that as you grow older and the future shrinks, you have only two choices: you can live in the fading past, or, like children do, in the bright full present.

Jenny would be here for nearly two more months—the rest of March and all April. Spring was Lee's favorite season in Key West: by early April most of the tourists would be gone, as well as the college students who had made the town noisy and dangerous with their rented mopeds and riotous intoxication.

The weather would be perfect: the nights warm and romantic. Almost every day, as soon as the conference was over, Jenny would come to the guest house, and sometimes late at night too, after Wilkie was asleep—as she had already done several times.

They would be together often as the island became steadily quieter, more beautiful, and more overgrown with flowers. Together they would watch the purple and white orchid trees unfold into bloom; they would see the stubby spread hands of the frangipani put out their pink and white and golden velvet whorls of petals, and the poinciana explode slowly overhead in drifts of scarlet confetti.